D0822205

Becoming
LADY
LOCKWOOD

A Regency Romance

JENNIFER
MOORE

Covenant Communications, Inc.

Cover Image: *HMS Victory* © Howat, Andrew (20th Century), courtesy Bridgeman Art and *Woman* © Susan Fox, courtesy Trevillion

Published by Covenant Communications, Inc.
American Fork, Utah

Printed in the United States of America
First Printing: July 2014

20 19 18 17 16 15 14 10 9 8 7 6

ISBN-13: 978-1-62108-689-5

For Frank—
Who gave me my own love story.
How lucky am I?

Acknowledgments

I'd always assumed writing a book would be a solitary endeavor—just me and my computer—but I couldn't have been more wrong. I could never have done it alone, and I owe my deepest gratitude to the people who've helped me along the way. It takes a village to write a book, and here are some of the people in my village.

Thanks to my parents, Ed and Penny, for teaching me to love books and not punishing me for reading with a flashlight under the covers.

Thanks to my groupies—Angela, Becki, Cindy A., Cindy H., Jody, Josi, Nancy, Ronda, and Susan (I put your names in alphabetical order because I love you all)—for slogging through pages and pages of garbage and not being afraid to tell me. And thanks to the friends who read the exact same pages and told me they were wonderful. I needed all of you.

Thanks to my late-night writing buddies: Josi, Nancy, Rob, Marion, and Cory. Your help and support and friendship mean more than you'll ever know. And thanks of course to the Bear Lake Monsters, who are some of the best people on the planet and who love me even when I'm weird and sleep deprived.

To Josi Kilpack, Nancy Allen, Sarah Eden, Carla Kelly, Dave Lunt, Mike Davis, Bruce Leavitt, and Marion Jensen—thanks for lending me books and answering research questions. You're all smarty-pants.

Kathy Gordon, thank you for giving me the Regency bug. And Stacey Owen, thanks for working over the rough manuscript and being patient with my liberal and seemingly random usage of commas. We're a good team.

Thanks to my fantastic husband, Frank. When I told you I wanted to write a book, you got me a laptop and a stack of "how to write" books. There has never been a time when you didn't believe in me.

And of course, thanks to my boys, James, Ben, Andrew, and Joey, for understanding when Mom wants to be left alone to type. Thanks for letting me drag you to a shipyard and a naval museum on our family vacation and allowing me to nerd out. And for the great brainstorming sessions—I'm still trying to work in the character that swallows a key.

Chapter 1

AMELIA WOULD RECOMMEND WIDOWHOOD TO anyone who inquired about it, though she supposed it would perhaps be more difficult on women who had actually formed an acquaintance with and felt some affection toward their husbands. As it stood, through a proxy wedding and her new husband's untimely death before their actual meeting, Amelia was now Lady Lockwood—widow to one Lord Lawrence Walter Drake, the late Earl of Lockwood—and she could not have been more pleased.

Since her father, Admiral Becket, was regularly absent from her life—typically at sea or in London—and she had no other family, widowhood had brought with it freedom from the requisite chaperones who had always had to accompany her upon venturing into society. Her new station also delivered her from the clutches of the well-meaning yet incessant matchmakers, who were determined to find a husband for every young woman within their range of influence in Spanish Town. At the age of twenty, Amelia was now a noblewoman with an inheritance to rival nearly any lady's on the island of Jamaica. Not to mention, with her dark hair, blue eyes, and creamy complexion, she looked rather fetching in black, if she did say so herself.

Pausing in her daily inspection of her family plantation, she set her parasol upon the ground, pulled a small blade from her reticule, cut a sliver from a nearby stalk of sugarcane, and popped it into her mouth. When the sweet taste was gone, she would need to discreetly spit out the chewed pulp, and the notion that nobody would scold the earl's widow for such an unladylike action caused her to smile.

She followed the dirt path between the high stalks and up a gentle rise to a hill where she could command a better view of the fields. Turning in a slow circle, Amelia noted with approval the dark smoke rising from the cane as the dried leaves were burned in preparation for harvest.

Amelia waved as the plantation steward approached. Mr. Ramsey was a short man with dark skin and a quick smile. He used a walking stick and wore a wide-brimmed straw hat that bounced as he walked.

"I believe we shall have most of the eastern fields harvested and pressed in the next month, miss—I mean, m'lady."

"That is good news indeed, Mr. Ramsey. And I should like to also remind you of our appointment with the sugar-press builder this afternoon."

"Such a thing will undoubtedly increase our production," he said, squinting his eyes and tapping his finger on his chin.

"True. But I'd like to hear the man explain the product more clearly, to understand the merits of such an investment before we commit the funding for a new press."

Mr. Ramsey nodded his head sagely. The wide brim flapped up and down. "A wise decision." He gave a quick bow and turned to walk back down the path toward the field.

Amelia felt a surge of satisfaction. Such an early harvest would yield a high profit. Cane sugar was always in high demand by the merchants who would be leaving for Europe before winter, and the trade embargo between England and France only drove the sugar prices higher. That was something for which she could thank the emperor Napoleon.

The sound of the workers' low voices singing as they tended the crops made its way across the fields, filling her with a comforting reassurance. She'd listened to the islanders' songs since she was a child, and they were as familiar to her as the sound of the ocean waves upon the beach or the calls of tropical birds.

Though it was still shy of ten o'clock in the morning, the late summer humidity caused Amelia's dress to stick to her skin, and drops of perspiration slid down her neck. Her parasol provided a scant amount of shade but no cooling. She pulled at the fabric of her bodice. The silky crepe reminded her of the fact that she was in mourning for a man she never knew; whose name she bore; and who, even after his death, controlled her destiny.

Lawrence Drake, the late earl of Lockwood, had been a great friend of Amelia's father, which, in itself, had been reason for her reluctance to sign the legal documents attaching her to a stranger. Though such things had never been discussed in her presence, she knew the type of man her father was: a force to be reckoned with at sea, but in port, a gambler, heavy drinker, and participant in various sorts of debauchery. Luckily, the admiral's less-than-stellar reputation had little effect on Amelia, an ocean away in the colony of Jamaica, where she'd been born and raised, first by her mother, then by her housekeeper after her mother's death. Her father had been away at sea when his wife had died nearly ten years ago, and he had returned just twice to see his daughter since. She could only imagine what sort of man the late Lord Lockwood had been in order for Admiral Becket to consider him a great friend.

It had been over a year ago that the admiral had sent word, ordering (the admiral always ordered) Amelia to sit for a portrait miniature, which was immediately conveyed to him by courier to London. She'd allowed herself to entertain a small hope that perhaps her father missed her and wanted a picture of his only daughter for himself, but she should have known better.

She walked toward the main house, admiring the way the white-washed stone pillars contrasted with the green of the fields and the deep blue of the sky. The plantation was her first love, and its care constantly occupied her mind. There was still plenty of work to do today. As usual, she had ledgers to review, and then later in the afternoon, there was the meeting with the merchant and Mr. Ramsey to discuss a new sugar press. However, in the tradition of the island, she'd retire to her cool room during the harsh midday heat. Today she planned to work on a dress she was sewing to wear when her full mourning period was finished. She opened her retractable lace fan and wafted it in front of her face, stirring up a breeze as she walked.

It had been only four months after she'd sent the small likeness of herself to her father that he'd arrived personally in Jamaica with a letter of proposal and marriage documents to be signed in the presence of a magistrate. Apparently the portrait had done its job, she had thought bitterly.

Amelia had put up a protest, but as she already knew, the admiral's word was law. He had assured her that her new husband would be occupied with his commitments in India for a minimum of nine months. It was the guarantee of at least a year of freedom from suitors and match-makers and horrid debutante balls before she'd even be in the same room with her husband that, in the end, persuaded her to reluctantly accept.

When the news of Lord Lockwood's death had come only a few months later, she was ashamed at the relief she'd felt. Her father had left the next day for London—no doubt to ensure that her widow's jointure settlement would be honored based on the date of her signature. And she hadn't been at all sad to see him go. He was harsh and demanding toward her, and his presence put the servants on edge, as he had a tendency for cruelty. Amelia didn't like anything to disrupt the morale and structured way she ran the plantation. Her father had constantly attempted to usurp her authority and make changes that frustrated not only her but everyone who worked for her as well.

As she came around a bend in the road, she saw two horses standing in the shade, where her stable boy had unsaddled them. He was brushing them down as they drank from buckets of water. She waved to the boy, slightly puzzled that the merchant had arrived so early. She'd need to send someone to the eastern fields to retrieve Mr. Ramsey.

Amelia stepped through the front door, removing her straw hat from her head and her reticule from her wrist. *Well*, she thought, *this has been a fine morning for introspection*. And the conclusion she had arrived at was thus: men married for beauty, and women, for money. The idea that love might somewhere enter into the picture was purely laughable.

Chapter 2

"BLAST!" CAPTAIN SIR WILLIAM DRAKE exclaimed under his breath. He clenched his hands together behind his back as he paced around the drawing room in the plantation house. Cleaning up his brother's mistake and running errands for the admiral—this was in no respect how the captain had wanted to spend his time in port. He had a ship to outfit, repairs to attend to, supplies to catalog, and a crew of over seven hundred men—either under guard or reveling in the infamous streets of Kingston—to get shipshape and ready to sail in two days. "Where is the infernal woman?"

"Why don't you just relax, William?" Sidney Fletcher said, his tone annoyingly amused. "Stop storming about the room. And try the cakes. They're actually quite delectable."

Captain Drake glared at his first lieutenant, who leaned back in a comfortable chair, rested an ankle on his opposite knee, and looked for all the world as if this was the most pleasant day of his life. The two men had sailed together since their first voyage as cabin boys eighteen years earlier, and Sidney had no qualms about addressing William so informally, though he'd never take such liberties aboard ship.

"Sidney, must I remind you this is not a social call?" William ground his teeth together as he turned from the window. What nerve this ignorant woman had. Not only had she presumed to swoop in and usurp his inheritance, she had the audacity to keep them waiting in the blazing heat of her drawing room.

"Perhaps not, William, but I'll wager it will be months before you have the prospect of such a lovely dessert again." Sidney deliberated for a moment as he selected another pastry. Then finally choosing one, he ate it and licked the icing from his fingers with relish.

William resumed his pacing. What did he know about this woman, Amelia Becket? From what his solicitor had determined, she had received a letter of proposal from his idiot brother and signed a marriage settlement nearly six months ago. She had done everything perfectly legally, which made her deception all the more appalling. She'd undoubtedly spent months, if not years, calculating and strategizing how to perfectly execute her plan. Well, now *William* was the earl, and if she thought she was going to commandeer what rightfully belonged to his family, she was sorely mistaken. He would find a way to disinherit her and expose her marriage for the fraud it was.

In his brother's effects, he had found a miniature painting of Amelia Becket. She was lovely to be sure, but beautiful women, in William's experience, weren't to be trusted.

His brother, Lawrence, obviously hadn't shared that opinion. He'd been a rogue. That was obvious from the rumors of intrigues and the gambling debts amassed over his time as the earl. Lawrence had no doubt been in India because of his love for the exotic, and even thousands of miles away, he had managed to nearly drive the Lockwood estate into ruin—what little of it his father had not managed to ruin himself. Lawrence, perhaps thinking himself invincible, had not provided a will before his death; at least, none had been discovered. This meant that if the marriage was indeed verified, his widow was entitled to one-third of his estates for life.

Voices from the front hall caught his attention.

"Is my appointment here so soon, Mrs. Hurst?"

"No, m'lady"—at this, William clenched his fists; the woman deserved no such title—"but two men in regimentals are awaiting you in the drawing room. I delivered iced tea and cakes not ten minutes ago."

"Thank you, Mrs. Hurst. As usual, I don't know what I would ever do without you."

A dark-haired young woman dressed in a black mourning gown entered the room. Sidney stood and walked toward the doorway while William remained near the window and took a moment to study her. She had light skin and deep blue eyes that sparkled with energy as she assessed her guests. She wore her shiny dark tresses piled atop her head, though a few strands had escaped and curled around her forehead and cheeks. Her face he recognized from the miniature. The artist had done her no favors; she was much prettier in person. He chided himself for the thought, resolving not to be taken in by Amelia Becket's attractiveness as was his brother.

"Good day, officers. My father, the admiral, is away from home now. I'm sorry you made the journey inland for naught."

"We've not come to see your father, Miss Becket." William managed to keep his voice calm.

Amelia's face clouded with confusion. She looked between the men before her manners took over. Her eyes moved to the gold epaulettes on William's shoulders and then to his face. "I'm afraid we've not been introduced, Captain." She stepped forward and held out her hand. "Lady Lockwood." Her boldness was unnerving, to say the least. What sort of woman introduced herself to a gentleman? William fought to subdue his anger at the presumptive manner in which she used the title.

"Captain Sir William Drake." He gave a sharp bow.

Amelia looked at him for a moment. Her eyes darted to the black armband he wore, and he saw understanding dawn on her face. "Captain Drake." He watched her closely for any expressions of guilt but was disappointed when she had the nerve to look at him with compassion in those blasted blue eyes. "I extend my deepest condolences on the passing of your brother, Captain."

"Thank you," William said. And hearing an impertinent cough from Sidney, he continued, "And please allow me to introduce my first lieutenant, Sidney Fletcher."

"A pleasure, Mr. Fletcher." Amelia bobbed in a small curtsy as Sidney took her hand and preformed a deep and exceedingly improper bow that caused her to laugh—a lovely sound that would have made a lesser man smile. But William was not so easily taken in.

"Please, won't you sit down, gentlemen? It is not often that I receive visitors and certainly not family. I am truly delighted that you would make the journey to visit me."

"Our pleasure, my lady," Sidney said as Amelia sat and motioned for them to do likewise.

William ground his teeth at the title. He sat on the settee directly across from her, and Sidney took an armchair next to him.

"And may I pour you some iced tea?"

"Tea would be lovely," Sidney said, smiling like a simpering dolt.

Leveling a look at his first lieutenant, William cleared his throat. "This is not a social visit, Miss Becket."

Sidney settled back into his chair with his glass of cool tea, as if getting comfortable for the entertainment that was undoubtedly to follow. He looked back and forth between them, eyebrows raised, and an expression of amused anticipation on his face.

"Oh, please excuse my assumption. And do call me Amelia, Captain. We are practically brother and sister." Her smile was so charming that it nearly caught him off guard. He might have been fooled had he not known it was only an act.

William sat ramrod straight on the edge of the settee. "I shall not speak to you so familiarly, Miss Becket."

Amelia's eyes widened. She opened her mouth and closed it again, looking toward Sidney with her brow furrowed. William marveled that she was able to feign such a look of distress in her wide eyes. He was indeed dealing with a master of manipulation.

"What the captain is trying to say, my lady, is that he would prefer to become better acquainted with you before addressing you by your given name," Sidney soothed.

"That is *not* what I am trying to say. And I'd thank you to not put words in my mouth." He shot Sidney a look that would have caused any other man in his command to quake in his boots. Sidney merely smiled, raised his glass in a salute, nodded his head, and gestured for William to continue.

William turned his gaze back toward Amelia. "Miss Becket, I'll not stand on ceremony. I am here on orders from your father, the admiral, who requests your presence in London."

"Oh." Amelia lowered her glass to hold it in her lap. But not before William noticed that her hands were shaking. "And did my father say why he wants me to come to London?"

"A matter of discrepancy in your jointure inheritance. His solicitor felt the matter was of such a nature as to require the presence of all concerned parties."

Amelia was silent for a moment, looking at a spot on the wooden floor. William supposed she was most likely squirming inside, as her deception was about to be exposed. Even if Admiral Becket was his superior, he would not let the man and his daughter take advantage of him in such a manner.

She leaned forward, setting the glass on the low table in front of her. "May I ask you a question, Captain?"

William nodded his head once.

"First, I must apologize. I regret that I know nothing of your family. Am I to assume that upon the death of my husband, you are now the earl?"

"That is correct."

"Therefore, sir, if there is a discrepancy in the marriage settlement, it exists solely between your lordship and my father. I cannot imagine that my presence in London will be of any use to either party in settling this matter." Amelia stood, and the men stood with her. "If you'll forgive me, I have no desire to travel to London to be a pawn in a discussion concerning financial negotiations, as it shall be decided with or without my input." She dipped in a small curtsy. "Good day, gentlemen. And Mr. Fletcher, do come again."

Amelia turned to leave but stopped when William spoke.

"Miss Becket, I'm afraid I did not make myself clear. I did not intend for you to understand that you had any choice in the matter. In spite of our disagreement, your father is my commanding officer and I am obligated to follow his orders, which are to ensure that you indeed travel to London." William pulled an envelope from his pocket and handed it to her.

She took it and studied it for a moment, reading her name on the front side. Breaking the seal, she slid out a folded piece of paper. Amelia glanced up at the men before walking a few steps away to read the message.

After a moment, she refolded the note and turned back toward William. "Very well, sir, you may tell my father that you did your duty, and I will send my steward to book a passage from Kingston to London at my earliest convenience."

From the corner of his eye, William saw Sidney cover his mouth with his hand in effort to hold in a snicker.

William took a breath, attempting to control his irritation. "As per the admiral's orders, you are to travel aboard my ship, the HMS *Venture*."

Amelia's eyebrows shot up. "A man-of-war?" Her eyes flashed and her voice rose. "I will not travel aboard a gunship and be a target for every French battle cruiser upon the sea. There is certainly no need to remind you, Captain, that we are at war. A loaded frigate is hardly safe transportation."

Her words rang more true than William would have liked. He understood firsthand the dangers of a sea battle, and under the command of the emperor, the French had become more violent in their strategy, no longer seeking to merely capture a British ship but to annihilate it completely.

"My lady." Sidney stepped around the low table and stood next to Amelia, speaking in a gentle voice. "The French are not discriminatory about which ships they strike. Your father must be convinced that you will be safest aboard a vessel built specifically to withstand such an attack."

Amelia looked at Sidney with a small smile.

"Surely," Sidney continued diplomatically, "he is concerned only for your protection."

At his words, she looked away but not before William saw an expression of disbelief. Perhaps Amelia Becket knew the sort of man her father was. Did the admiral really mean to protect her? Or only her inheritance? For a moment William almost felt sorry for her.

She stepped away from the men, standing at the window and holding the sheer curtains aside. "Jamaica is my home." She spoke softly as she looked across the fields almost as if she had forgotten she wasn't alone. "I have no desire to leave her and the plantation; it is harvest season, and I am needed here." Turning around, she lifted her chin as she faced the men. "I am sorry, Captain, but you must convey my decision to my father. I absolutely refuse to travel to London."

"Then I am afraid I will have no alternative than to bodily force you to comply and convey you to London in chains."

Amelia's face drained of color, but she held her head high. Her eyes narrowed. "You would not dare."

"Miss Becket," William said coldly. "I think it would astonish you to find out what I would and would not dare to do."

Sidney stepped toward Amelia and took her hand, turning her slightly away from William. "My lady, the *Venture* is beautiful. The sea is calm this time of year, and it will be a delightful voyage. The Gulf Stream current will be full of dolphins and flying fish; perhaps we shall even see an iceberg in the North Atlantic. You will hardly want the journey to end once we reach London." He bowed again, to William's irritation. "I should dearly love your company."

Sidney's words had their desired effect, as Amelia's features softened.

William ground his teeth and rolled his eyes. This had already taken enough of his time. He had dreaded this encounter since reading the admiral's message in Haiti. The message had been enclosed with their new mission assignment, which was nearly as troubling in itself. "We make sail at high tide in two days. A detachment will be sent to fetch you, with orders that should you resist—"

"It shall truly be a delight to have you aboard, m'lady," Sidney spoke over the captain's words—an infraction punishable with lashings aboard ship.

She turned away from William, leaving no doubt that she was speaking only to Sidney. "I think we shall be fine friends, Mr. Fletcher. You are very gentlemanly, despite your misfortune of having a poorly mannered beast for a captain." She looked directly at William, raised one eyebrow slightly, then walked past the two men toward the door. "If you'll excuse me, I have travel preparations to make."

With that, Amelia exited the room, leaving William and Sidney staring after her.

Sidney was the first to break their astonished silence. He laughed heartily, slapping his friend on the shoulder before walking back to the low table and selecting one last finger cake. "William, I think your final voyage promises to be the most entertaining yet."

William did not appreciate the reminder that this would be his last voyage. Their course and mission assignment would be difficult enough without the added turmoil a woman aboard the ship would undoubtedly produce. He did not reply.

Chapter 3

Amelia stood at the railing of the second-story balcony and watched as a hired carriage accompanied by two marines on horseback approached the plantation house. The soldiers sat tall in the saddle; their red coats, white breeches, and black boots looked strict and official.

She turned and walked back into her bedroom, quickly glancing around to ensure that she'd not forgotten anything. Her gaze moved over her bed and the canopy of mosquito netting. She had indeed led a sheltered life, she thought, realizing that she'd slept in this very bed every night for nearly twenty-one years.

Her father's note had left no room for argument. And though it was terrifying, once she had gotten used to the idea of traveling to London, the prospect of an adventure thrilled her down to her toes. The population of colonists in Jamaica was small but growing. Not wanting their children to be deprived of British culture, the colonists raised the children with a British education—which included finishing school for the girls. But Amelia's duties at the plantation had kept her from many social events. She could not wait to meet new people in London and to learn new things.

Picking up her reticule, parasol, and straw hat, she walked out of her room and down the steps to the front hall, where the two marines stood at attention.

"Good day to you, gentlemen," she said.

The soldiers touched the brims of their hats.

"Miss Becket?" the taller of them said and, seeing her nod, continued, "Captain Drake sends his compliments."

"Thank you, sir," she replied, certain that the soldier was merely speaking out of politeness. She very much doubted the captain had thought to impart any niceties toward her. Especially since he must have instructed his men to refer to her by her maiden name, flatly refusing to acknowledge her marriage to his brother.

"Corporal Ashworth, at your service, miss." The soldier touched the brim of his hat again. Amelia noted his loose-fitting jacket hanging from narrow shoulders on a rather thin frame. The corporal was tall and quite lanky, and he moved with a stiff awkwardness. But his smile was genuine, and she couldn't help smiling back.

"And allow me to introduce Corporal Thorne." The corporal indicated his companion. Amelia turned her attention to the other soldier. Corporal Thorne was shorter and stocky. His dark eyes were set in a serious expression, and Amelia assumed he was the sort of person that spoke infrequently. Corporal Thorne touched the brim of his hat and nodded his head once smartly.

Corporal Ashworth continued. "It will be our pleasure to escort you to the HMS *Venture*, miss. If you're ready."

"Thank you, Corporals," she said, and the men stood aside. She placed her hat upon her head, tying the ribbon beneath her chin as she walked past them, out the door, and down the steps to the grassy expanse in front of the house, where the entire household staff waited to bid her farewell. The hired driver and Mr. Ramsey were attaching her trunk on to the carriage.

Mary, her lady's maid, curtsied. "Bon voyage, madame." When she looked up at Amelia, her dark brown eyes were wet. She continued in French, "I told you I would come with you." While she spoke she placed her hands over her expanding belly.

"*Merci*, Mary." Amelia felt her own throat begin to constrict. She placed her hand over Mary's. "I cannot allow your child to be born at sea. You must remain with your husband. It will be but a few months and I will return to cover this baby's cheeks with kisses."

She exchanged well-wishes and good-byes with each of the staff and finally arrived at the housekeeper, Mrs. Hurst, who was dabbing her eyes with a handkerchief. Amelia looked into the older woman's familiar face and blinked at the tears that filled her own eyes.

Mrs. Hurst pulled her into an embrace. "You'll have a lovely voyage, m'lady, and 'twill be but a short time before you're back with us."

Amelia fought the urge to break into sobs and run back into the house. Since her mother had died, the staff—and especially the housekeeper—had been her only family. An ache began to spread in her chest as she understood how much she had come to love these people. She returned the embrace, kissed Mrs. Hurst on the cheek, and squared her shoulders. Holding on to Corporal Ashworth's hand, she climbed into the open carriage and sat on the seat, arranging her skirts and opening her parasol.

The marines mounted their horses, and the carriage started forward. Amelia waved at the small group gathered in front of the house.

As they drove, her gaze traveled over the green hills, tall palm trees, and fields of sugarcane, and Amelia wondered when she would see her home again. The drive through Spanish Town was a familiar one, although the uncertainty of when she might return caused Amelia to make an effort to commit each detail to memory. The carriage passed the colonial offices; the governor's home, where balls and social events were held; and then crossed the Río Cobre on a new cast iron bridge that had been built a few years earlier.

All around were the sounds of insects keening and birds chirping and the heady perfumes of fresh flowers combined with decaying undergrowth—the sounds and smells of home. A group of native women dressed in brightly colored blouses and knee-length skirts walked in the other direction, talking and laughing. They sauntered on their bare feet with an easy grace, each carrying bunches of bananas piled high upon their heads. The women smiled and waved, and Amelia waved back. Everyone waved in Jamaica. She wondered how different it would be to travel through the streets of London.

Many of the ladies she knew traveled to England for the Season nearly every year, but Amelia had never joined them. As the war with France had continued, sea voyages had become dangerous, and the colonies had become more and more isolated. This suited Amelia perfectly. Besides, her mother had hated London, though she'd never told Amelia why. Amelia had assumed that it was because her mother loved the casual, friendly society of Jamaica, but now that she was older, she realized it was most likely because of her father and his lifestyle.

It had been surprisingly easy to get the plantation affairs in order for Amelia's abrupt departure. She was a fastidious ledger keeper, and Mr. Ramsey kept the entire operation running smoothly. It appeared that Amelia would miss the plantation more than it would miss her. And the idea made her heart sink a bit.

Her mind turned toward the ship and what awaited her on board. Or more precisely, whom. Captain William Drake reminded Amelia a great deal of her father. The captain was presumptuous and demanding, and he even walked with a similar rolling gait, as one who is more accustomed to the decks of a moving ship.

When she had seen him at her house, she'd noticed he was tall and that his broad shoulders were accentuated by the blue regimental coat. His hair was thick and dark, and his attempt at controlling it by tying it back with a leather string had little effect. But the thing that reminded her most of her father was the way the captain had looked at her. His dark eyes had been calculating, scrutinizing her words and actions for weakness. Testing her. He undoubtedly believed she had manipulated the entire marriage as a way of claiming his family's inheritance. She didn't think Captain Drake possessed the smallest bit of compassion.

It would indeed be unpleasant to spend the next few months in the company of such a man, but on a vessel carrying over seven hundred sailors, she was fairly certain she would be able to avoid the captain. Especially since he'd given every indication at their brief meeting that he would avoid her as well.

As the party neared Kingston, they encountered more people traveling toward the markets with merchandise of every kind pulled in donkey carts or piled in baskets upon their heads. The carriage rode through the crowds, finally stopping at the noisy docks, and Corporal Ashworth held her hand as she stepped out of the carriage and into the bustling crowds.

Hearing her name, Amelia turned to see the smiling face of Sidney Fletcher as he pushed through the throngs toward her. "Miss Becket," he said as he reached her, "I am so pleased that you are here."

"Thank you, Mr. Fletcher." Amelia's relief at seeing him must have been evident in her expression. She was a little annoyed that he had not called her Lady Lockwood, but she could manage being Amelia Becket for the voyage. Aboard the ship, she did not think her title would carry much weight anyway, and her father would sort out the arrogant captain soon enough.

Sidney paid the carriage driver, instructed the marines to return their horses to the livery and report to the ship, and made arrangements for Amelia's trunk. Then he offered his arm and led her toward the harbor.

Merchant ships of various types dotted the blue water, but the HMS *Venture* surpassed every other vessel, not only in sheer size, but she was quite obviously the latest advancement in nautical engineering—and the Royal Navy didn't skimp when it came to design.

"She's beautiful," Amelia said, admiring the striking wooden hull and contrasting black trim. The bulkheads on the upper deck were blue, with red-and-gold painted frames around the doors. The entire rear, or stern, of the ship was covered with windows that sparkled with the reflection from the water.

"That she is, Miss Becket. A finer ship you'll not find in the world. A feat of beauty and state-of-the-art design. It's easy to forget that she's carrying five hundred tons of artillery on her decks."

Amelia laughed at his enthusiasm. "One would think you enjoyed your life at sea, sir."

"It's true. I'm never so much at home as I am on the deck of a ship."

"It seems to me, Mr. Fletcher, that you are the type of person who possesses the temperament to be at ease wherever you are."

Sidney inclined his head in agreement, the wide smile never leaving his face. "Once you've spent some time in London, Miss Becket, I'll wager you will be longing for the smell and the feel of the sea breeze and the sound of the waves slapping against her hull. Mark my words."

They walked down the long pier and climbed into a waiting boat. Sailors manned the oars on each side of the smaller craft, and once Amelia and Sidney were aboard, the men began to row toward the magnificent vessel anchored offshore. As they neared the HMS *Venture*, Amelia could indeed see how such a ship would intimidate her enemies. Three enormous masts rose from her decks, the sails tied neatly to the "yards," or crossbars, from which they hung. Ropes supporting the mast and controlling the sails crisscrossed the main deck in a complicated but orderly pattern. From this angle, she could see the figurehead on the bow—an intricately carved and painted shield bearing the British coat of arms.

"Now comes the exciting part," Sidney said, a mischievous twinkle in his eye as they neared the hull. He pointed to the sailors on deck, busily extending cranes, which Sidney identified as davits. "They're going to raise our boat onto the ship!"

"Excuse me?" Amelia demanded, but no one paid her any attention.

Ropes were lowered from the deck above, which Sidney and a few others attached to the rowboat's sides, and the sailors on board began to haul the boat out of the water with a pulley system. Amelia closed her eyes and held on to the sides of the rowboat, afraid that if she moved, it would tip and dump all of them into the sea. The boat swung in the air, ascending steadily and finally reaching the davits, where it was secured hanging off the side of the ship.

She tried to reason how she was to cross onto the ship's deck but saw only the davits raised nearly upright.

"Now this might be a bit frightening your first time, Miss Becket. I assure you I'll not allow you to fall." Sidney helped her to stand in the swaying boat and showed her how to step around onto a davit. His foot rested on one of the evenly spaced blocks on the narrow surface, and he climbed down it like a ladder to the deck.

Amelia handed her parasol to Sidney and held on to one of the sailor's hands as he helped her gain her balance enough to step around the davit and place her foot onto a block. She made the mistake of looking down to the sea fifty feet below and closed her eyes as she clung to the wooden crane, willing her pounding heart to slow. When she was able to calm her breathing, she slid her foot down to find the next block, wishing she wasn't so encumbered by the full skirts that impeded her view of where she needed to place her feet. One more step, and she felt Sidney's hand on the small of her back, and the other sailor released his grip on her gloved fingers. Two more steps and she stood firmly on the deck of the HMS *Venture*.

She thanked the sailor who had held her hand, but he looked away rather than answer. Before Amelia had an opportunity to think much about the cold reception, Sidney led her away from the railing on the side of the ship, which he explained was called the gunwale, and told her that she was standing upon the main deck on the forecastle—the area of the deck in front of the main mast. He pointed out the companionways that led below deck and the gangways leading up to the quarterdeck, which was where the officers were typically stationed.

Although her father had spent most of his life at sea, Amelia knew little about the workings of a ship and was determined to learn more. Perhaps the knowledge would entice a bit of affection from the admiral when she arrived in London. At the very least, it might give them some common subjects to talk about.

Men and supplies continued to board the ships as a constant stream of small boats made their way to and from the shore. As she watched the ordered chaos, Amelia caught a glimpse of Captain Drake at the railing of the quarterdeck. He stood tall, his legs spread apart, his hands clasped behind his back, and his eyes surveying the crew as they made preparations for the voyage. He motioned to a young cabin boy, who ran toward him, listened for a moment, and darted off, apparently on the captain's errand. Captain Drake's gaze continued to sweep the deck and met Amelia's briefly before continuing past, not giving any further sign of recognition or acknowledgement. Amelia felt a flush heating her cheeks that he'd found her watching him.

Sidney's raised voice recaptured her attention, and she turned toward him as he continued to describe the ship over the din. "The *Venture* is one of the most powerful warships in the world, but she's also a small city. We've livestock aboard, a surgery theater, a well-stocked galley, an officers' wardroom, a schoolroom for the trainee officers, and a hold the size of a giant warehouse." His excitement was contagious, and Amelia put the captain and his superior manner from her mind.

"You're speaking as if persuading me to embark upon a leisurely voyage, Mr. Fletcher. Why the effort to convince me of the ship's merits when, as you know, I have no choice in the matter?"

"Merely to show that you will indeed enjoy the journey, no matter the circumstances that led to—"

A shrill whistle interrupted Sidney. He looked toward the quarterdeck and spoke quickly. "Please excuse me, Miss Becket. I must man my post. You'll want to remain on deck as we make sail. It's spectacular; however, portside aft will be a safer position to observe." Seeing her confused expression, he pointed to a spot to the left and close to the upper deck before he pulled on the brim of his hat and hurried off.

Amelia made her way to the corner he had indicated.

The pipes whistled shrilly again, and the quartermaster's voice called, "All hands on deck!" A thunderous pounding followed this order as hundreds of feet ran across the wooden planks. Amelia felt a moment of terror as so many wild-looking men gathered around her, but it was short-lived, as Corporal Ashworth moved closer to stand between her and the crowd.

As she peered around him, she saw that most of the men were unshaven and barefooted. Many wore no shirt. Their hair was long and dirty, and their skin was dark from hours spent in the sun. Amelia cringed away into the corner when one particularly frightening man scowled at her. It was a stark contrast between these sea dogs and the marines who wore full regimentals and stood at attention around the decks. Their job was not only to fight the enemy but also to protect the officers from the other sailors.

"Man the capstan!" the quartermaster's command boomed. Amelia watched as both sailors and marines carried heavy wooden bars and inserted them into the large circular winch on the deck. Once the bars were in place, they stuck out like spokes on a wheel. Six men manned each bar, and on the quartermaster's command—"Weigh anchor"—the men began to heave, pushing to turn the capstan slowly as the heavy anchor was raised from the ocean floor.

Amelia was thrown slightly off balance and placed a hand upon the gunwale to steady herself. Once the anchor was secured and its heavy cable properly stowed, the quartermaster called out through his blow horn, "Hands to sails!" Sailors scampered up the riggings, running gracefully along the yards, and at the quartermaster's command, they loosed the main sails, climbing and swinging and dropping from the ropes high above the decks like monkeys. Amelia was terrified at the thought of the men falling and breaking their bodies on the decks or plunging into the sea. But the sight was equally exhilarating, and she felt a rush of excitement when the wind caught the sails, bowing them out. The ship surged forward. The men cheered, and although Amelia wanted to cheer with them, she had to remember that proper young ladies didn't behave in such a manner. She was unable to stop herself from applauding, however.

The *Venture* moved down the channel through Port Royal Bay, past the location where, decades earlier, an earthquake had devastated the city. As the ship navigated through the narrow passage, Amelia's gaze moved to the mouth of the bay, where many pirates—most famously, Calico Jack—had been hanged for their crimes. She loved her island home and its strange history, and her anxiety was returning at the thought of leaving behind a place she knew so well. The ship continued south past Mosquito Point and, with that, emerged into the open sea.

The crew released more sails as the breeze quickened, and Amelia watched, craning her neck as her island home, Jamaica, the pearl of the Antilles, gradually became no more than a small mound on the horizon. A wave of homesickness washed over her. The ship rolled on the larger ocean waves, and she realized that her discomfort was not strictly limited to nostalgia. She was growing increasingly seasick.

Just as she reached this realization, she heard steps coming toward her. Turning, she saw Captain Drake approaching.

"Miss Becket, you are looking most unwell. I must insist you take to your quarters and lie down."

Even though he was completely correct, and her stomach was threatening to empty itself, the lack of compassion in his demeanor put her on the defensive.

"Indeed, Captain Drake. While I am touched by your concern for my well-being, I have no intention to retire, as I am feeling quite well." The ship pitched again, and Amelia's stomach pitched along with it.

"I assure you, my concern is for the deck of my ship and for my crew charged with keeping her in shipshape condition."

Did the man's arrogance know no bounds? Amelia felt her head spin in a wave of dizziness, and the captain grabbed her elbow.

"Your face is green, Miss Becket. I insist you take to your berth." He spoke sharply, turning to the marine next to her. "Corporal, fetch Dr. Spinner to Miss Becket's quarters."

She wrenched her arm from his grasp. "Captain, I am not in the least ill." She spoke through clenched teeth, afraid that if she opened her mouth, the contents of her stomach would make a most unwelcome appearance. In a manner that she hoped appeared casual, she rested her hand against the netting of hammocks lining the rail of the ship. But truthfully, besides her determination not to allow the captain to order her about, the netting was the only thing holding her up.

Amelia nearly swooned with relief as Sidney Fletcher hurried toward them. "Miss Becket, are you unwell?" He held her elbow in the same manner as had Captain Drake a moment before, and Amelia leaned against him. "Will you allow me to escort you to your quarters then?"

"Thank you, Mr. Fletcher. That would be most welcome. How very gentlemanly of you." She looked at Captain Drake and narrowed her eyes.

A slight smile tugged at the corner of the captain's lips, and Amelia found that it infuriated her. But when she opened her mouth to tell him so, her stomach betrayed her, and she was horrified to see her breakfast splatter over Captain Drake's shiny boots.

Amelia and Captain Drake stared at each other in disbelief for one mortifying instant before she felt her stomach clench again and pressed her gloved hands against her mouth.

"A bucket!" Captain Drake bellowed.

Luckily the bucket arrived just in time, and Sidney held it as Amelia heaved into it. He lowered her gently onto the deck, with the bucket in her lap. She accepted his offered handkerchief and wiped her mouth with a trembling hand. "Captain, I'm so dreadfully sorr—"

But the captain ignored her and continued to shout for a crew to swab the deck and someone to find a cabin boy to clean his boots. Amelia hung her head over the bucket, waiting for the next wave of nausea to overtake her. She was too weak to fight back the tears of embarrassment. She hoped Captain Drake would just forget about her and leave her to her humiliation, but she heard his voice once again. "Lieutenant Fletcher, see to it that Miss Becket remains in her quarters until such time as she is no longer a threat to the cleanliness of this ship."

Amelia heard the captain's footsteps as he left, presumably to change his boots, and when she felt well enough to stand, she permitted Sidney to lead her down the companionway and to her quarters on the deck below.

Chapter 4

THE MORNING AFTER THE HMS *Venture* set sail, Captain William Drake leaned over the table spread with rolls of maps, charts, and navigational instruments in the captain's sitting room. He had called a council of the lieutenants to discuss the particulars of the voyage. Some of the officers were gathered around the table; others stood or sat on the captain's sofa or wingback chairs. Sidney sat on one of the padded bench seats that ran beneath the windows covering the stern end of the room. The men looked up as a knock sounded and Riley, a young cabin boy, entered.

"Sorry to disturb you, Captain; I've finished polishing your boots."

From the corner of his eye, William saw a few of the officers steal glances at one another, each maintaining a straight face, but the captain was certain the years of discipline in the British military was the sole reason they were able to contain their grins.

He gritted his teeth in irritation as he took the boots from Riley.

"And is there anything else you'll be needing, Captain?"

"No."

"Aye, aye, sir," Riley said, saluting energetically as he turned to leave.

William felt a swell of affection for the boy. Riley was a reminder of himself eighteen years earlier, when he had signed on as a cabin boy on his first voyage at the age of ten.

"Master Riley?"

"Aye, Captain."

"Well done. I imagine it wasn't a pleasant chore."

A noise resembling a muffled cough came from Sidney's direction, but William ignored it and continued talking to the cabin boy. "You did a fine job."

Riley's face broke into a grin. "Thank you, Captain."

When the cabin boy had left, William turned his attention back to the map spread on the table.

"And, Captain, what is your opinion of this curious route?" Sidney asked.

William looked at the men spread around the room before he answered. Each of these men trusted him, had sailed with him for years, and had fought alongside him. They would follow him to the ends of the earth, yet he saw unease in many of their eyes.

"My opinion, Mr. Fletcher, is that the Lords of Admiralty, in consultation with the cabinet, dispatched the orders, setting our course and assigning our mission. It's not my job to have an opinion."

"But the Bay of Biscay brings us within an easy distance of France. And the entire French navy. We've no armada for support. Surely there has been a mistake."

Lieutenant Wellard spoke up. "We always follow the north Atlantic Gulf Stream. In all my years at sea, I've never seen such a course as this one. And to pass through enemy waters seems folly. It shall be nearly impossible not to encounter any French ships in their own territory. Even with the blockades in place, we will certainly meet runners."

William looked at Lieutenant Wellard. Though lower in rank, the lieutenant was well experienced, and the captain trusted his judgment. "True, Mr. Wellard. It's not the typical route. I can only assume the admiralty has a reason for laying this course. And speculation as to their purpose will do us no good."

Lieutenant Wellard nodded his head in acceptance.

"And as for the French navy," Captain Drake continued with a smirk, "not only do we have superior weaponry and warship, but the discipline of the British military is second to none. The best strategy is to continue to train these sailors and marines for the inevitable."

The men agreed, nodded, and began discussing their drill schedules for the upcoming week.

Sidney remained lost in thought, not participating in the discussions but staring out the stern window.

"And are we in agreement then, Mr. Fletcher?"

"Aye, aye, Captain," Sidney replied in a dull voice. His face remained impassive, and William knew his old friend well enough to recognize his apprehension.

When William dismissed the officers, Sidney had asked to have a private word with the captain—as William knew he would.

"I'll speak plainly, Captain. This appears to me to be a trap or a ploy of some sort; I suspect there is a piece to the scheme that we have not been made privy to."

"Be that as it may, Mr. Fletcher, as soldiers, it is our duty to follow orders."

Sidney began to pace. He ducked his head to avoid a hanging lantern and stopped at the table, studying the map for a moment before jabbing his finger at the area in question. "This course comes at the end of our voyage, when we are most vulnerable. Not to mention the unpredictability of the seas this time of year. We could hardly find a more dangerous situation if we sought it. I suspect for whatever reason, we're being unwittingly played as a decoy."

"You believe we are being sent to our doom by our government? That the Lords of Admiralty intend to sacrifice the lives of nearly eight hundred men and an expensive warship?"

"I'm saying it doesn't sit right with me. The orders are—"

William's voice was a growl as he cut off what Sidney was going to say. He stepped closer. "I suggest, Mr. Fletcher, that you lower your voice lest we both find ourselves accused of insubordination or even treason."

"Aye, aye, Captain." Sidney forced his eyes away from the map and, letting out a deep breath, schooled his features into his characteristic jovial expression. His lips curled in a smirk. "I wouldn't want anything to prevent your lordship from assuming your position as the earl. It would be a pity for the House of Lords session to commence without Lord Lockwood in attendance."

William let out a groan and rubbed his eyes. "You know I have no aspirations to such a thing. I would much rather be fighting a losing battle with the French than sitting in Parliament."

Sidney placed his hand on William's shoulder, and his eyes sparked with mischief. "I have a feeling, sir, that notwithstanding the French, your final voyage as captain of the HMS *Venture* will indeed be memorable. Why, a lovely young lady and a certain pair of boots have already made it most unforgettable."

"Why must you bring up that woman?" William scowled and walked to the window. "Miss Becket is insolent and stubborn, to say the least. You saw how she defied my order to retire to her berth, even when she was so ill that she could barely stand."

"Yes, she is stubborn. But you must know that a woman responds more favorably to a polite suggestion than a direct order."

"I am the captain, and as long as she is aboard my ship, I expect her to follow orders."

Sidney had the audacity to laugh. "Captain, you are in for a long, miserable voyage if you cannot understand how to behave toward a woman."

"I *know* how to behave toward a woman."

"Threatening to kidnap her if she refuses to sail with you, then once she's aboard your ship, telling her she looks sickly and demanding that she get to her quarters? This is not the way to a lady's heart, sir." William could tell Sidney was jesting, but there was an undercurrent of truth in the subtle reprimand, which served only to make William more defensive.

"I'm not interested in Miss Becket's heart. I only want her to remain as far away from me *and my boots* as possible until we are in London and I am able to discredit her claim to my brother's jointure."

Sidney raised his eyebrows, surprised. "You must realize how difficult this is for her. She has left a home she loves, a veritable paradise." He picked up a mango from a bowl of fruit on the sideboard and held it out toward William for emphasis. "She has never been to sea before. She does not know what will happen when she reaches London. Her future is unpredictable, and to make matters worse, she is at the moment lying on a pallet on her cabin floor, since the doctor deemed her too ill to even rest comfortably in her hammock."

William felt a twinge of guilt that he didn't like one bit. Just because he entertained unpleasant feelings toward the woman was no reason not to treat her well while she was under his care. She wouldn't be able to hold it over him or claim that he had not acted like a perfect gentleman when they reached London. And then he would see to it that Miss Becket relinquished her claim to his family, and he would wash his hands of her permanently.

Chapter 5

It was two days later when Amelia awoke and felt a curious sensation in her stomach. The constant nausea was replaced by the welcome rumblings of hunger pains. Tentatively she sat up on the pallet Dr. Spinner had procured for her and waited for the dizziness that had plagued her. But the light-headedness was conspicuously absent.

Dr. Spinner had attended her regularly, and she was grateful for his ministrations and the ginger tea he had brought, which had been the only thing that her stomach hadn't rejected.

She stood and walked to the small basin of water the doctor had left for her, and with a cloth she cleaned herself as completely as she was able. It felt wonderfully refreshing to wash off the sticky sweat and smells of sickness. She dressed in a fresh gown and brushed her hair, fastening it in place on top of her head.

A small mirror hung on the wooden bulkhead above her traveling trunk, and she stepped around the cannon, which occupied the majority of the space in the small cabin, to peer at her reflection. Aside from a bit of paleness, she was pleased to see that she looked much the same as she had before she had taken ill.

Once she was presentable and her cabin straightened as much as possible, Amelia felt a bout of indecision. If she went in search of breakfast, she might happen upon Captain Drake. The memory of their last encounter filled her with the deepest embarrassment. She couldn't get the image out of her mind of the shocked and repulsed expression he'd worn as he had watched her befoul his boots. But what was her other option? She couldn't hide in her cabin for the next few months. Finally, her hunger made the decision for her.

With a fair amount of trepidation, she opened her door and peeked out.

Corporal Ashworth stood outside her door. When he saw her, he thrust his rifle to arm's length in front of him and then pulled it back to his shoulder quickly, snapping his heels together.

"Good morning, Corporal," Amelia said. "Do you know where I might find something to eat?"

"If you're feeling better, miss, I'm to show you to the officers' wardroom. You'll find Dr. Spinner there, taking his breakfast."

"Thank you." Amelia followed the marine, grateful for the railings on the sides of the wet stairs in the companionway. The boots she wore had a difficult time finding any traction, and she slipped more than once.

Corporal Ashworth stopped outside the door when they reached the wardroom. He again presented his rifle and clicked his heels as he took up his position.

"Aren't you coming in, Corporal?"

"No, miss. Aside from the surgeon, only commissioned officers eat in the wardroom. But I assure you, you'll be quite safe."

Amelia smiled, amused at the corporal's assumption that she was afraid. "I thank you for your concern."

"Just following orders, miss."

And what orders might those be? she wondered.

A few officers and Dr. Spinner were seated at the large table that took up nearly the entire room. They stood when she stepped inside.

"Miss Becket." Dr. Spinner stepped toward the door. He escorted her to the table and held a chair out for her. "I am so pleased to see that you are feeling better." Dr. Spinner was probably near the same age as Amelia's father. His gray hair was beginning to thin on his crown, and he wore it pulled back and tied at the nape of his neck. His thick glasses magnified his eyes, giving him the appearance of someone who was constantly surprised.

"Thank you, Doctor," Amelia said.

Once she was seated, he introduced her to the other men who sat around the table, and while they exchanged greetings, a steward placed a basket of biscuits and a plate of eggs and sausage in front of her.

The officers returned to their meals, and the silence was uncomfortable, as if they had been interrupted by Amelia's arrival and now hesitated to return to their former conversations. They had removed their gold-buttoned blue coats and hung them upon the backs of their chairs. Many of them had loosened their collars and rolled up their sleeves, but the mood of the room was definitely not in accordance with the men's casual appearance. Amelia felt as though her presence had made them self-conscious.

As the daughter of an admiral, she was aware that many sailors considered it bad luck to have a woman aboard the ship. It would probably take some time for the men to feel at ease with her, but it would be a long, awkward voyage if everyone aboard continued averting their eyes and avoiding her company.

Amelia picked up a biscuit from the basket. She noticed the officers hitting their biscuits against their plates before biting into them. When she asked Dr. Spinner about it, he explained. "A few solid raps should shake out any weevils making their home in the biscuits."

She looked closer at the doctor, trying to judge whether he was joking, but the eyes behind his thick glasses were serious. Amelia examined her biscuit and hit it against her plate, watching to see if anything tumbled out before she was finally satisfied and took a small bite. If she hadn't been so hungry, the idea of weevils in her food would have banished her appetite. As it was, she found that even though the hard biscuits were bland, a bit of marmalade made them quite palatable. The eggs tasted fresh and warm, but she avoided the sausage. Her stomach was not ready for such a thing. "Dr. Spinner, tell me how you came to be on the crew of the HMS *Venture*?"

The doctor pressed his cloth napkin against his mouth before he replied. "It was nearly four years ago, during the battle of Cape Ortegal. I served aboard the HMS *Euphrates* with Captain Drake, although at the time he was still Lieutenant Drake."

Amelia noticed the other men in the room listening, some of them nodding as if they remembered.

Dr. Spinner continued. "In an altercation with a French battleship, the captain was hit by a round shot and killed. Lieutenant Drake assumed command immediately. It was his strategy to lure the French ship within the range of a British squadron under the pretense of fleeing. In the heat of a spectacular battle, Captain Drake led the charge, boarding the ship, and after fierce fighting, the French ship was defeated.

"During the battle, Captain Drake was wounded on the shoulder by a bayonet but refused to leave his men and retreat for medical care. He lost so much blood that he nearly died. Lieutenant Drake not only retained his promotion to captain but was knighted by the prince for his bravery."

Dr. Spinner reached out and lifted his wooden cup. "I treated his wound directly after the battle, and weeks later when he had fully recovered, Captain Drake sought me out and requested that I be the surgeon aboard his ship, the *Venture.* And after sailing under him, I shall never sail under another."

Amelia tried to imagine Captain Drake fighting in a sea battle with a bleeding shoulder wound and found it was not too difficult. Whatever her other feelings toward the captain were, the idea that he lacked courage had never entered her mind.

"I have heard of the Battle of Cape Ortegal, of course, but I had no idea Captain Drake was involved," she said.

"He was more than involved, Miss Becket. It is the opinion of many, including myself, that the captain is responsible for the eventual shift and victory in the battle of Trafalgar."

She considered this appraisal of Captain Drake. He was a war hero; however, that didn't make him any more likeable. But she felt that she was alone in her opinion. And did the captain's dislike for Amelia affect the other officers' opinions of her? Or were they just unaccustomed to a woman aboard the ship? Amelia tried to engage some of them in conversation. They answered politely enough, but their discomfort was still evident. She pursed her lips in frustration.

She finally turned back to the surgeon. "Dr. Spinner, I thank you again for the care you gave me these past days. I truly appreciate it, and the ginger tea was the perfect thing to soothe an uneasy stomach."

"You can thank the captain for the tea. He insisted it would help, although I myself do not hold to such outdated remedies."

"Perhaps the captain hopes for his boots to smell like ginger when we next meet," Amelia said.

One of the officers snickered, followed by another, and when Amelia giggled, the entire room erupted in hearty laughter. The interactions between Amelia and the officers throughout the remainder of the breakfast meal became much friendlier, and it didn't take long before they were telling her their own stories and asking about her home in Jamaica.

Amelia began to think that it might be possible to win the favor of her shipmates and change the reputation that she had unfortunately earned in her first hour on the decks. The first order of business, however, would be to convince them that she was an asset instead of just the admiral's spoiled daughter.

The sound of the ship's bell ringing eight times sent the officers grabbing their jackets, tying their cravats, and hurrying to their second watch duties. Amelia left the wardroom with Dr. Spinner.

"How are you planning to spend the rest of the day?" The doctor asked her as they walked toward the companionway stairs.

Corporal Thorne had replaced Corporal Ashworth outside the door. He presented arms in a salute, and Amelia waved to him before she answered. "I'll admit I hadn't given much consideration to how I'd pass my time aboard. I should very much like to learn more about the workings and management of the ship. And to assist in any way I am able. Perhaps I'll venture—"

Her words were cut off when they encountered a group of sailors hurrying down the stairs. Two men were being carried as gently as possible by their companions. Based on the pained looks on the faces of the men being carried, they were injured.

"What happened?" asked the doctor, checking one man's leg.

"Rope snapped," a sailor answered, grunting under the weight of his injured shipmate. "Loose barrels smashed into the two of them."

"They'll both need to be conveyed to the operating theater immediately." Dr. Spinner led the group down the stairway.

Amelia watched them for a moment, and when she turned to continue to the upper decks, she saw a boy with his hand pressed against his other arm, looking disoriented. Blood seeped between his fingers and dripped onto the deck. She rushed to him and put her hand on his shoulder to steady him. "You've been hurt too."

The boy's expression was confused.

She gently pulled his hand away to reveal a deep gash. Amelia began to lead him carefully down the stairs, following the same direction the doctor had taken. "Do you know where the operating theater is?" she asked Corporal Thorne, who stood in the companionway.

"Orlop deck, aft," he answered. "Follow me."

"Come," she said to the boy. "Dr. Spinner will mend your arm right away."

The orlop deck, it turned out, was below the lower gun deck. And also below the waterline. With no windows for light, the deck was cast in shadow. When they all arrived in the operating theater, the doctor was splinting one of the injured men's legs. The other man lay upon a table. Swaying lanterns hung from the ceiling, giving the room its only light.

"Dr. Spinner," Amelia said. "This boy has been injured."

The doctor looked up for a moment. "Have him sit. And apply pressure to his wound. I'll tend to him when I've finished with these two."

Amelia led the boy to an overturned half barrel that sat against a bulkhead. She helped him sit. She searched the room and returned with a clean-looking rag, which she pressed against his arm. Sitting on a barrel next to him, she studied his face for a moment. He was quite pale, and she worried that he was in danger of fainting. He looked so young, and she determined to remain nearby to care for him.

"What is your name?" she asked him.

The boy looked at her blankly for a moment before his eyes focused. "Riley."

"My name is Amelia Becket. Pleased to meet you."

"Miss Becket. You . . ." He seemed to be searching for words. "The captain's boots . . ."

Amelia laughed. "Yes, one of my more humiliating moments. Thank you for reminding me, Master Riley."

His mouth turned up in a weak smile. "Just Riley, miss."

"Then you must call me Amelia." She moved the cloth and checked his injury. It was dark and quite deep. It still bled but not nearly as heavily as before. She'd had some experience treating wounds on the plantation and knew that one of the things she should be most concerned about was the boy losing consciousness.

"Riley, I think your wound will probably require stitches." Seeing his face get even paler, she continued. "Did you know that Captain Drake had an injury on his shoulder? Similar to yours, I would imagine. And Dr. Spinner stitched it up for him so nicely that the captain asked him to be the surgeon aboard this ship."

Riley blinked and raised his eyebrows. "Is that true?"

"True as I'm sitting here. I heard it from the doctor himself." She put her finger in front of her lips and leaned closer, as if to share a confidence. "And though a proper lady would never speak of such a thing, I myself required stitches once." She lifted her curls and pointed to a scar on her hairline.

Riley's eyes moved to her forehead.

"The scar is quite faint now, but at the time, it bled so much that my mother was convinced I would die before we could reach the doctor." Amelia proceeded to tell him about the day she had taken one of the worker's machetes, determined to harvest some of the sugarcane herself.

The machete had become stuck in a heavy stalk, and she had pulled so hard that when it was finally freed, the handle had struck her in the head. "Luckily I was not strong enough to injure myself very severely," she said.

When the doctor finished setting the broken limbs, Amelia watched as he sutured Riley's wound. Dr. Spinner complimented her on the fact that she hadn't broken down into hysterics upon seeing the blood. Amelia laughed at the notion. She had seen plenty of injuries among the workers who harvested the sugarcane with sharp blades. While she helped the doctor clean the injury, she distracted Riley with more stories of Jamaica.

"In the evening, the entire sky fills with bats. When I was young, my grandfather and I would sit outside on the balcony and watch them flitting through the sky."

Riley looked wistful. "The other ship's boys and I did not go ashore while we were in port. Captain Drake said Kingston was not the place for young gentlemen."

"That was quite sensible of him, Riley. I think the captain kept you out of a great deal of trouble. I myself have only been to Kingston a handful of times, though it is merely an hour away from my home outside of Spanish Town."

She asked the doctor questions about the placement of and distance between stitches, and seeing her interest in the procedure, he showed her how to tie off the knots and cut the thread between each individual stitch. With Riley's permission, the doctor even allowed her to apply the last two sutures. Amelia did her best to keep her hands from shaking, as she was sure each stitch caused the boy pain.

When the doctor was finished, Amelia took Riley's damaged shirt to wash out the blood and repair the tear.

All three patients had been given doses of laudanum for their pain and now rested comfortably. The men were moved to the sick bay, and Riley was taken to his berth with orders to sleep for the remainder of the day. He could return to his duties in the morning.

Amelia felt satisfaction in the fact that she had found a way to be useful. She determined to assist the crew in any way she could and banish any notions of her bringing bad luck to the voyage.

Amelia helped the doctor rinse the blood out of the shirt and rags, hang them to dry, and put away the medication in the dispensary cabinet. When they finished, it was nearly time for their midday meal. Dr. Spinner escorted her up the companionway. They were followed again by Corporal Thorne, who took up his post outside the wardroom with his usual display of ceremony.

As Amelia entered the room, she was delighted to see Sidney Fletcher among the officers seated around the table. He bounded toward her with a pleased smile and grasped her hand with both of his.

"Miss Becket, it is wonderful to see you back in good health."

"Thank you, Mr. Fletcher."

"The men have been telling me what a delight it was to eat breakfast with you this morning. I am disappointed that my duties kept me away."

Amelia smiled at the lieutenant's contagious good humor and allowed herself to be led to the table. She exchanged greetings with some of her new friends before Sidney captured her attention again.

"You recovered just in time." Sidney said. "This afternoon we shall have quite a show. You won't want to miss it."

Amelia tipped her head, trying to think of what he might mean. "What kind of show might I expect to see aboard a British man-of-war, Lieutenant?"

Sidney's eyes glinted. "A full gun-training drill."

Chapter 6

William stood on the quarterdeck next to the helm. A glance at the compass in the binnacle box assured him that the quartermaster was keeping to course. The captain walked to the railing that overlooked the main deck and then turned, his eyes landing upon the large gold letters painted upon the afterpart of the quarterdeck: *England expects every man to do his duty.* The words appeared on every ship that was with Admiral Nelson at Trafalgar, and it was the motto by which William directed his crew.

He was reluctant to admit it, but he had thought often of Sidney's concerns the past few days. Their orders and the course laid for the voyage were so unusual that he worried about what the Lord Admirals had in mind when they assigned the *Venture*'s mission. Was Captain Drake's ship being used as a decoy? Were they sailing toward certain death? The responsibility for the men under his command weighed heavily on him. The importance of the gun drills became even more crucial as he wondered what dangers they would encounter. The best way to ensure the safety of the ship and the men was to drill until there was no doubt as to their capability in battle. The men needed to know precisely where to go and what to do and to work seamlessly together in a manner that could be achieved only by practice.

As William watched the deck, Sidney emerged from the companionway with Miss Becket. She opened a light yellow parasol and held it as she pointed and gestured with her hand. She appeared to be asking Sidney questions, which he answered in his usual animated fashion. Watching her, William perceived genuine interest in her inquiries and the explanations Sidney gave. She seemed to consider his answers before asking another question, and William wondered what it was that she found so interesting.

But he didn't allow himself to wonder for long. He signaled to the boatswain, who sounded the bell five times and then repeated the pattern. A marine began to beat his drum, and the boatswain called the order, "Hands to quarters!" The command was repeated and called down the companionways until the ship erupted into action.

William watched as Sidney quickly led Miss Becket to the portside aft corner and under the overhanging deck, out of the way of the guns and the traffic. The officers moved purposefully toward their assigned positions, but he noticed many sailors moving slowly or hesitating as the gun decks were cleared. Some appeared to be waiting for instruction, and in the heat of battle, there was no time to think. William ground his teeth, frustrated.

He knew that the lieutenants would be supervising the dismantling and stowing of the panels that separated the cabins on the lower levels. Ship's boys ran over the wooden planks, sprinkling sand from buckets to keep the sailors from slipping on sweat or blood while they hauled the huge cannons back and forth.

Each cannon required a crew of six men to prime, load, aim, and fire. A boy was assigned to each crew as a powder monkey, running the cartridges of gunpowder from the handling chamber deep in the hull of the ship. The powder was carefully passed through damp curtains to guard against sparks and then carried to the gun crew as cautiously and quickly as possible.

William waited on the top deck until each lieutenant's runner had reported that their guns were loaded and battle stations ready. Once he was satisfied, William gave the order to the boatswain, who cried, "Up ports!" The noise of chains being cranked to raise the coverings of the gun ports sounded throughout the ship. "Run out!" yelled the boatswain, and any further noise was drowned out by the thundering of ninety-eight cannons rolling across the decks until their muzzles protruded from the sides of the ship.

William waited until the noise stopped then turned to where Sidney watched for his signal. "Mr. Fletcher," he called. "Portside." The men on the left of the ship tensed. "Open fire, first division!"

Sidney yelled to his crews, "Stand clear!" then "Fire!" The men simulated the noise of a cannon, yelling, "BOOM!" and immediately pulled their guns back to swab them out and reload.

"Open fire, second division!" called the captain, and for the next hour, the officers called orders and sent runners to the captain with their reports. The men grunted as they pulled the cannons back and forth, and boys ran up and down the companionways.

William watched for mistakes and speed and made note of the crews who needed extra practice.

He walked down to the gun decks, noting the clumsiness of some of the crews as well as the apologies of the officers in charge of their companies.

Sidney yelled at a sailor, "Swab out that cannon completely, man. Do you want your hand to get blown off when you reload?"

William knew it would be important to modify the drills, perhaps blocking a section of the companionway or pulling men off their guns to simulate losses and prepare them for any eventuality. Today he had gotten an idea of how the sailors would handle a battle, and despite the fact that all the officers were experienced, most of the crew had fought in few, if any, altercations. There was quite a lot of work to be done to get this crew trained.

When the call of "Cease fire, all!" finally came, the men sagged in relief and began to put the ship back together. After supper, William would need to discuss with the lieutenants the shortcomings he had spotted. The drill had left him feeling discouraged and anxious about their safety in battle.

As he pondered on this, his attention was captured by Miss Becket, standing in her position at portside aft, and for a moment his anxiety spread to include her. How would he protect her in a battle? He quickly banished the thought, angry at himself for even entertaining it in the first place.

His father would have chastised him for his weakness in worrying for a woman. The entire reason his father sent him to sea in the first place was because of William's worry for his mother and newborn sister. His mother was so often the object of his father's harshness, and one particular night, William had tried to defend her during his father's drunken rampage. He had been too young to do anything but enrage his father, and the next day, William found himself on his way to London, apprenticed to a captain on a ship sailing for Australia.

He gritted his teeth, angry for letting himself stew in old memories. He hadn't realized he was still watching Miss Becket until he saw her standing on her toes, trying to see over the high breastwork of the gunwale to the sea below. She looked around with an expression of frustration and, seeing a line of rigging, grabbed hold of it and stepped onto the ropes. She only climbed a few feet off the deck, but she was on the windward side of the ship. A strong gust would take her into the ocean. And William hadn't given her permission to go aloft. It was time this woman learned who gave the orders on this ship. Where was the corporal assigned to her? William stormed down from the upper deck and marched toward her.

"Miss Becket, what exactly do you think you are doing?"

She looked toward him. Her blue eyes sparkled with excitement. "Captain, there are dolphins in—"

"I demand that you get down from there at once. This is hardly how a lady behaves." He was well aware that his anger was completely out of line, but his frustration over the drill and the feelings dredged up by thoughts of his father were only intensified by Miss Amelia Becket and her insubordinate attitude. He reached up his hand to assist her, but she glanced at it and then looked pointedly at him. The delight in her eyes was replaced by coldness. She pressed her lips together and raised her eyebrow in her infuriating fashion before stepping down without his aid.

"It was my understanding, Captain, that the entire reason I am aboard your ship is to be transported to London in order for you to prove that I am not worthy of that title." She picked up her parasol from where it leaned against the breastwork and walked back toward the companionway, catching herself as she slipped on the newly cleaned deck, once again leaving William completely speechless.

He stood for a moment, watching her storm away before he went after her, calling her name but having to repeat himself before she turned.

Her eyes were damp, and for a moment he wondered if she had been upset by his reprimand. He quickly pushed aside his surge of guilt.

"Miss Becket, I'd appreciate it if you would remain in your cabin tonight. We're in for a storm . . . I'd say in about four hours."

She cast her eyes around the skies, finally settling on a collection of clouds in the distance. "And how can you tell, Captain?"

"The barometer has dropped," he said, though it was only part of the reason. How could he explain that after eighteen years at sea, he could sense a storm as accurately as any instrument? "A storm at sea can be frightening. If you would prefer to remain in my sitting room, I will assign some officers to attend you."

"I am not afraid of a little rain, Captain. But I thank you for your concern." Her eyes lifted to his, and he couldn't help but notice how blue they were. The bright blue of the Mediterranean in full sun. And the lashes framing them were dark and thick. *Where are these thoughts coming from?*

"If you change your mind . . ."

"I shan't. Good afternoon, Captain." She dipped in a slight curtsy before turning and walking down the companionway.

"Good afternoon, Miss Becket."

Chapter 7

Amelia lay upon the narrow mattress, bracing herself as well as she could as the hammock swung back and forth in her cramped quarters. The captain had been mistaken when he'd said a storm at sea was frightening.

It was absolutely terrifying.

The ship tipped back and forth like a toy on the water. Amelia had found herself thrown from one side of the cabin to the other and had finally climbed into her hammock to avoid crashing into the cannon or falling against the wall.

She had endured many tropical storms in Jamaica and even a hurricane, but nothing could have prepared her for this. Her cabin was pitch-black. Water leaked through the edges of the port opening in the bulkhead, dripping on Amelia, her nightclothes, and her bedding. The ship creaked and groaned with every wave that smashed into her. Every sound convinced Amelia that the ship would sink. The sounds of men yelling, sails flapping, and objects shifting on the decks became suddenly loud then muted and silenced as another wave hit the ship. And on top of it all, she was sick again, but this time there was no nicely placed bucket next to her nor a pot of warm ginger tea.

Endless hours passed before the sea tired of pummeling the *Venture*. The waves remained choppy, but finally the constant sound of rain beating against the hull lulled Amelia into a restless sleep, where her dreams were haunted by maggoty biscuits, cannon blasts, and a handsome captain swinging a sword while his shoulder bled.

She was awakened by a knock at her cabin door. "Miss Becket—Amelia? It's Riley, miss."

She looked around, realizing that the sun was shining through the gap in the edges of the porthole cover. Awkwardly scrambling out of her hammock, she opened her trunk and found a wrapping to cover her damp nightclothes. "One moment, Riley." She quickly looked into the mirror and saw that her hair was partly wet and resembled a rat's nest. Her red, swollen eyes indicated that she must have been crying at some point during the night. She was pale and had been sick. Though she'd attempted to clean herself up, her appearance—and she suspected her smell—definitely left much to be desired.

Smoothing down her hair, she opened the door a bit and saw Riley standing next to Corporal Thorne.

"If you please, miss. Captain sent me to inquire after you."

Amelia felt a rush of warmth in her cheeks as she remembered that moments earlier she had been dreaming about Captain Drake. "You may tell the captain that I am quite well. Thank you, Riley."

The boy's glance strayed to her hair, but he wisely said nothing about her appearance. "The storm, it hit us something fierce, and Captain thought you might like some fresh rain water to wash your clothes and take a bath." Riley's face colored as he said his last words. He stepped aside and indicated a large half-barrel tub behind him. "The cook's heating up some water, and he'll send it straight away."

Amelia thought there was nothing on the earth that had ever sounded as wonderful to her as the idea of a hot bath did right that instant. She opened her door wide, and Riley rolled the tub into her cabin and set it upright. He pulled a sheet of linen sail into her room, and she helped him use it to line the inside of the tub.

She fetched Riley's repaired shirt from her trunk and gave it to him. Then the two of them sat upon the trunk as Corporal Thorne supervised the men carrying bucketful after bucketful of hot water to pour into the tub.

"Riley, please tell Captain Drake how much I appreciate this."

"I shall, miss. And thank you again for mending my shirt. I would have done a poor job myself."

"Your injury—is it still painful?" she asked.

"It's tolerable." He lifted his chin higher.

"Spoken like a true hero, Riley." Amelia winked at him, and he smiled. She bid him good-bye and closed the door behind him.

Hearing a quick knock, she opened the door again and took the thick chunk of soap Riley handed her.

Amelia spent the morning soaking in a hot bath, washing her hair, her clothing, and her bedding. She combed her wet hair and pulled it back in a braid to dry. She dressed and was about to pull on her ribbon-laced boots when she remembered how often she had slipped on the wet decks and stairs the day before. All of the sailors she had seen—and even some of the officers—walked the decks in bare feet. Feeling brave and a bit defiant, she pulled off her stockings and put them back into her trunk. No one would even notice with her long skirts. The wood was smooth beneath her feet, and her heart skipped at the thought that she was doing something so scandalous. *What would the stodgy matchmakers in Spanish Town think?*

When Amelia emerged from her cabin, she felt like a new woman and vowed never to take the simple pleasure of a hot bath for granted again. She set off to find some breakfast but, upon discovering the wardroom empty, asked Corporal Ashworth to direct her to the galley.

She entered the large kitchen and saw various men working throughout the area. One man cut meat with a cleaver, and another cooked the smaller pieces on a stove. Two men peeled potatoes, and some boys were in the process of counting biscuits and separating them into buckets. Amelia asked a boy for a biscuit, which he happily gave her. She sat on a stool and rapped the bread on the wooden table before eating it.

A man with a peg leg and a dirty apron stretched across his belly limped over to her.

Amelia hesitated for a moment. Propriety would dictate that a lady should not speak to a man to whom she had not been properly introduced, but in the circumstances, she decided not to stand upon ceremony.

"Good morning, sir," she said, waving at him.

"I suppose ya must be Miss Becket," he said with a smile that exposed a mouth full of missing teeth. "Oliver Crenshaw, head cook. But ya can call me Slushy. Everyone does."

"It's nice to meet you. I wanted to thank you for heating water for me this morning. I cannot tell you how much it was appreciated."

"It was no trouble at all, miss."

Amelia looked around the large kitchen. "I was just noticing how very orderly your galley is managed. It must be an enormous undertaking to feed so many men each day."

"I thank ya, Miss Becket." Slushy beamed, and his neck reddened. "These lads finding ya all what ya need?"

"Yes, thank you. I was just after a biscuit."

"Feel free to help yerself. 'Tis a true pleasure to have a lady aboard, and yer welcome in my galley anytime ya like."

"Thank you, sir."

"Not sir. 'Twouldn't do. Just Slushy." She noticed now that the redness had spread to his cheeks.

"And do you have time to show me around the galley, Slushy?"

"'Twould be my pleasure, miss."

Amelia followed Slushy and saw the racks where the cheese was kept; the tubs where salted pork was soaked before it was cut and cooked; and the steward's room, where the dried goods were housed. She listened with interest as he explained the metal tags on the cuts of meat identifying which mess they belonged to. The cook for each mess was in charge of his group's daily rations. The short tour led Amelia to a massive stove, where oatmeal or soup could be cooked in large vats. Beneath the stove, cooks continually tended a hot fire, and above the fire were metal boxes used as ovens. On the table near the stove was a heaping basket of browning bananas.

"When ya came in, I was just tryin' to figure what I might do with these here before they grow too ripe." He waved toward the basket and grimaced. "I haven't much practice with island fruit. I thought maybe I'd try and make the officers a banana pudding . . ." He shrugged his shoulders.

"Well, Slushy. It's fortunate indeed that I arrived in the galley this morning. With the fresh spices and treacle you brought aboard from Jamaica, and if you have a bit of cream and butter, I could help you make Banoffee Pie."

Slushy squinted his eyes and tilted his head, "What's that ya said, miss? Bawfee Pie?"

Amelia laughed. "It's made with banana and toffee, you see. Ban-offee."

Slushy shrugged. "Can't say it sounds too appetizin', if ya know what I mean, but 'twill be a pleasure to have yer company."

He found her a clean apron, which she tied on, and then she headed into the steward's room to take an inventory of the ingredients they would need for the pies. It was a relief to do something she was comfortable with. After her mother had died, Amelia had spent a large amount of time with the plantation servants, who had taught her to cook and sew and operate the sugar press and nearly everything in between.

As she and Slushy worked, he told her about the cannon blast that took off his leg. He had been certain he'd never work again—until Captain Drake had offered him the position of head cook.

"There's not many jobs in the navy where a man don't need both legs, Miss Becket," he told her solemnly. "A great man, our Cap'n Drake."

Slushy's conversation reminded Amelia that she planned to find Captain Drake and thank him for such a thoughtful gesture that morning. When the last pie was finished and the preparation table cleaned, Amelia excused herself. "I had a lovely morning, Slushy. And thank you for the company."

Slushy's face was red again. "Come again, miss. And perhaps ya could teach me some more of them island recipes."

It was early afternoon, and Amelia still felt a bit weak after her bout of seasickness the night before. She decided that a stroll on the upper deck in the fresh air might help her feel better. Stopping at her cabin, she checked to make sure her newly cleaned clothes were drying, and she put on her straw hat. Corporal Ashworth followed her up the companionway. He stood at attention on the deck as she strolled. There was a slight breeze, but not a wisp of cloud remained in the sunny sky from the storm the night before.

The captain wasn't at his usual post on the upper deck, and Amelia decided against searching for him. He might even be asleep after the tiring night he'd undoubtedly had in the storm.

Amelia was unused to sitting idle. She was constantly occupied with some task or another on the plantation, so she began looking around for something she could do to help the crew. She was determined to be involved and make herself useful. It had felt good to help Dr. Spinner and Slushy, and there must be more tasks aboard this ship that she was capable of doing. She remembered what Captain Drake had said about her behaving in an unladylike manner, and she admitted to herself that her intentions were not completely pure. She wouldn't mind irritating him a bit.

She walked around the upper decks, where she paused and watched the sailors feed and clean up after the livestock. Pens held cattle and pigs and goats, and inside the ship's boats, small cages housed chickens and geese.

Amelia made her way to the forecastle of the main deck and saw a group of sailors climbing in the rigging and running along the yards to release a torn sail. Once the enormous sheet was lowered, the men spread it out on the deck to assess the damage. A man wearing a striped shirt and a red handkerchief tied around his neck was apparently in charge. His beard was as white as his midcalf-length trousers, and he walked around the edges of the sail, instructing men, who immediately set to work with needle and thread. He was quite soft-spoken. When he talked, the men had to lean close to hear him.

He stopped near Amelia, looked toward her, and nodded.

"Is the sail repairable?" she asked, looking at the shredded mess.

"Aye, miss. We'll set it to rights."

"And what is your name, sir?"

"Tobias Wheeler, miss," he said in his soft voice.

"Amelia Becket. If you'd like, I could help mend the sail."

Tobias stepped closer and peered at her. "Do you know how to sew?"

Amelia was a bit taken aback. She hadn't thought she would need to present qualifications. "Yes. Well, tolerably. I made this dress."

He looked closely at the dress. "Sewing on a heavy linen sail is much more difficult than making dainty stitches on garments." He lifted one of her hands and stared at her palm. "Your hands are small and soft." He sighed as if disappointed. "But the storm last night was brutal on the sails. I could use the help. Very well then, miss."

She sat on the deck where he indicated and arranged her skirts around her. Tobias showed her the thick three-sided needle and handed her a sailmaker's "palm." It was a strap of leather with a hole that fit over her thumb. At the base of her thumb was a heavier piece of rawhide that she would use to push the needle through the thick linen. Tobias fastened the brass buckle of the palm on the back of her hand and set about teaching her how to make the stitches on the sails.

He gave her a stretch of sail to mend, and she pulled the section into her lap.

"This here's a trial basis, miss. I mean no disrespect, but if 'tisn't done properly, I'll just have to unpick yer stitches and start again."

Tobias had been right. It was difficult work. The leather chafed against her hand, and the thick waxed thread cut her fingers, but Amelia kept at it and eventually had a nice row of stitches in the sail where a jagged tear had been earlier.

"Ya did well, miss," Tobias said as he inspected her work. His light gray eyes were shrewd, and the wrinkles around them fanned out across the leathery skin of his face as he squinted to peer closely at the seam she made. He ran his fingers along both sides of the sail, checking her stitches.

Amelia looked up and realized it was nearly evening. She bent her head from side to side, rubbing her neck. She unbuckled the palm and handed it back to Tobias.

He stood and offered his hand to her. "Thank you for your help, miss. You do good work, and I'd be pleased to have you anytime you like. Sails always need mending."

She took his hand and rose to stand next to him. "You are quite welcome, Mr. Wheeler."

"Please call me Tobias, miss."

"Then if we shall be working together, you must call me Amelia."

After saying good-bye, Amelia walked slowly down the companionway and toward the wardroom for supper. Corporal Ashworth trailed behind. In spite of the fact that sewing the sails was tedious and difficult and her hands and back ached, she felt a swell of pride. She couldn't remember ever before needing to prove herself, and the fact that Tobias Wheeler had judged her work competent enough to meet his standards made her want to impress him again.

Chapter 8

When Amelia emerged from her cabin the next morning, Corporal Ashworth was waiting for her.

"I'm to take you to the captain's sitting room this morning, miss. You'll find your breakfast waiting for you there."

"And why is that, Corporal?" Amelia wondered if she had done something to offend the officers in the wardroom the day before.

"Friday morning is ship's discipline. Captain Drake worried you might feel, um . . . uncomfortable, miss."

He was right. Amelia had heard tales of the corporal punishment that was typical on a ship and was glad the captain didn't expect her to be present as he meted out the sentences.

She followed the corporal up the companionway to the main deck then to the quarterdeck, where he opened the door to the captain's cabin and stood aside for her to enter.

"The entire crew's required to attend discipline, miss, but I'll remain outside the door here should you have need of me."

Amelia sighed. The captain's lack of trust in her was beginning to be exasperating.

"And does Captain Drake truly consider me such a threat to the ship?"

"Miss?"

"It is not necessary for you to pretend, Corporal. Since I came aboard, I've remained under constant guard. I only wondered the reason that the captain fears to leave me unattended."

The corporal tipped his head and squinted his eyes. "Miss Becket, I apologize for giving you such an impression. My orders are to ensure your safety. You are to be permitted to go anywhere you like, and I assure you the captain does not consider you a threat. But you must realize that the only woman on a ship of nearly eight hundred men . . ."

"Oh." Amelia felt her cheeks redden as she realized how mistaken she had been. And how naïve. "I misunderstood. In that case, thank you, Corporal Ashworth."

He closed the door behind her, and she heard the sound of his heels snapping together as he stood at attention.

Amelia stepped farther into the room. As with the rest of the ship, the space was used efficiently; however, that was where the resemblance ended. An entire wall of the room at the stern of the ship was windowed, which gave it a bright, warm feel. The ceiling contained skylights between the heavy wooden beams. There was a round table covered in maps and charts, a desk with the top closed, and a comfortable-looking sofa flanked by wingback chairs.

A door stood slightly ajar on one side of the room, and peeking inside, Amelia saw that it led to the captain's private sleeping cabin. From her brief glance, she saw that everything inside was tidy and orderly. The sheets were stretched tightly across the captain's berth. A pair of buckled shoes sat on a sea trunk with the name *Drake* painted on the side, and an oilskin coat hung above it. Against one bulkhead was a simple washstand with a basin and a mirror. Shaving implements and a hairbrush lay in an open box that sat next to the basin. A lantern hung on a hook above a small table. Not a thing was out of place.

She turned away, feeling uncomfortable for snooping, and walked around the sitting room. Glass-fronted cabinets lined the far wall, and she spent some time looking at interesting objects that the captain had apparently acquired in his travels, as well as perusing his books. Selecting a book, she walked toward the sideboard table and took a biscuit, some eggs, and a cup of tea. Sitting at the round table, she took care not to get any crumbs on the captain's maps. She studied the charts and measuring instruments while she ate her breakfast, trying to make sense of the equations and markings. When she had finished, she returned her plate and cup to the sideboard and settled with her book on the bench below the window, but she did not read.

The seat was comfortable, the sun warm, and the view of the sea mesmerizing. Amelia turned and pulled her feet up onto the bench, leaning her back against the wall. This was undoubtedly her favorite spot on the ship, she decided. As she watched the rise and fall of the waves and the way the light played upon them, her mind turned to the man whose quarters she was occupying. It seemed that every time she thought she understood Captain Drake, she found herself surprised by the man. The accounts she had heard from crew members presented his character as kind and thoughtful. She'd even seen evidence of this in the bath he had arranged for her and the fact that he had thought to spare her from the unpleasantness of ship's discipline by allowing her to wait in his private quarters.

Perhaps it was best to stop assuming the worst when it came to him. But as soon as she had the thought, she remembered these dealings were so unlike her personal encounters with Captain Drake. He had yelled at her, accused her of deceit in her marriage to his brother, and called her character and behavior into question. How could she make sense of it all?

As she pondered on this, a knock sounded at the door, and the man himself entered, leaving the door slightly open behind him. She saw the corporal present his arms.

Amelia stood, and the captain's gaze moved to linger momentarily upon her bare feet, which were exposed briefly as she swung her legs from the bench.

"Good morning, Captain," she said, tucking her feet beneath her skirts.

"Good morning, Miss Becket." He rubbed his eyes, and she saw for a brief moment evidence of the strain of a captain's responsibilities.

"I thank you for allowing me use of your quarters, sir. They are very comfortable."

"You are welcome." He indicated for her to join him in the sitting area before he sank heavily into a chair.

"And I haven't had a chance to thank you for sending Riley to my cabin with hot water yesterday. It was much appreciated."

He glanced at her then rubbed his eyes again.

"I should leave."

"I apologize, Miss Becket, for my lack of conversation this morning. As you can imagine, I am rather unused to company."

"Why do you not take your meals in the wardroom then, sir? There is plenty of company to be had."

He turned his head to look at her. "It is not my job to be popular, miss. A captain who tries to be friendly with his crew quickly loses their respect. The wardroom is for the officers."

"I understand, sir." She stood and began to walk toward the door. The captain's life was indeed a lonely one, and she felt a wave of sadness. She knew all too well how it felt to be alone. She stopped and turned back toward him. "Was it so terrible this morning?"

"Discipline is always terrible." Captain Drake stood and took a breath then schooled his expression into one of polite interest. "And what did you find to occupy yourself?" He nodded toward the seat she had vacated on the window bench and the book lying upon it.

"I examined your charts for a time, but I found to my dismay that no amount of study would help me understand them on my own."

The captain's eyebrows rose slightly, and his lips twitched. "Would you like a tutorial?"

Amelia smiled, glad that she had found a way to shake the captain's melancholy mood. "If you have the time, sir."

***

After nearly an hour of instruction, Amelia and Captain Drake leaned over the chart, where he had placed the compass. She concentrated, trying to make sense of the equations they had used.

"For this exercise, we shall assume that we've remained at a constant rate of ten knots for ease of calculation. And so based upon our starting point and our heading indicated by the compass, we now use the dividers to determine—" Amelia and the captain heard a knock at the open door and looked up from the table as Sidney Fletcher entered.

Sidney paused, blinked, and opened his eyes wide before his face resumed its typical smile. "Please excuse me. I did not intend to interrupt."

"Mr. Fletcher," Amelia said. She took a step away from the captain. Sidney's presence had made her realize just how close they had been standing and made her feel the need to explain herself. "Captain Drake was giving me a lesson in charting a course."

"And how do you get along then, Miss Becket?" Sidney asked, his smile growing as he looked between them.

"It's much more difficult than I had imagined." She set down the dividers she still held. "Perhaps I should have paid more attention to my mathematics in school."

"Is there something I can help you with, Mr. Fletcher?" Captain Drake's voice sounded irritated, and Amelia worried that she had overstayed her welcome.

"If you will excuse me, gentlemen," Amelia said. "I have occupied enough of the captain's time this morning." She hurried past Sidney and out the door to where Corporal Thorne awaited her. She pondered on the captain's kindness in humoring her in her attempts to study the charts. He undoubtedly considered it a waste of time for both of them but had taken her request seriously. Not once in their time together—as she struggled to understand the complicated equations and asked endless questions—had he become annoyed or spoken to her in a patronizing manner. In fact, he had been quite pleasant, considerate even.

As it was nearly time for the noon meal, she walked to the wardroom, hoping that the soldiers would assume her flushed cheeks were merely a result of the sea wind.

Chapter 9

Amelia sat next to Tobias on the deck. It was the third day she had worked with him, and the two of them had lapsed into a comfortable rhythm as they folded and stitched the seam on a sail.

She paused for a moment to rub some of the blisters that had developed on her hands. "Tell me about your family, Tobias."

Tobias was quiet for a moment. "My son and his wife both died nearly five years ago. I've one granddaughter, Anna. She'll be about your age, I suspect. If you don't mind my asking how old you are . . ."

"Certainly not. I shall be one and twenty on the twenty-ninth of this month, though I confess that I've quite lost track of how many days we have been at sea and am not exactly sure of today's date."

"Ah, September 29, the feast of Michaelmas. You've a lucky natal day to be sure."

Amelia smiled. "When I was young, I believed the feast in the governor's mansion was held each year to celebrate my birthday."

Tobias chuckled. "My Anna just turned nineteen this past spring. Bright girl, inquisitive, a hard worker. You remind me of her, you know."

Amelia was surprised how much such a simple statement touched her. "And tell me, sir. Does Anna live in London?"

"Aye. She works as a chambermaid in a grand house in the West End—for a Miss Regina Foster."

"She'll be glad to have you home for a visit, no doubt."

"This is my last voyage, miss. I've not been back to London for over a year. I plan to retire and take care of my Anna. And my old bones."

Amelia laughed. "You seem quite healthy to me. But returning to your family will be a welcome reprieve after such a long time away, I'm sure."

"And what of you, Miss Amelia? Do you journey toward family?"

"My father lives in London, and he sent for me to join him." Even as she said the words, she knew she was not destined for a loving reunion. Her father didn't desire her company. He would not greet her arrival with open arms. She was a nuisance to him that had to be borne for the sake of a business arrangement with the Lockwood estate. But she had long since finished shedding tears over the lack of affection between them. She could only hope their business would be conducted promptly and she could return home to Jamaica.

Once she had finished the seam she was working on, she decided to stroll around the edges of the deck and enjoy the warm breeze before supper. Thinking about Tobias and his undoubtedly loving relationship with his granddaughter produced an uncomfortable ache that she hadn't felt for a long time. Since her mother and grandfather had died, she had been quite alone in a house of servants who treated her well but weren't her family. She stopped and absently held on to a rope of rigging as she looked across the waves.

Perhaps it was being so far from home in an unfamiliar environment that had dredged up old memories and left her feeling off-kilter. She wondered what awaited her in London. Her father would no doubt ignore her most of the time she was there—except for an occasional battery of words when he'd had too much to drink. What would it be like to return home to a father like Tobias, who was warm and loving and whose eyes saw only good in her? Her own father was cold and criticized her at every opportunity. She swallowed against the obstruction in her throat and swiped at the moisture in her eyes.

Turning, she nearly walked into Captain Drake, who had approached without her notice.

"Miss Becket. Pardon me, but are you well?" His brow was furrowed, and the concern she saw in his eyes only served to increase her bout of tears.

"I am well, sir." She attempted to laugh, but it sounded more like a sob. "Just a spell of homesickness. Please excuse me." Turning back toward the gunwale, she chided herself and tried to get her emotions under control.

Captain Drake stepped next to her and offered his handkerchief.

She took it and wiped her eyes. "I'm sorry, Captain. I am behaving ridiculously." She folded the handkerchief and handed it back to him.

He looked down and took the handkerchief from her. His gaze moved to her face and back to her hand as he lifted it, leaned closer, then reached for her other hand. "Miss Becket, what has happened here?"

She attempted to pull away, but his grip on her wrists was firm as he examined the blistered palms and swelling, punctured fingers, as well as one particularly large slash where her needle had slipped and dug into her skin.

"It's nothing, Captain, just—"

"Is this a result of mending the sails?" he asked.

"Yes, sir."

She saw a muscle working in his jaw and wondered that such a thing would make him so upset.

Captain Drake called for Riley, who hurried over. "Fetch a balm from Dr. Spinner for Miss Becket's hands."

"Aye, aye, sir."

The captain did not release his grip, even after Riley had scurried away.

"Are you angry with me, Captain Drake?" Amelia asked, more surprised than anything.

"I am angry at myself for letting such a thing happen. It is my duty to be aware of what takes place on this ship. I should have never allowed a lady to participate in this type of activity. The responsibility for your injuries is mine, Miss Becket."

"No, Captain." She pulled her hands away with a bit of effort. "I am responsible for myself. I chose to help Mr. Wheeler and intend to continue—"

"Miss Becket, I forbid it."

Amelia felt her temper begin to rise and struggled to contain it. She took a breath and let it out slowly, contemplating the best strategy to convince the captain to change his mind. A battle of wills would surely be won by the man in control of the ship, and challenging his authority was the quickest way to a permanent refusal.

Riley returned with the jar of salve, which the captain opened and began to spread over Amelia's hands. She felt instant relief as the ointment covered her abrasions. But the relief was soon replaced by a rather unnerving feeling. Captain Drake's touch was surprisingly gentle, and Amelia felt her pulse speed up at the intimacy of his ministrations. He moved slowly, making sure to cover each blister and wound with the salve, spreading it carefully. His hands were warm, and she was fascinated by his long fingers and the way they held her own hands so tenderly. She did not dare to glance at his face, sure he would see the blush that she could feel upon her cheeks.

"Dr. Spinner asked me to instruct Miss Becket to apply the salve before bed and to sleep with her gloves on," Riley said.

"Thank you, Riley," Captain Drake said. He was still examining Amelia's hands. "You're dismissed."

"Aye, aye, sir."

"Thank you, Riley," Amelia said and smiled at him. He bowed to her and left.

"Captain," Amelia said, taking her hands from his and folding them in front of her. She knew it wouldn't do to be stubborn. "Will you please allow me to help the sailmakers? I enjoy the work, and the friendship, and—Please do not forbid it." She swallowed again, frustrated that her emotions were attempting to make a reappearance and frustrated that she had to ask for permission. She'd never needed to ask for permission to do anything on the plantation.

Captain Drake looked at her for a long moment, and she struggled to hold his gaze and to blink back her tears. The captain needed to be the one to make the decision, and she must wait patiently for his verdict. At last he spoke.

"If I notice that your fingers become more damaged or if you feel any sort of pain, you must discontinue sail mending. Do you understand?"

"Yes. Thank you, Captain." Her face relaxed, relieved.

"And you must promise to apply the salve often."

"I promise, sir."

"Very well, Miss Becket. Carry on."

Chapter 10

William stood on the upper deck as he did every day, supervising the sailors and officers as they performed their duties. But he found that as the time went on, more and more often his eyes strayed toward Amelia. She sat with the sailmaker and his mates upon the foredeck as they showed her how to attach ropes to the sails. He knew the knots were quite complicated, and even from this distance, he saw her face set in concentration.

It seemed that in the three weeks she had been on the ship, he had noticed she'd been involved with nearly every task aboard.

When he'd asked Slushy about the variety of dishes that came out of the galley on nearly a daily basis, the cook confessed that Amelia had shown him some new recipes while she spent many mornings assisting him. William had heard from Dr. Spinner that she regularly aided him in the infirmary and also that she had from time to time mended clothing and acted as scribe for sailors who did not possess the education to write letters themselves.

He clasped his hands behind his back and paced back and forth in front of the rail, watching Sidney and a group of lieutenants as they led marines in a bayonet exercise. The soldiers were definitely improving, as were the sailors with their battle drills.

His mind returned to Amelia. Sidney and Riley both spoke of her as if she walked upon water, and each jumped at any chance to stroll the decks with her in the evenings. William had often seen her chatting with Mr. Wheeler or standing beside him on Sunday mornings as the entire crew turned out to hear the captain read from the Bible and narrate the Articles of War.

He'd seen her more than once as Sidney or another lieutenant had conducted weapons training or timed the men as they climbed up and down the riggings. She was always cheering or complimenting them on their progress. There was possibly no greater incentive for any of the sailors to perform than that of her smile. It was as if she held nothing back in her expression.

The women he knew in England were trained to be demure and only occasionally raised the corners of their lips in a slightly pleasant manner. Amelia's smile not only lit up her face but elevated every person around her. Men worked harder, acted friendlier, and were in greater spirits when she was near. She was easy and pleasant and open. In this respect she was unlike the young ladies of his acquaintance in London, who strove to portray a perfect façade. But Amelia was still refined and ladylike. Her manners left nothing to censure—although he had noticed that she had adopted the habit of walking on bare feet. Truly, he'd been unable to get the image of her dainty pink toes out of his mind since he'd chanced to glimpse them in his sitting room.

William walked back to the rail and surveyed the main deck again. He himself looked forward to the short charting lessons they had each Friday after he had overseen the ship's discipline. In fact, it was the bright spot of his week. Amelia was attentive and interested and asked thoughtful questions. There were quite a few junior officers who could take a page out of her book when it came to applying themselves to their studies. For her, learning to chart was the ultimate in pointless causes. It was information she would never use, and it was difficult and time-consuming. What did she hope to gain from such an exercise? In William's case, he had to admit that he simply enjoyed spending time with her. Was it the same for Amelia?

As he watched, he saw one of the sailors say something to her and then heard her laughter. For someone who made a life off embezzling other people's family fortunes, she had a lovely laugh. Anyone within hearing couldn't help but smile.

It was difficult for him to reconcile this intelligent woman with the fraudulent colonist he'd envisioned in Jamaica. If she managed to charm the magistrate as easily as she had his crew, William would have a difficult time discrediting her and her claim to his brother's jointure. Perhaps it was time to get to know Miss Becket a little better; surely it would help him in his case against her and her father.

He strode down the gangway and onto the main deck. The group around the sail didn't see him approach, and he watched their interactions for a moment.

Amelia had finished tying a knot and was showing it to one of the sailors.

"Nearly there, miss. But ya see this end needs to go around and through, or else—" The man speaking glanced up, noticed William, instantly stood to attention, and saluted. The men around him did the same. Tobias took Amelia by the hand and helped her rise to stand with the others.

"As you were, men," William said. "If you don't mind, Miss Becket, I was hoping to have a private word with you."

"Of course, Captain." She stepped carefully over the ropes that spread over the planks of the deck, and when she reached William, she rested her hand upon his offered arm.

They strolled around the edge of the deck in silence until William finally spoke. "Miss Becket, I am afraid I have been amiss in my duty toward you."

"And how so, Captain?"

"In the time we have been at sea, I have never once invited you to dine in my cabin."

Was it his imagination, or did her fingers tighten on his arm? "I hoped you might join Mr. Fletcher and me for supper tomorrow evening." He felt her hand relax slightly and wondered if the mention of Sidney joining them for dinner was a relief to her. The spark of jealousy this idea produced surprised him.

"I would be delighted to take supper with you tomorrow."

"Shall we say the end of the first dogwatch—four bells?"

"Certainly, Captain."

***

The next evening, William nodded to his steward when he heard a knock on the door—precisely on time as the ship's bell rang four times.

The steward opened the door, and Amelia entered wearing a lavender gown with a gray floral design and lace around her neck and sleeves. Her appearance surprised him, as he had only seen her in black mourning dresses. He thought she looked quite lovely and resolved to tell her so.

"You look quite lovely," Sidney said, and William shut his own mouth before making a fool of himself.

"It's not every day one gets invited to supper with the captain." She smiled at Sidney and then turned her gaze to meet William's. He noticed that the gray accents on her dress changed her eyes to the color of the sea beneath a cloudy sky. The effect of a different shade of gown was startling, and William found himself still pondering on it when Sidney cleared his throat.

"Captain, if you'd like we can adjourn to the table?"

He glanced at Sidney, who was watching him with a grin. William pulled his mind to the matter at hand, remembering his duty as host. "Of course. If you please, Miss Becket." He led her toward the table and pulled a chair out for her. As she sat, he caught Sidney's glance and the slight raise of his eyebrows. William scowled back at him, which only made Sidney's smile widen.

Once they were seated and the steward had served them, William resolved to take control of the supper and stop acting like such a fool.

But before he had a chance to speak, Sidney once again captured Amelia's attention. "And how do you like your journey thus far, Amelia?"

Did he call her Amelia?

She set her goblet down and dabbed her napkin on her lips before she spoke. "I have enjoyed it quite a lot, actually. More than I would have guessed."

"Splendid," Sidney said.

"And, Captain," she said, turning to him, "I assume this voyage is to be your last, as you will need to replace your brother as the earl. Am I correct?"

"Yes."

"Will you be sorry to leave the sea?"

William felt a pang in his chest whenever he allowed himself to dwell on his inevitable departure from his ship, and this time was no exception. He cleared his throat. "I shall indeed miss my life at sea."

"I am truly sorry, sir," she said, and for a moment he was taken aback by the compassion in her eyes. "But you will make a good earl."

"I am inclined to disagree with you, as I know nothing about being an earl or the administration of an estate. The entire concept is foreign to me."

"Nonsense." Amelia laughed. "You are an expert in the management of people. I have seen for myself the way you run this ship."

"I hardly think it is the same thing."

"It is precisely the same thing. It is difficult to strike a balance between appearing too fearful or too friendly to those in your employ, but once it is achieved, their respect is won. It is a skill my grandfather often pointed out to me. Years ago, the steward at the plantation was harsh with the workers and unpredictable with his punishments. They were afraid and nervous, and they spoke about him behind his back. Since they had no respect for him, the entire plantation suffered. But when my grandfather replaced him with a new steward, who was firm but kind, the steward's fairness and genuine concern for the workers earned their trust. They worked harder because they wished to please him." Her gaze focused on William, and he felt his chest tighten at the approval he saw reflected in her blue eyes.

"Sir, you inspire the same loyalty on the ship. Slushy and the doctor are devoted to you because of the way you've treated them. Once Riley learned that his wound was similar to yours, he was no longer afraid of receiving stitches because of his admiration of you. Such a talent of inspiring people is rare and will make you a fine earl."

William listened to her, astonished. Did she truly feel this way? He stuttered, searching for words that would convey how much such a thing meant and finally settled upon, "I thank you, miss. Your words are very . . . generous."

He remembered the fork that he held in his hand and bit down on the piece of chicken that had not quite made it to his mouth while he'd been listening to Amelia.

"And the captain will look resplendent in his white wig when he attends the House of Lords—we mustn't forget that," Sidney said, laughing.

Amelia laughed with him. "Yes, he will look very handsome indeed."

As she said this, William caught her eye and she looked away quickly, but not before he noticed her cheeks coloring. Sidney must have noticed it too because he was swift to change the subject.

"Is it difficult to manage the entire plantation with your father gone so often, Amelia?"

There it is again. Why is he calling her by her given name?

"It is difficult, certainly, but my father has nothing to do with it. The plantation was my mother's, and she bequeathed it to me upon her passing. My father has only come to Jamaica a few times. More often when I was younger, but since my mother's death when I was ten, he's visited but twice. Once to attempt to figure out a way to discount my inheritance and take control of the plantation—in which effort he was unsuccessful—and the other to . . . encourage me to sign the marriage documents attaching me to your brother, Captain."

"And so the plantation is yours, Miss Becket?" William asked.

"Yes. According to my mother's solicitor, my father was quite surprised when he discovered this fact. My grandfather did not have a high opinion of my father and did everything in his power to keep the property out of his hands. Although, I suppose that for a time it belonged to your brother while he was my husband, until he passed away."

William and Sidney exchanged a glance, which Amelia did not fail to see.

"You had assumed that I married your brother because my own financial situation left much to be desired, did you not, Captain? I assure you that was not my design in signing the marriage documents, though I cannot speak to my father's intentions."

"Then what was your design, Miss Becket?" He had not imagined there would be other factors that might induce a woman into matrimony.

"Being a married woman was a relief. I was suddenly freed from the constrictions society places upon a single young lady. I would never have been able to travel on your ship without a chaperone, Captain, if I was not a widow. And business dealings became much simpler when merchants were no longer dealing with a young, unattached girl.

"I mean no disrespect to your brother, Captain. Your argument over the jointure is between you and my father. I have no desire for the money, for a husband, or to live in England. From what I know of it, I will most definitely never belong to the society of London. Once the business with the solicitor is concluded, I intend to be upon the next ship sailing west."

Amelia spread some butter on her bread. "And I am sorry I have monopolized the entire conversation. Captain, if I might ask, tell me what awaits the Earl of Lockwood when he returns home?"

"My mother and younger sister live at the manor," William said, still thinking about Amelia's words. If the plantation was hers alone, why would her father attach her to Lawrence? For his title? *Is she manipulating me? Is she being manipulated by her father?*

"And they will no doubt be thrilled to have you home," Sidney said.

"Oh, I should have loved to have a sister," Amelia said. "What is her name?"

"Emma. She is a few months shy of eighteen. Probably near to your own age."

"And tell me about her," Amelia said. William noticed she did not make any comment in regard to her age, which, from his brother's marriage document, he knew would be twenty-one years at the end of the month.

"I have been at sea since Emma was but a few months old and have only spent time with her a few weeks out of the year. I regret that I do not know her well enough to describe her properly."

"She is lovely, Amelia. She looks nothing like her brother," Sidney said.

William sighed and set his fork down loudly. Amelia giggled.

Sidney continued, managing to speak with his infuriating grin. "On the contrary, her hair is light, and her eyes are blue. She speaks softly and is quiet and very reserved, but her laugh is delightful, if one is able to coax it into the open. She has a sharp mind and a subtle wit that make her a joy to talk to."

Both Amelia and William stared at him, and he shrugged and smiled. "Somebody needed to spend time with your mother and sister while you brooded about your family estate, examining ledgers and arguing with your brother."

"I should have never invited you for Christmas," William said, rolling his eyes. And Amelia laughed again.

As they had all finished their meals, William offered Amelia his arm and led them to the sitting area, where they could visit more comfortably.

"And what of your family, Sidney?" Amelia asked.

Sidney?

"Well, as it happens, I was not bequeathed a sugar plantation in Jamaica, nor did I inherit an earldom. I am merely the third son of a viscount and shall inherit a very small manor in Cheshire. Not far from Lord Lockwood's earldom, actually."

"Why did you join the navy?"

"By the time my father inherited the viscountship, the estate had fallen upon hard times. I was enlisted at eight years old as a cabin boy to spare my family the expense of raising another child." Sidney smiled, but it lacked its usual joviality. "The other factor in the decision was obviously the abundance of delicious sea biscuits," he said in a half-hearted attempt at humor.

"And when the war ends, what do you intend to do?" Amelia asked.

"If I still have breath in my lungs, I should like to rebuild what was once a grand estate. Neither my father nor my brothers have a head for business, and the viscounty has suffered from their neglect." Sidney's smile did not reach his eyes. "But I do not think I shall have that opportunity, as my family is quite dependent upon the living the navy provides."

"And why did you go to sea, Captain?" Amelia asked, turning toward William. "I assume that your family was not in financial troubles."

"You speak very boldly, Miss Becket," William said. "What makes you assume such a thing?"

"I'm sorry; I did not mean to offend you. I only supposed that my father would not go to the trouble of connecting me with your brother if he didn't think there would be a financial gain as a result. My father does nothing without an economic benefit. I only wondered why you decided to enlist in the navy."

William wondered if she was merely curious. Did she actually care? Or was she digging for information about his situation? He studied his hands as he spoke. "At the time, my father was a merchant marine, and there was no indication that he ever would be the earl. It was through a series of events that he inherited the estate from a distant cousin. He became Lord Lockwood after I had been at sea for quite some time." William was silent for a moment. He looked up at Amelia before he continued. "Perhaps I went to sea for the same reason you desired marriage. The life we are born with is not always the life we would choose, and so it is up to us to make of it what we will."

"Well spoken, sir," Sidney said. "You each made the best of a difficult situation. Amelia was coerced into marriage, and—"

"And I have my father to thank for my profession in the navy," William concluded.

"Your father convinced you to go to sea?" Amelia asked quietly. "How old were you?"

"Ten. The same age you were when your mother died. And I think *convinced* is rather a mild term." For an instant, they shared a look that spoke of years of loneliness and longing for a family, which would be unrecognizable to anyone who had not experienced the same anguish.

"It seems we have much in common, Miss Becket," William said softly.

Amelia looked away, and when she looked back, her expression was composed. "Not the least of which is the same surname, Captain." She raised an eyebrow and tipped her head.

"That is still to be determined, miss," he said with a wry smile.

"I warn you; my father does not concede easily, sir. You shall have quite a fight on your hands. And while the two of you argue in front of the magistrate, Sidney and I will be sitting home drinking a nice glass of guava nectar."

Sidney laughed. He leaned back in his chair and laid his ankle upon his other knee. "It sounds wonderful, Amelia. However, there are no guava trees in London."

Amelia's eyes opened wider. She tapped her finger against her lip, as if contemplating the problem. "I had not considered that. Tea, then?"

"Tea it is."

Amelia bid the men good night, and after she left, William and Sidney returned to sit in the chairs.

"Well, Captain, it was an interesting evening. And I think we can rightly say that the information we learned has blown an enormous hole in your theory about Amelia and her efforts to pilfer your family's fortune."

"And since when do you call Miss Becket by her Christian name?"

Sidney grinned and raised his palms, shrugging. "Since she asked me to. You may not have realized that I have quite a way with the fairer sex."

William scowled. Why had she not asked *him* to call her Amelia?

"And it turns out you are not alone when it comes to having a harsh father."

Hadn't he given her plenty of chances to invite him to call her by her first name? Was she still angry that he had rebuffed the suggestion when they first met?

"We can definitely put to rest any theories about whether or not Amelia looks fetching in colors other than simply black."

William looked up at Sidney's grinning face and narrowed his gaze. "You're dismissed, Mr. Fletcher."

Chapter 11

AMELIA FINISHED THE SEAM SHE had spent the past hour stitching and unbuckled the sailor's palm from her hand, noticing the callouses that had developed where the leather rubbed against her skin. It was better than the pain, she decided, though she was a bit sad that her hands weren't as soft as she would have liked. She also noticed that her arms were becoming quite brown. And even though she took the precaution of wearing a hat, when she had peered at herself in the mirror in her cabin, some freckles had begun to make a most unwelcome appearance on her nose and cheeks.

She stood shivering in the coolness of the evening as the heavy sail slid off her lap. Tobias came to stand next to her, and they watched in a comfortable silence as the sailmaker's mates folded up the large sheets that had been mended, preparing to return them to the hold for storage.

The bell rang for the first dogwatch, and Amelia bid Tobias good evening as she turned to go to supper.

"If you don't mind, Miss Amelia, I wanted to speak to you for a moment."

"Of course, Tobias."

"Since today's your natal day, miss, I've a small gift. Nothing grand, mind you." He handed her a folded piece of sail linen.

She looked at him as she took it and then, upon opening it, gasped in delight at the image that had been stitched onto the heavy fabric: A dolphin leaping above blue waves. She was touched by the gift. Not only because Tobias had remembered her birthday but because she realized that it must have taken him hours to create. "It's beautiful. Thank you, Tobias. I had quite forgotten that today is my birthday."

"I'm glad you like it, Miss Amelia. You're a right clever girl, and I feel pleased to call you a friend. Many happy returns." He bowed his head quickly and hurried away.

Amelia walked down the companionway to her room. She lit the lantern and studied the embroidery on the scrap of fabric more closely. It was truly remarkable. To think that Tobias had spent his precious spare time creating this for her stirred tender feelings in her heart. She was indeed fortunate to have made such dear friends aboard the HMS *Venture*.

She opened her trunk, laid the gift carefully inside, and retrieved her thin shawl, wrapping it around her shoulders. Her feet were quite chilled, and she donned stockings and slippers, which felt strange and constricting, as she'd not worn anything on her feet for weeks. When she stepped outside, she handed the lantern to Corporal Ashworth. Fire was regulated closely on board the ship, and it was potentially disastrous to leave a candle burning unattended. She made her way to the wardroom with a smile as she thought on the kindness of her friend.

The dinner meal was pleasant. The officers did not seem to feel the chill in the air as keenly as she did, as most of them had taken their regimental coats off and wore only their white cotton shirts.

Sidney sat on one side of her, with Dr. Spinner on the other, and she found herself laughing at their conversation and listening with interest at the stories they and the other officers told.

When the meal ended, Amelia began to stand, but Sidney placed his hand on her arm.

"You'll not want to leave just yet, Amelia."

She raised her eyebrows and moved her mouth to inquire as to why, when Slushy entered, limping into the room with a large Jamaican ginger cake. He set it on the table in front of her, and the officers cheered.

One of the midshipmen—Sergeant Fairchild—was admitted into the wardroom. He produced a fiddle and began to play.

"And a happy natal day to ya, miss," Slushy said as he began cutting slices of the cake, placing them upon wooden dishes, and passing them around the table.

Amelia was astounded. "Thank you," she said when she had found her voice. She felt a prickling behind her eyes and blinked rapidly. She took a bite of cake. "Delicious, Slushy. Just like home."

Slushy tipped his hat. The men applauded and called out well-wishes.

When they had finished their cake, Sidney led Amelia to the far side of the room. Officers lifted the large plank of wood that was used for the table, turned it on to its side, and leaned it against one of the bulkheads. The rest of the chairs were lined up around the edges of the room between the cannons.

"What is this, Sidney?" Amelia asked.

"The men and I decided that for your birthday, we would throw a ball. You'd not want to celebrate your natal day without a dance or two, would you?"

Amelia raised an eyebrow. "A ball with only one woman in attendance? I wonder if I should be able to fill my dance card."

Sidney laughed, and Amelia realized that he was indeed serious about dancing.

"But it would be impossible for me to perform each lady's position."

"Never fear, we have devised a way that you should not be required to. Before you arrived, the group of us drew lots, and the winners—"

He was interrupted by some of the men grumbling but raised his voice to speak above their protests. "The *winners* shall pose as ladies, so as to not leave you the lone female in the set."

Judging by the faces of the officers, it was not difficult to deduce which men had drawn the short straws.

Sidney turned to face her. He extended his leg, pointed his toe, and placed his hand over his heart, bowing with much aplomb. "And now, Miss Amelia Becket, as I outrank every man here, I should like to claim your hand for the first dance. That is with your consent, of course." He held out his hand, and she took it, following him the few short steps it took to arrive on the "dance floor."

Amelia watched as another officer bowed and took the hand of a particularly sullen-faced lieutenant. For all his gallantry, the man was shoved to the other side of the room by his partner and returned with fists raised, prepared to repay the favor.

"Now, Mr. Brenton, that is not how a young lady should act," Sidney chided, and the room rang with laughter.

Dance partners were finally established, and Sergeant Fairchild began to play a familiar country dance. Bitterness at being the "ladies" seemed to be quickly forgotten as the officers smiled and began to enjoy themselves. The men who weren't dancing clapped their hands to the music.

When the song ended, Sidney declared that it was Amelia's turn to choose a tune.

"Bonny Charley," she said, and her hand was quickly claimed by a different partner. Amelia laughed at the men's good-natured teasing as a different group took their turn as the "ladies." She couldn't believe that the officers had conceived such a plan in secret—and all to make her happy. Certainly she had friends in Jamaica but none so thoughtful as these men, who would spend their supper hour dancing about the room because they knew it would please her.

Another dance began, a quadrille this time, and the four couples spread out as well as they were able in the small space. They had danced but for a moment when the music abruptly halted, and every eye turned toward Sergeant Fairchild and then followed his gaze to Captain Drake, who stood in the doorway of the wardroom.

The soldiers immediately stood at attention and saluted.

William's eyes traveled around the room, taking in the scene before he spoke. His voice was calm, betraying no emotion, but there was a dangerous glint in his eyes. "The bell for second watch rang a full three minutes ago. And can you imagine my surprise when no officers took up their positions?"

Amelia heard Sidney curse under his breath. She could feel the tension stretching in the room and knew she must do something.

"Captain Drake, if you please, it is my fault that the officers did not hear the bell."

William's gaze moved to Amelia as she spoke. He did not take his eyes from her as he dismissed the men. They grabbed their coats and hats, rushing past him out the door.

"Not you, Fairchild," he said, his eyes still on Amelia's face.

Sergeant Fairchild stood at attention on one side of the room, clutching his fiddle.

William stepped slowly toward Amelia, and she struggled not to shrink under his scrutiny. "Miss Becket, tardiness at the watch is punishable by lashings."

"Captain, you see, today is my birthday, and the officers were only doing something nice for me. Please, sir. Do not discipline them." She felt the prickling behind her eyes return and blinked quickly to dispel any tears that might leak. "You must punish me instead, sir."

"You claim to be responsible for detaining the men from their duties?"

"Yes, sir."

"Ship's discipline is very severe, Miss Becket." He had stepped so close that Amelia had to tip her head back to hold his gaze. "And the penalty for hindering the watch is especially serious."

Amelia forced herself not to look away. She clenched her jaw to stop her chin from trembling and waited for the captain to hand down her sentence.

"However, I will take into consideration that this is your first offence." He slowly rubbed his chin, thinking. "And it is, after all, your birthday."

The heaviness in Amelia's chest began to lighten.

"In place of your punishment, Miss Becket, I should very much like to dance with you."

She blinked and opened her eyes wide, examining his expression but finding no indication that he was teasing. If he had ordered her to walk the plank, she could have not been more surprised. "Captain, I do believe you are flirting with me."

He quirked an eyebrow, and the corner of his lips lifted in a small smile. He turned his head slightly toward the sergeant, who still stood against the wall. "A waltz, if you please, Mr. Fairchild."

"Captain," Amelia gasped. "A waltz is so . . . vulgar."

William looked down at her. "Miss Becket, I happen to know that the prince himself commissioned a waltz at his own ball last year."

Amelia felt the heat rise to her face at the very idea of waltzing with the captain. "But, I do not know how—"

"I am a very excellent teacher." He took her hand and bowed over it, then placed her left hand onto his right shoulder before taking her right hand in his. She chided herself for not wearing gloves to supper, feeling self-conscious at the roughness of her palms. Various partners had held her hands at different times during the evening, but the way his hand enfolded hers caused heat to spread over her skin.

William placed his right hand on the small of her back and pulled gently with his left hand, leading her in a simple series of steps, which she quickly mastered. She focused on the captain's shoulder, where her hand rested tentatively. He moved lightly, but her movements were stiff. She was afraid of relaxing when he was practically holding her in his arms.

After a few turns around the room, Amelia felt her tension ease. The music was beautiful, and Captain Drake had a way of drawing her across the floor as if she were floating. When she finally braved a glance at his face, she met his eyes, and her nervousness returned.

"And is your punishment so dreadful, Miss Becket?" he asked. "I have yet to see you smile."

Amelia allowed herself a small smile. "It is a very nice punishment indeed, sir. Is it one you utilize regularly?"

"Perhaps I shall, if you believe it will keep the men in line."

Amelia laughed. "I do not know what they would think if you waltzed with each sailor who failed in his duty."

"I imagine it should be quite effective at discouraging rule breaking, don't you?" William looked thoughtful, as if considering the idea.

"Perhaps. Until some of the men develop a taste for waltzing. You might begin to worry when the same men continually require discipline."

William laughed. Amelia had only heard his laugh a very few times and found she quite liked it. Especially knowing she was the one who had inspired it. She also realized that the sound had caused her heart to trip ever so slightly, and to her dismay, she found that she quite liked that as well. She lowered her eyes, suddenly finding the gold buttons on the captain's coat fascinating. She was extremely aware of the captain's arm, the way it wrapped around her, and his hand resting on her lower back. The hand that held hers was strong, and she felt each movement of his fingers and the subtle tightening around her own hand. And had he always had such a pleasant smell?

"How do you find the waltz, Miss Becket? Is it as scandalous as you had supposed?"

Amelia prayed that the captain could not read her thoughts and attempted to school her expression into one of polite disinterestedness that she thought a genteel lady of London might wear. "No. It is very agreeable, sir. And you are a fine dancer."

"As are you, when you loosen up a bit." His lips quirked, and he lowered his voice, although Sergeant Fairchild was the only other person within hearing distance and Amelia didn't think he could hear much of anything with the fiddle so near his face. "Your expression does not fool me, miss. It is not in your nature to feel dispassionate about learning new things. And besides, your cheeks are quite flushed."

"Perhaps, sir, I have danced too much this evening." Amelia's mind reeled as she attempted to understand her feelings or, more accurately, to explain them away. Undoubtedly, it was the excitement of trying something new, of her birthday, of her dear friends who had surprised her that caused her skin to heat and flustered her thoughts.

The captain stepped back, and Lieutenant Fairchild brought the song to an end.

Amelia felt the loss of William's heat immediately. He bowed overhand, and she automatically curtsied.

"You are dismissed, Mr. Fairchild." William offered his arm to Amelia. "It's been nearly two years since I've had the pleasure of a dance, Miss Becket, and I thank you for indulging me."

"Thank you, sir." She slipped her hand into the crook of his elbow, and he led her out of the room. Corporal Thorne presented arms and snapped to attention when they exited the wardroom; then he followed them to Amelia's cabin.

As they walked, she searched her mind for something to say to return the mood to its easy friendliness but came up with nothing.

They arrived at her quarters, and Corporal Thorne handed Amelia her lantern and then took his position next to the door.

William took her hand from his arm and turned it over in the light of the lantern, studying her palm. "I see you followed my orders, miss. You are applying the salve regularly then?"

"Yes, every night."

He shook his head and made a soft tut-tut sound. "It is a pity. I should have very much liked to discipline you again."

Her heart tripped, and she gasped as the captain pressed a soft kiss on her hand and bid her good night.

Amelia shut the door behind her; her pulse was pounding. She could still feel his kiss on the back of her hand. What nerve the captain had. Such impertinence, such cheek to—her mental ranting was interrupted when she spied a parcel upon her hammock. She set the lantern down upon her small washstand and brought the parcel closer. It was wrapped simply in a piece of sail and tied with a length of rope.

Moving the lantern to the deck, she settled next to it and untied the rope. She pulled away the canvas and discovered a cream-colored blanket knitted from thick, soft yarn. The blanket was beautiful and warm, and as she unfolded it, an envelope fell to the floor. Amelia picked it up and opened it, sliding out a note.

Miss Amelia Becket,

As we near Europe, the air becomes increasingly cold, which I imagine should prove most uncomfortable for a lady accustomed to the warm sun of Jamaica. I shall set Riley to the task of procuring for you an oilskin coat in a small size from the purser's stores so that we will not be denied your company upon the upper decks as the weather changes.

This blanket was made for me with love by my younger sister, though I have rarely felt the need for it. I think that you might make good use of it.

I apologize for the practicality of this birthday gift, but as there is no shop aboard where I would have found a trinket to dangle from your wrist or a bouquet of wild flowers, I hope this will do.

Many Happy Returns,
Captain Sir William Drake

Amelia read and reread the short note until she had it committed to memory. As she wrapped herself in the warm blanket in her hammock that night, her mind was filled with the heart-fluttering memory of her first waltz, the gentle kiss on her hand, and the thick blanket that she found smelled deliciously, like the gift giver himself.

She realized that if she wasn't careful, she was in danger of falling very much in love with Captain William Drake. And if her father was to prove that she was indeed the widow of his brother, William was the one man on earth that it would be completely inexcusable for her to develop such feelings for.

Chapter 12

William walked slowly up the gangway to the quarterdeck, his hands clasped behind his back. He kept his posture, though it was a challenge. His shoulders would have preferred to slump. The typical pall hung over the men after ship's discipline. They went about their duties quietly, almost afraid of looking at each other. All aboard were affected by the punishments. None wished to appear unsympathetic by returning to their regular temperaments too quickly. It was one of his least favorite duties as captain. But his heartbeat gained speed as he neared his quarters, where he knew Amelia would be sitting in her usual spot upon the window bench.

He imagined how it would be when he opened the door. She would turn her head, and upon seeing him, her face would light up in her enchanting smile. He looked forward to her smile as much as any beautiful vista he'd seen. And he'd had his share of spectacular views in his eighteen years at sea.

Once they had exchanged pleasantries, she would ask about the discipline. She worried about the men, cared about them, but she also worried about him and how heavily he carried the weight of his responsibilities. Just being near her would lift his mood, and he began to step more quickly. He acknowledged Corporal Ashworth, who stood at attention outside the captain's quarters, but paused before opening his door.

William suddenly realized he was behaving like a prat. It was unnatural for a man in his position to seek comfort in such a way. He was turning to Amelia to mend his spirits, the same way a child ran for comfort to his mother, or a husband to a—He shook his head and cut the thought short, angry with himself for how quickly it came to mind and how often it had of late.

Amelia was out of his reach. If the admiral's suit won out in front of the magistrate, she would legally be his sister-in-law, which, in the sight of the law, was the same as being his sister. And his sister was the last thing he wanted Amelia to be. It was becoming even more imperative to discredit his brother's marriage.

Turning from the door, he paced back toward the rail overlooking the main deck. He needed a firmer control over his emotions before he entered his quarters.

In the week and a half that had passed since their waltz, he had thought of little else. He wondered if Amelia had noticed how perfectly she had fit into his arms. The candlelight had created golden highlights on her dark curls, the light had flickered in her eyes, and her cheeks had glowed. He shook his head. This train of thought wasn't helping.

He had wondered if their relationship would suffer after dancing together. But he should have realized that Amelia was not like a typical young lady who made too much of things. Or who would think one thing and say another. The time they'd spent together since her birthday was as friendly and comfortable as before. Perhaps too comfortable, he thought. They had seemed to gravitate toward each other whenever on deck, and somehow, he knew, without looking, the moment she stepped out of the companionway from below.

The cold in the air had done little to diminish Amelia's spirit, though he noticed that she regularly wore her heaviest dress—not that it was much heavier than any of her other gowns—and layered on her shawl and coat when she was on deck. While she had watched the gun drill the day before, she'd stood hugging her arms around herself in her usual spot, her hair escaping its binding and whipping around her face. The frigid sea wind had been bitter, but she had held her post as any sailor aboard was expected to do.

Finally, William decided that the more he attempted to distract himself from the young woman awaiting him in his quarters, the more anxious he became to join her. It was a hopeless case. Saluting once again to the corporal, William knocked gently on the door to announce himself and then entered. A warm glow spread from somewhere around his diaphragm when he saw her wrapped up in her blanket, sitting upon the window bench. It thrilled him to see her using his gift.

It was just as he knew it would be. Her smile lit up the room. "Captain, I was beginning to wonder if you had decided to remain on deck today." When she stood, she pulled the blanket tighter around herself and joined him in the sitting area. "And how are you, sir?"

An image of Amelia and her smile greeting him at the door of his townhouse at the end of a long day in Parliament slipped into his mind, but with some effort, he pushed it out again. "I am well, Miss Becket, due mostly to the fact that at the conclusion of the ship's punishment, such pleasant company awaits me in my cabin."

He had the pleasure of seeing her cheeks grow pink. "I look forward to Friday mornings as well, sir."

"And are you ready for your charting lesson, then?"

"Whenever you are, Captain."

He stood aside and indicated for her to precede him, and they adjourned to the table. "Today your assignment is to plot our current location. We shall be using the sighting determined by the quartermaster's sextant this morning at dawn. I shall give you our assumed latitude, and here is the chronometer for reference." He stood and watched as she pulled the instruments closer.

Amelia drew her brows together as she studied the chart, the listing on the chronometer, and the sextant reading. William could see her mind working as she wrote the calculations carefully, set the compass, and used the dividers to measure.

It was nearly a half hour later when she pressed her finger at a spot on the chart, wrote down its latitude and longitude upon a slip of paper, and handed the slip to William. He looked at it, studied her calculations—he had long ago figured out the answer in his head—and finally handed it back to her. "Miss Becket, I believe we shall have to change your title to 'ship's navigator.' This is precisely correct."

She gasped and looked at him for a moment. Disbelief was evident in her wide eyes. "I cannot believe I did it."

"I do not know why you should be surprised. I did not assume that you were a person who failed at anything once you set your mind upon it."

Her face broke into a wide grin that shone with pride. And then without any warning, she stepped close, placed her hand upon his chest, and stood upon her tiptoes to kiss his cheek.

William stood frozen to the spot. His mind temporarily emptied, and his heart felt as though it would explode from his ribs. If he could have predicted that those words would have caused such a reaction in Amelia, he would have uttered them endlessly each time he saw her.

Amelia had turned back and bent over the chart again, and it was a moment before the captain realized she had asked him a question.

"I beg your pardon?" he said, tipping his head and forcing a look of attentiveness onto his face.

She furrowed her brow. "I was merely wondering what the reasoning is behind this choice of course. It seems as though it would be much safer to travel northeast." She trailed her finger in a line from Jamaica to England. "But we are much farther south." Her finger tapped on the location that she had pinpointed a moment earlier. "Does this course not bring us too near Spain and France?"

"The admiralty sets our course, miss. Our mission orders us to follow this route, taking the current into the Bay of Biscay, where we are to appraise matters pertaining to ships patrolling the area, note the position of the blockade, and return any reconnaissance to London."

"But your orders were issued months ago, sir. Surely there is a more effective method for the admiralty to determine the state of its ships so close to England."

"Our duty is not to question, miss," the captain said quietly.

"But the French . . . Moving into their territory in such a manner is only asking for trouble." Amelia's voice was rising.

William remained silent. She was expressing the same fears that he and Sidney had discussed from every possible angle since their voyage began.

"What shall we do about it, Captain?"

"There is nothing to do but prepare as well as we are able for the possibility of battle."

"Possibility? It is an inevitability." Amelia's eyes were flashing. She understood the situation too well for her own good. She turned her gaze back to the chart. She was breathing heavily, and he could see that she was trying to school her features. Her finger reached to brush at her cheek. Was she crying?

William stepped toward her and placed a hand on her shoulder. With the other, he lifted her chin and saw moisture pooling in her eyes. Amelia blinked and a tear escaped. He used his handkerchief to capture it before pulling her to him and wrapping his arms around her.

She laid her head against his chest and pulled the handkerchief out of his hand to wipe at her face.

"I will do all in my power to keep you safe, Miss Becket."

Amelia pulled back until she could look up into his face. "You mistake me, sir. It is not for myself I fear. I worry for the men at the cannons and the marines with their muskets and the officers who will not leave their stations; for Tobias and Slushy and Riley and the corporals; and for Sidney and all my friends and shipmates." Reaching up, she laid her hand upon his cheek. "But mostly, I fear for the captain, who must stand upon the deck, carrying the weight of his men's lives on his shoulders, his uniform making him a mark for every French bullet."

The tears streamed unstopped down Amelia's face now, and William again found himself completely speechless. She was worried about *him*? He pressed her head against his chest and pulled her blanket more snuggly around her shaking shoulders. Then it was really only a matter of bending his neck down slightly to press a kiss to her hair—convenient, really. He was reminded again just how perfectly she fit into his arms. As her shaking calmed and her breathing slowed, he realized that while he had entered his cabin intending to be the one comforted, the awareness that he possessed the ability to do the same for her was infinitely more satisfying.

A knock sounded at the open door, and Sidney stepped inside. When he took in the scene, his ridiculous grin was enormous. "My apologies, Captain. The quartermaster sends his compliments, and asks . . . but I shall tell him you are otherwise occupied. And quite agreeably, I might add."

"Mr. Fletcher." William sighed, knowing that Sidney was finding a polite way to tell him he was late in his required calculations to determine local noon. "I would ask you to please escort Miss Becket to the wardroom for the midday meal."

Amelia had stepped away from the captain, which annoyed him terribly.

Sidney looked toward her, his eyes narrowed in concern, and his smile diminished. Even with his miniscule brain, he was apparently able to see that the lady had been weeping.

"But Amelia, are you unwell?" Sidney's brows were drawn.

"No, I . . ." She attempted to smile. "I am well, thank you." She looked down, concentrating on folding William's handkerchief.

Sidney continued to study Amelia. "Of course, Captain. It would be my pleasure." He stepped closer and offered his arm, his irritating grin beginning to grow on his face once again. "And Amelia, I see that you are distributing embraces. I should like to be next in the queue if you don't mind."

William's eyes darted to Amelia. How would she respond? Sidney was undoubtedly teasing in his tactless manner as usual. But for him to even mention such a thing was gauche, to say the least. Not to mention, the image of Amelia embracing his first lieutenant gave William a most sudden desire to plant his fist into Sidney's idiotic face.

Amelia's eyes darted briefly to William's and then back to Sidney's, and the captain was relieved to see her expression had regained a semblance of its typical cheerfulness. "Oh no, Sidney. It is the captain who is distributing embraces, but I am sure he will oblige you happily."

Sidney laughed heartily at this, and Amelia joined him, though a bit less enthusiastically.

"Perhaps if Mr. Fletcher proves himself to be as adept at navigational equations as you, miss, he shall escape punishment for his ill-timed arrival." William inclined his head toward Amelia. "Farewell, Miss Becket. I do hope you shall not be troubled further."

"Thank you, Captain, for the lesson. And for . . ." Her face colored again, and she curtsied quickly then took Sidney's arm, following him out the door. It closed behind her only to open a moment later, just enough for her to step back through the doorway.

"Captain, I would very much like for you to call me Amelia." She set his handkerchief on the sideboard table, turned without waiting for a reply, and swept out the door.

William stepped toward the table, pausing for a small moment as he held the handkerchief before heading above deck.

Chapter 13

AMELIA SAT IN THE GALLEY with the ship's boys, counting and dividing eggs into the buckets for the different mess cooks. Slushy tended the chicken that boiled in large vats on the stove. While Amelia did not particularly care for the smell, the galley was the warmest spot on the ship. She had also learned that Slushy liked to sing as he cooked and that the sound of his discordant harmonies drove the boys into fits of laughter. Slushy tolerated it good-naturedly, and Amelia laughed along with them as he favored them with a particularly terrible performance of "Sally in Our Alley." By the time he reached the last chorus, Amelia and the boys joined in:

There is no lady in the land
Is half so sweet as Sally;
She is the darling of my heart,
And she lives in our alley.

The group applauded, and Slushy bowed with a flourish, holding onto the preparation table to steady himself. Once he stood up straight, he grinned. "Get on with ya, boys. Tend to those chickens up on deck, and fetch the dried peas from the steward. I've work to do and can't spend the entire day delightin' the likes of you with my melodious talents."

As the boys left, Amelia saw that Riley had stepped into the galley and, upon seeing her, began to walk in her direction.

"Good morning, Riley," Amelia said.

"And to yourself, Miss Amelia. Captain sends his compliments and requests your presence on deck right away, miss."

"Very well, Riley. And how is the weather on deck this morning?" she asked, hoping that she sounded casual even though the news that the captain wanted her had set her stomach fluttering. She felt a sudden urge to grin and start up another rousing rendition of "Sally in Our Alley."

"Cold, miss. But the sun is shining."

They left the galley, followed by Corporal Thorne, and Riley wrinkled his nose. "We're to have boiled chicken again, I see."

"Chicken and pea soup tonight," Amelia said. "And for a little added excitement—sea biscuits!"

Riley smiled. After so many months at sea, the men regularly grumbled about the lack of variety in their menu. The two of them stopped at Amelia's cabin. Riley waited as she put on her shawl; then he chivalrously held her coat as she slid her arms into the sleeves.

"And what vittles do you prefer to chicken?" she asked, tying her warmest bonnet beneath her chin and putting on her gloves.

"Beef, miss. How I'd love a large slice of beef with plum pudding and roast potatoes and gravy everywhere."

Amelia smiled. "We do not have many cows in Jamaica. But I miss fresh fruit." She stepped out the door and toward the companionway. The cool breeze that flowed from the decks was already chilling her through her coat. "And who is waiting in London for you, Riley? Do you have family there?" She prayed that he had someone.

"Aye, Miss Amelia. My mum and three younger sisters. My pa's dead. It's been more than a year since I saw them last."

"I'll wager you're a great help to your mother."

Riley's shoulders straightened as they walked up the companionway.

When they stepped onto the deck, they spotted a group of sailors crowded around the gunwale on the starboard side. William hailed her and rushed toward them. "Thank you, Riley. Amelia, you must see this." He grabbed her hand and pulled her toward the group, who parted to allow her to step through their midst and to the side of the ship, where they all pointed at something in the water.

As she watched, a fountain spouted from the sea, followed by the enormous body of a whale that surfaced and plunged back into the water. Its tail, nearly as large as the ship's mainsail, crashed into the water, sending up a spray. She turned to say something to William, but he turned her back around and pointed. "Just wait," he said.

A moment later, a smaller spout shot up, and a miniature version of the huge whale bobbed on the water and then dove, its small tail hovering for an instant before it smacked down into the sea.

Amelia pressed her hands to her mouth to suppress the glee that threatened to burst forth in a most unladylike squeal. "A baby whale!" she finally squeaked. She looked at William—whose arm she had just noticed was around her shoulder—and fought the thoroughly compelling urge to lean against him.

He watched her face with an excited smile of his own. "In all my years at sea, I've rarely seen such a sight and never so close to the ship." Squeezing her closer, he pointed again, and they watched the sequence of bursting forth with a spray and then plunging back into the sea, first by the large animal then repeated by the smaller.

A cool breeze caused Amelia to shiver, and William pulled her against him, wrapping his other arm around her. She leaned her head back against his chest and felt his chin rest on the top of her bonnet.

Amelia imagined that she would remember this as one of the most perfect moments of her life. The sun shone brightly in the blue sky, she was watching a miracle that few people would ever experience in their lifetimes, and she stood in the arms of the man she loved.

There it was. She loved William. She thought about him constantly when they were apart and felt as though she would burst with happiness when she was with him. He was everything she had ever dreamed of: handsome, kind, witty. William listened to her, respected her opinions, and felt pride in her. He was her other half.

A wave of sorrow drifted through her blissful moment, reminding her that if her father had his way, William would also be her brother-in-law. And if such was the case, would she be able to return to Jamaica? Or would she be expected to spend her life under his care, living in the dower house on his estate, near enough to see him every day but unable to be with him? William would undoubtedly marry, and she would be nearby to watch him and his bride and their children. That was, unless she married herself and went away with her own husband.

Her contemplations became unbearable, and with some effort, she forced the thoughts from her mind. She wouldn't ruin this moment. Not when the future was so unpredictable. Right now, she was precisely where she wanted to be, and she would accomplish nothing by fretting about the unknown.

Chapter 14

William stood on the quarterdeck. Despite the bitter chill, he hoped Amelia would venture up on deck today. He paced in front of the railing, and hearing the four bells signaling the middle of the forenoon watch, he joined the quartermaster. The man looked ill at ease, as did all of the officers as they sailed through the French seas. The sailors were unaffected as, per the captain's orders, they knew naught of their location and only understood that they were mere days from home.

Sidney was the worst of all. He remained in such a state of agitation that William was nearly ready to force the lieutenant to his berth with a dosage of laudanum to calm him. William patted the quartermaster on his shoulder. "Keep to course, Mr. Michaels."

"Aye, aye, Captain."

When William returned to the railing, he looked down to the quarterdeck, where Amelia stood, her arms wrapped around herself, speaking with Mr. Wheeler. When her gaze met his, she smiled and shook the older man's hand. He patted hers in a fatherly manner.

William had seen a friendly affection develop between the sailmaker and Amelia, and he marveled at how she was able to soften the hearts of everyone around her. She had undoubtedly softened his, he thought with a wry smile.

Amelia walked toward him, and he stepped down the gangway to meet her. Linking her hand through his offered arm, she allowed herself to be led slowly as they strolled around the edges of the main deck.

"And how do you do this morning, Amelia?"

"Quite well, sir. And yourself?"

"Smashing. It is a fine day to be at sea." He stopped at the gunwale and walked around, turning to face her. "However, there is a matter which I would like to discuss with you."

Amelia raised her eyebrows. "It sounds serious, sir."

"Precisely so, Miss Becket." Her eyebrows rose even higher as he addressed her formally. "It has come to my attention that you were seen at dawn this morning with the junior officers as they sighted our position. Furthermore, I am told that you even had the audacity to use a sextant yourself in an attempt to understand the process."

Amelia stared at him. Her face was a myriad of expressions ranging from curiosity to anxiety.

William leaned closer. "As I can find no other explanation, I am forced to assume that you are attempting to take control of my ship, miss." He winked, and Amelia's face relaxed into a somewhat relieved smile.

"It is true, sir. You have discovered my nefarious scheme. Just this morning I evaluated the size and cut of your jacket to see how I should look in regimentals."

"I hardly need to explain that mutiny is a severely punishable offence." He lifted her hands, wrapping his fingers around her wrists. "I wonder if we are carrying shackles in such a small size. But maybe returning you to London in chains is not a sufficiently serious punishment for a crime of this nature. I think I shall employ . . . *the waltz*."

Her eyes widened in mock terror. "Captain, no! I shall reform. Such punishment is inhumane."

"You should have considered the penalty when you—"

They were interrupted by a call from the riggings, which was repeated across the deck. A cold ribbon of fear wrapped around William's heart. *Please let them be mistaken.* He pulled Amelia behind him as he rushed to the gangplank and up onto the quarterdeck.

Sidney handed him a spyglass, and he peered through it, his heart sinking at the sight of the white, pointed sails that practically screamed "blockade runner." William waited a moment longer for the ensign to catch the wind, and when it unfurled, his fears were confirmed. Dread spread through his limbs, and he took a deep breath so as not to alarm the men. He must maintain a façade of calm if he hoped to inspire courage in them.

"William, what is it?" Amelia asked, slipping her hand back into his.

Not now. Not with her. He closed his eyes and let out a breath. "It is a French warship, Amelia."

"No," she whispered. Her eyes darted from the ship to his face, and he found he could not bear her look of fear.

He gripped her hand more firmly, hoping to lend her courage that he himself did not feel. He must keep her safe.

"Corporal Thorne," William called.

The marine rushed to him. "Sir?"

"Please see Miss Becket safely to the stern hold at once, and then quickly resume your position."

"Aye, aye, Captain."

William's training took over, and he turned to Sidney and began to give orders. "Mr. Fletcher, give my regards to the boatswain and ask him to please call for action stations. At your posts, officers." The bell was rung five times and then repeated. The drum began to sound, and feet pounded upon the deck at the shrill of the boatswain's whistle and the call, "Beat to quarters!" All around them, the entire ship had broken into an ordered chaos that normally set William's heart racing in anticipation, but today he was nearly panicked at the thought that Amelia could get hurt—or worse.

"William," Amelia's voice shook. "Can't we outrun them? Please, we must do something."

"We shall do something, Amelia." He pursed his lips tightly.

"But . . ." The color had drained from her face, and tears began to fill her eyes.

The captain's steward stepped onto the quarterdeck with William's dress uniform and helped William into his full-metal jacket, bicorn hat, and perfectly polished boots. The sound of cannons rolling across the deck filled the air. The marines marched to their positions, muskets loaded and at the ready. William glanced toward the other ship and saw it bearing down on them quickly.

"William." Amelia's voice was little more than a terrified sob.

The sound pierced his heart, leaving behind an ache. He brushed his fingers gently across her cheek. "Be safe and brave, my Amelia," he said then nodded to Corporal Thorne, who tugged on her elbow and guided her down the gangway.

William knew that he must put Amelia from his mind if he was to have his wits about him during battle. So many lives were in his hands, and he did not take the responsibility lightly. He permitted himself one last glance toward the opening to the lower decks, where Amelia and Corporal Thorne had begun to descend the companionway. She turned her head and briefly met his gaze and just as quickly was gone below.

He turned his attention to the starboard bow, where the warship drew ever nearer. Stepping to the quartermaster, he said, "Three points to starboard, Mr. Michaels. Let's bring her around and show those Frenchies what they're up against."

He waited for all of the lieutenants' runners to indicate that their squadrons stood ready, and then he signaled to the boatswain, who gave the order, "Up ports!"

The sight of the HMS *Venture* with her gun ports open and the absolute silence the English navy maintained before a battle must have struck fear into the hearts of the French sailors. Many enemies—or at least those few who had survived to tell the tale—had reported how unnerving and even eerie it was to face such a force. It was indeed part of the strategy to intimidate the enemy before the first cannon even fired. It was also quite a demonstration of the discipline necessary to control men at a most volatile moment.

At the captain's signal, the boatswain cried the order, "Run out!" and as one, the cannons on the starboard side emerged from their ports.

"Stout hearts, men!" William bellowed. He knew that they were watching the cannons aimed toward them with the same apprehension as their enemies.

"Mr. Fletcher, at your command. Open fire, first division!"

Sidney stood at the other end of the deck. At the captain's signal, he cried, "Stand clear!" and lifted his arm into the air. The entire ship held its breath, and time stood still as Sidney brought his arm down and yelled, "*FIRE!*"

Chapter 15

THE ROAR OF THE CANNONS and the jerk of the ship as the entire side fired as one sent Amelia into a panic. She huddled in a ball next to the grate that Corporal Thorne had moved for her. She had climbed into the hull but just as quickly climbed out again when she heard the sloshing of water and the scampering of rats. The ship shuddered, and Amelia fell against the bulkhead in the small, dark section of the deck. Righting herself, she covered her ears against the screams, crashes, and explosions and loosed the emotions that she had attempted to hold in check. The idea that her beloved ship, her beloved crew, and especially her beloved William were facing a warship intent on their destruction caused her stomach to clench. She breathed rapidly as she fought back waves of nausea and tears and terror. And there was nothing to be done but wait.

More rolling of cannons across the deck; the smell of smoke; and the sounds of running, yelling, and injured and dying men crying out penetrated her attempts to push the horror out of her mind. The ship jolted again as it was hit, and she pressed her hand against the bulkhead to steady herself. She hated hiding, helpless, knowing that men she cared about were being hurt.

Amelia stood up and brushed off her skirts. She was disgusted with herself. There was plenty she could do, and she'd not behave like a coward and desert her shipmates. She fought down her terror and hurried toward the operating theater to assist the surgeon. He would definitely require extra hands at a time like this.

When she entered the familiar room, the scene she saw before her could only be described as a nightmare.

By the shadowy light of the lanterns, she saw carnage all around. Men—and parts of men—lay on tables and on the deck. Some men had gaping wounds; others, only blood where their limbs should be. The surgeon's mates stoked a fire in a portable stove, where a pail of tar bubbled. Amelia watched, horrified, as two of the mates held an injured man upon the table while a third removed the sailor's mangled leg with a saw. The stump of leg was dipped into the boiling tar to seal the wound and stop the bleeding. Amelia grabbed the doorframe for support. Her head was swimming. The noise of the groans and sobs and screams of agony filled her ears, and her first instinct was to run back to the dark corner above the stern hold.

She took a steadying breath and remembered that these were her shipmates. Fighting the upheaval in her stomach, she stumbled through the madness toward the surgeon. She would not let these men see her become sick or repulsed by them. It was their darkest hour, and they needed all the comfort she could give. Dr. Spinner looked relieved to see her, equipping her with a curved suture needle and catgut thread.

He pulled her toward the edge of the room, as far out of earshot as was possible. "Miss Becket, I do not mean to appear uncaring toward the men, but there will be many who we shall not be able save. If given a choice, our services will be most valuable to a man with a chance of survival. My design is to help as many men as possible, but sometimes this requires difficult decisions, and often they seem cruel. Please follow my advice."

"I understand, Doctor."

He turned back toward the supply cabinet. "You shall also want this," he said, handing her an apron.

Amelia took off her coat and put the apron over her head, tying it behind her back as she followed Dr. Spinner. The surgeon's mates were already attending to various patients, and the doctor led her to a man with a bloody cloth pressed to his face. Moving the cloth, the doctor revealed a gash torn in the man's cheek. He looked it over quickly then motioned to Amelia.

"I have given him pain medication. If you please, suture the wound."

"Yes, sir."

The medicine had obviously done its job well. The man did not move as Amelia closed his wound. Initially, she attempted to work as carefully as possible, but as the cannons continued to fire, the room became increasingly crowded, and she realized speed was more beneficial than caution.

When she had finished, the man was carried away and replaced by another. Dr. Spinner instructed her as to the dosage of laudanum and set about removing the large splinter of wood that had wedged itself into the man's leg. The sailor screamed out and attempted to rise, so Dr. Spinner called one of his mates to help hold the patient in place.

Amelia held the wounded man's hand and brushed the hair from his brow. His eyes darted about, pain and fear evident. "You'll be all right, sir. The doctor only needs to remove the splinter, and we shall have your leg repaired in no time." Her words and the sedative had the desired effect, and the man relaxed.

"Suture, if you please, Miss Becket." The doctor moved on to the next patient, and Amelia set to work sewing up the leg.

She concentrated hard, lest the swaying of the ship cause her to lose her balance during the delicate procedure. When Amelia had boarded this vessel, she'd never imagined she would come to sew up both sails and men upon its decks.

The man was moved, and his place was taken by a younger man. His shipmates laid him gently upon the table. A shirt had been tied around his torso in an attempt to stop his bleeding, but the makeshift bandage was saturated, and blood seeped onto the table and dripped onto the floor.

Dr. Spinner lifted the shirt, and his face fell. He caught Amelia's gaze and shook his head ever so slightly. As she moved to follow him away from the table, the young man opened his eyes and lifted his hand toward her. Stepping back to him, she grasped his hand. It was cold, and she noticed that his face was growing paler by the moment.

"It's bad, isn't it, miss?" he asked.

Amelia nodded and blinked back the tears that had sprung to her eyes. "Yes. It is bad." She laid her other hand on his. "What is your name, sir?"

He grimaced against the pain that must have been unbearable. "Nicholas."

"I'll stay here with you, Nicholas." She smiled. "I'm Amelia."

His eyes rolled, as he blinked and struggled to focus on her face. "Amelia . . . pretty." His voice was getting weaker.

"Thank you."

"Amelia, I'm scared," he whispered, closing his eyes.

"There's nothing to fear, Nicholas." She leaned forward and kissed his forehead. His hand clenched briefly and then dropped from hers.

With the corner of her apron, she wiped the tears from her cheeks, placed Nicholas's hand gently upon his chest, and rejoined Dr. Spinner where he was attending to the next patient. If she paused and allowed herself time to think, she would undoubtedly fall apart, so she kept busy.

It seemed like hours later, as she rinsed a rag out in a bucket of formerly clean water, when Dr. Spinner paused and turned to her. "Do you hear that, Miss Becket?" She sat silently for a moment listening and then realized that the cannons were no longer firing.

"And did we win then, Doctor?"

"We'll know soon enough, miss, but as we aren't having this conversation on the bottom of the ocean, I take it as a good sign."

Amelia listened as she hung the semiclean rag to dry, hoping to hear William or someone reporting that the French had turned tail and run. She moved a pile of bloody rags, making room as the next injured sailor was laid upon the table. Turning back to her patient, she froze. The rest of the world seemed to fall away, and she pressed her fist to her mouth to stop the sob that fought its way free.

Tobias.

He lay unconscious upon the table. His head lolled to one side. The doctor stepped to the other side of the table and lifted his shirt. Ugly, purple bruising covered his torso in splotches that grew as she watched.

The doctor set the shirt back down and shook his head.

"Please, Doctor. We must do something." Her voice was shrill, but she didn't care. "Please."

"I'm sorry, Miss Becket. I know the two of you were friends. You'd best say your good-byes quickly." He patted her on the arm and moved away to attend to another sailor.

Were? It couldn't be. Not this. The cannons had stopped. It was Tobias's last voyage. He was going home to rest his old bones and see his granddaughter, Anna.

She blinked against her tears and took his hand. "Tobias," she said softly. "Please wake up."

He groaned and rolled his head. His eyelids fluttered opened. "Miss Amelia," he whispered.

She choked on a sob and attempted a brave smile as she laid her hand on his bearded cheek. Her eyes burned with unshed tears.

Tobias began to cough, the pain of each movement evident on his face. He struggled to speak.

Amelia smoothed his gristly white hair away from his face. "Just rest, Tobias."

"I'll have plenty of time for that soon enough, miss." He coughed again, and Amelia poured him a cup of water. When she offered it, he shook his head. "My trunk . . ." Another fit of coughs wracked his broken body.

Amelia stroked his face, "Shhh. It will be all right, Tobias."

His voice was barely a whisper, and she leaned close to hear. "A pouch for Anna . . ."

"Of course, Tobias. I'll deliver the pouch myself. And I'll make sure Anna's taken care of—I promise. Please, do not worry anymore." Amelia couldn't stop the tears that dropped from her eyes.

Tobias strained as if trying to sit up. "Pocket," he whispered.

Amelia searched his pocket but found only the sailmaker's "palm."

When he saw that she held it, he closed his hand around hers. Tobias's face relaxed. "I'm fond of ya, Miss Amelia . . . Like a daughter . . ." His soft whisper trailed away, and Amelia knew he was gone.

A small cry of "no" escaped her lips, and she lay her head upon his chest. Blood pounded in her ears. Tears streamed down her face, soaking his shirt, and Amelia felt a piece of her heart crumble away.

Minutes later, still standing at Tobias's side, Amelia felt a hand laid upon her shoulder. It was with extraordinary effort that she lifted her head and tried to focus on the new movement around her. She turned to see Sidney standing over her. His face carried none of its usual joviality; rather, his expression was drawn. He pulled her to him in a gentle embrace before stepping back and looking into her face.

"I'm so sorry, Amelia." She noticed that his eyes were weary and lines had formed around the sides of his mouth.

"I'm glad you're unharmed, Sidney."

"Thank you. The captain sent me to fetch you from the stern hull. I should have known you'd be in the midst of things." Sidney attempted a small smile. "My friend Amelia Becket would not hide in the bowels of the ship when she could be doing something vital."

"And the captain? Is he . . . ?"

"He is well, Amelia. Attending to the interrogation and processing of prisoners."

Hearing his words, Amelia let out a breath she hadn't realized she was holding. Relief flowed over her, and her shoulders sagged. She allowed Sidney to lead her to the side of the room, and she leaned against him as he rubbed her arm. Sidney's words and touch brought Amelia comfort, but it wasn't his embrace she ached for. How had William fared in the battle? He was unharmed, but she could imagine the burden of watching his men and his ship under assault. She longed to comfort him, ease his troubles.

As they watched, the doorway filled with marines, who took positions around the room. Injured French prisoners were led or carried into the theater for care.

Amelia turned down Sidney's offer to escort her above deck. "This is where I'm needed." She patted him upon the cheek. "I am grateful that you are well, Sidney. I should not have been able to bear the loss of another so dear to me."

Sidney's face softened. "Thank you, Amelia. And I shall ease the captain's mind and tell him you are safe also. I believe he half expected you to don regimentals and lead the musket charge."

"How did the ship fare?" Amelia asked.

"Not well," he said, his jaw clenched, and he looked away. "The extent of the damage is still being assessed."

"It is a good thing we are so close to England, isn't it, Sidney?"

He turned back to look at her, and she saw the strain had returned to his face. "Yes, Amelia. It is a *very* good thing."

Once Sidney had departed, Amelia realized that she still held Tobias's ship maker's palm in her hand. She put it carefully away in her skirt pocket and turned her attention to the injured prisoners. Dr. Spinner was attempting to calm a man who had a bleeding wound on his side. As the doctor obviously spoke no French, his voice only increased in volume, and the prisoner became more agitated.

"Remain still, ya cursed Frenchie," the doctor said, his teeth clenched.

Amelia stepped closer and spoke to the man. "*Et comment allez-vous, monsieur?*" Both the doctor and the prisoner looked at her with relief evident on their faces. "*Le médecin va vous aider, mais vous devez rester immobile.*"

The man calmed, and after the doctor's examination, Amelia set to work suturing his wound. She continued to speak in French to him, imagining that he must be quite frightened aboard an enemy ship where he was unable to understand anything.

"What is your name, sir?"

"Pierre."

"Pierre, I assure you, you are quite safe aboard the *Venture*. Captain Drake is a good man, and he'll not mistreat you. Please tell your shipmates not to fear."

She worked side by side with the surgeon for hours, translating when necessary. Once the prisoners were treated to Dr. Spinner's satisfaction and then transferred to the sick bay, Amelia sank onto one of the overturned barrels. She leaned back against the bulkhead and closed her eyes, thoroughly exhausted.

The doctor joined her. "Your help was invaluable today, Miss Becket."

Amelia didn't think she could lift her head if she tried. She spoke without opening her eyes. "I am sorry for how I acted today, sir. When I saw Tobias upon the table, I did the very thing you warned me against."

The doctor patted her hand. "I have rarely seen a woman with such compassion. I don't begrudge you for caring about your friend."

Amelia allowed herself to relax, and she may have even fallen asleep in the awkward position, but her head jerked up quickly as her mind filled with the dreadful images and sounds of the battle and its aftermath. She looked to her side, where the doctor's head was slumped forward in sleep. She realized he still held her hand, so she gently pulled away, stifling a groan, and stood. She left the room and saw Corporal Ashworth outside the door. He presented arms and snapped to attention.

"Corporal, I am glad to see you," Amelia said quietly, not wanting to wake the doctor.

"And I am glad to see you too, Miss Becket."

Amelia turned, knowing the corporal would follow. Tobias had begged a favor of her, and she intended to see it fulfilled. Walking across the deck onto the companionway, she saw evidence of the battle all around her. The air still stank of smoke and powder and sweat. The companionway stairs were covered in a mixture of sand and blood. When she reached the upper decks, she saw jagged holes where cannonballs had blasted their way through the bulkheads. The carpenter's mates were boarding up the damage as quickly as possible by candlelight.

The attack had begun in the morning, and she realized that it was now past dark.

Amelia found the sailmaker's mates on one of the decks, surrounded by sail canvas. One of the men, Mr. Croft, pointed and directed the others. He must be Tobias's replacement. She did not allow her mind to fully form the thought and turned to the man instead.

"Mr. Croft, are we to repair the sails?"

"Aye, Miss Becket. But first we've a task of a more unpleasant nature. Sailmakers are charged with preparing our dead for burial. Sewing them into shrouds." He rubbed his eyes with his fingertips. "If you're not up to the task, miss, none of us will hold it against ya."

Amelia's stomach turned, but she did not let her apprehension show on her face. These were her shipmates. "I am up to the task, sir. But I should like one of you to fetch something first, if you please."

Once Mr. Croft had dispatched a man to retrieve the pouch from Tobias's trunk, Amelia steeled herself and reached into her pocket for Tobias's palm. She strapped it on her hand and buckled it. "Show me the way, sir."

Chapter 16

William stepped through the dark doorway of the operating theater, lifting his lantern, but saw only Dr. Spinner fast asleep upon a barrel. Where was Amelia? Sidney had reported searching the stern's hold and then discovering that the woman had apparently spent the entire day assisting the surgeon with the wounded. The lieutenant had recounted the events of his interaction with Amelia and even confessed to embracing her when he had seen her devastation at the death of her friend, Mr. Wheeler. How William wished he had been the one to comfort her.

William raked his fingers through his hair. Why hadn't he ordered Corporal Thorne to remain with her and shield her from the unspeakable things she must have seen? She should never have been exposed to such atrocities.

In all his years at sea—most of them during war time—William never ceased to be amazed by the depths of violence men were capable of inflicting upon one another. There were no words for the depravity and horror of battle, and to think that his joyful, softhearted Amelia should be a witness to men's most savage acts caused him immeasurable sorrow.

He shook his head to clear the thoughts in order to focus on what needed to be done. It was crucial that he get this ship out of the French waters immediately. But it was not only the French that concerned him.

He had spent the last hours in conference with the lieutenants discussing a letter found in the captain's quarters of the enemy ship. The marines and officers had stormed the damaged French vessel, continuing with their swords the fight begun by cannons. As she sank, Sergeant Fairchild had the presence of mind to search the French captain's documents.

When the missive was delivered to him, William had read it and felt as if he'd been struck a blow. The message detailed the *Venture*'s mission and course and even went so far as to offer a reward should the frigate be defeated. A betrayal.

Very few people would have had access to the information concerning the mission. Which of them had designed this trap? He'd questioned the French captain relentlessly, but the man had revealed nothing.

A theory began to niggle itself into William's mind. Amelia's father, the admiral, would have known their course. He was likely the man who had chosen it. And he had a personal interest in at least one of the passengers. Amelia had mentioned that her father had been surprised to find that the plantation had not become his property upon the death of his wife. Would he have gone to such lengths to obtain it? Admiral Becket was a ruthless man. William might even go so far as to question the admiral's ethics, but the man would not endanger the lives of eight hundred men and a vessel worth nearly eighty thousand pounds, would he? And the very thought of the admiral killing his own daughter to obtain her inheritance—that was far too reprehensible to consider.

Besides, the theory did not take into account the suit for her jointure after Lawrence's death. The admiral would receive nothing from the Lockwood estate should Amelia die. It could not be her father. William stopped his train of thought and pushed it from his mind.

He left the room and walked up the companionway. The carpenter and his mates were removing damaged wood from the bulkheads and hammering new boards in place. William walked along the starboard side of the middle deck, watching the men's progress by the flickering light of the lanterns. The deck was slowly being returned to its orderly state. Sailors reassembled the partitions to section off the individual cabins.

William stopped at Amelia's partially reconstructed quarters. Next to the porthole, an enormous, jagged opening had been blown in the bulkhead. Blood and sand covered the deck, and splinters of wood were strewn everywhere. Though it was only a matter of time before the men cleaned and scrubbed the floor and repainted and repaired the damage, he wouldn't allow Amelia to return to such a reminder of the violence that had occurred here.

He walked to the stern, searching for her trunk, which had been moved and stowed with all the other items from the various cabins. Once he'd located her belongings, it was just a matter of shifting a few other trunks, and he was able to open it.

A soft feminine smell greeted him as he lifted the lid, and he paused a moment to experience it, inhaling slowly. He immediately discovered what he was searching for—her blanket. When he found her, she would no doubt be cold. He removed it and began to lower the lid, but something caught his eye. A pink ribbon tied in a bow wrapped around a letter—his birthday letter—and a scrap of sail. Holding it closer to the lantern, he studied the picture embroidered upon the canvas and realized it must have been a gift from Mr. Wheeler.

Would Amelia ever be the same after witnessing her dear friend's death? She was a strong woman, but how would she recover from something like this? He carefully replaced the items then stood and continued up the companionway to the lower gun deck.

Corporal Ashworth saluted as he neared, and William found Amelia nearby. She kneeled upon the one spot of cleared deck with the other sailmaker's mates. By candlelight, she was carefully stitching shrouds of the thick sail canvas around the dead men's remains.

Amelia's jaw was tight, her face set and grim. Her hair had begun to fall from its braid and hung in wavy strands around her face. When he approached, she looked up. William's stomach hardened. Dark circles stood out beneath her red eyes. She was exhausted.

He stepped toward her and helped her to her feet, leading her a short distance away from the other men—and the bodies. After setting the lantern upon the deck, he pulled her to him, wrapping the blanket around her shoulders. She stood in the circle of his arms, resting her head against his chest. For an instant the horrors of the day melted away, and there was only the two of them.

"William," she said softly, and he held her tighter.

He pressed a kiss on her soft hair. "Come, Amelia. You must sleep. This chore is . . . gruesome. Please, leave it to the men."

"I cannot."

He stepped back and pulled the blanket tighter around her shoulders. Cupping her chin, he lifted her face. Her eyes looked back at him dully. It was painful to see her expression devoid of its typical liveliness.

"I wish I could somehow cause you to unsee what you saw today. It has stolen the light from your eyes."

The sides of her lips lifted in an attempted smile. "A lady might take offense to such a statement."

"When did you eat last?"

She shook her head; the loose curls swayed around her face and brushed her shoulders. "I do not remember." Her gaze moved toward where the men continued to work and then back to William. "But the task at hand does not lend itself to an increase of appetite."

"Won't you allow me to take care of you, Amelia? Please, come away from here."

She nestled back against his chest. "Tobias would want the job done well. I feel like I cannot abandon it, William. Please understand."

They stood silently, and he found that he did understand. Amelia felt as though she was paying tribute to a person she had been very fond of, and if it helped her to heal, he would not stop her.

He stepped back and put his hands on her shoulders. "I must return to the quarterdeck. Send for me if you need anything."

"This is what I needed. I feel much better now." Her words warmed his insides in much the same manner as a hot cup of tea.

He left Amelia and walked quickly up the companionway, realizing he had been gone too long from the upper deck. With the state of the rigging and the damaged mast, he needed to check how many knots the ship was capable of in her condition. He vowed to leave the Bay of Biscay as quickly as possible.

***

An hour later, he and Sidney stood over the charts, studying the readings. The results were not good. Tomorrow, the riggings would be repaired, and William hoped that within two days the sails would be completely mended. But in the meantime, the ship moved at the whim of the tide, and that was not necessarily a good thing. Earlier, he had found himself quite discouraged and felt the task of repairing the ship and returning to England nearly insurmountable, but the brief encounter with Amelia had rejuvenated him. It was amazing, the effect that particular pretty lady had on him.

"Captain, I find your schedule optimistic. I believe it will take us at least a week, possibly two, to get out of these cursed waters." Sidney rubbed his palm over his cheek. Though the lieutenant tried to hide it, William could see the despair on his friend's face.

"Melancholy spreads like a plague, Mr. Fletcher. You and I both know this. And I'll not allow it to take hold. Our rations are low; the men's spirits are even lower. If they feel that we can get the *Venture* ready to sail at full speed in merely a few days, they will work hard to accomplish it. And I believe they can do it." It was imperative that the officers appear positive, as the men would follow suit.

"But in her current state, we shall not be able to withstand another attack."

William looked thoughtfully at Sidney. His first lieutenant had been correct in his assertions this entire voyage. They had been led into a trap, and Sidney had every reason to worry that another warship might come upon them while they wallowed in enemy waters. "Then it is essential to get this vessel in shipshape condition. And it will not happen unless the men believe it is possible." He placed his hand upon his oldest friend's shoulder. "Mr. Fletcher, it seems to be a particular talent of yours to remain lighthearted in the most unsuitable of times. I trust that you will put your skill to use and maintain a façade of optimism in these dire circumstances."

After leaving his quarters, William made another round, inspecting the progress of the repairs. The carpenter reported the ship was taking on more water, so with a great clanging, the men began to run the pumps.

When he reached the main deck, the captain saw that the sailmaker and his mates had carried the shrouded bodies up the companionway and had arranged them on the deck in preparation for the burial service. The site of nearly thirty men wrapped and sewn in heavy canvas was sobering, and he knew there would be more in the days to come as men succumbed to their injuries. He scanned the deck, hoping to see Amelia, but she wasn't there.

The ship's bell rang six times. It was nearly dawn. William walked to his quarters and donned his full dress uniform. He sat at his desk and, opening the drawer, drew out the Bible that rested inside. The cover was worn and cracked. Sea air was not discriminatory in its harshness to objects, even those of spiritual importance.

One other object lay in the drawer, and he picked it up. He studied for a moment the portrait miniature of Amelia that he'd found in his brother's effects, tracing his fingers around the frame. He noticed now that the picture portrayed her with a reserved smile. She looked out of the frame with gentle eyes. Obviously the artist failed to capture her intelligence or her passionate spirit. The image was a subdued imitation of the real thing, a ghost of the lively person he had grown so fond of. He dreaded the idea that Amelia would become a wilted shade of herself. He must not let her despair rob her of her enthusiasm for life. A feeling of nervous urgency began to grow inside him. The *Venture* must leave French waters without delay, before this blasted war stole another piece of Amelia's vitality.

He crossed the sitting room and paused at the door, breathing in one deep breath and setting his hat upon his head. Then he stepped out onto the quarterdeck.

The sky was beginning to glow, but they would not be able to take bearings this morning. The only indication that the sun was rising was a lightening of the heavy fog from dark gray to not-as-dark gray. The gloom was not going to help the men's moods.

Sidney stepped up onto the deck. The dark bags beneath his eyes and the day's growth of whiskers indicated that he hadn't taken the opportunity to sleep or shave.

"I don't like this fog, Captain," Sidney said in a low voice. "The Frenchies could be anywhere, and we'd not see them until they were on top of us. If only the ship could be repaired silently." He grimaced. "They'll hear us hammering and running the blasted pumps for miles."

William nodded. "We'll forego the gun salute this morning, Mr. Fletcher, but remember, if we can't see them, they can't see us either."

At William's signal, the boatswain summoned the men with the call, "All hands bury the dead!" The ensign was lowered to half-mast. The sailors silently walked up the companionway and filled the main deck.

The men stood in their divisions. Amelia had positioned herself next to Riley, and as William watched, the boy patted her arm, whispering something to her, and she smiled gratefully at him in return. William was growing fonder of Riley by the minute.

The first body was laid upon the platform and covered by the flag. Sidney, as the deceased man's division commander, stood at attention next to the captain.

The sailors bowed their heads.

William opened the Bible and read the verse, even though he could have repeated the words of the ceremony in his sleep.

"For I know that my Redeemer lives, and at the last he will stand upon the earth. And after my skin has been thus destroyed, yet in my flesh I shall see God."

"Edward Baker," Sidney quietly told William the dead man's name.

The captain continued. "We commit the body of Edward Baker to the deep."

The boatswain and one of his mates tipped the platform. The body slid from beneath the flag and plunged into the sea.

The marines held out their guns, and each sailor saluted.

The ceremony was repeated twenty-seven times.

When Tobias Wheeler's body was released, William looked to where Amelia stood. Her jaw was clenched, and she maintained a stoic countenance—just like any good sailor. He rather wished she would cry—it was terrible to watch her stare at the deck and struggle to keep her emotions in check.

As she stood, she trembled. Even in the darkness of the fog, he saw the weariness in her pale face. She had been awake for an entire day and night. In that time, she had worked as constantly as anyone aboard the ship. And he was certain she'd not eaten. He thought how she must have looked as a young girl at her own mother's funeral, and now she had lost Tobias, whom William suspected was a father figure to her. Her weariness and pain tore at him, and he wished he could take it from her.

The gun salute was conspicuously absent, but it was wiser not to alert potential enemies to their position.

When the service ended, William commanded the lieutenants to dismiss their divisions. He and the other officers stood at attention until the last man had left to return to his duties. Amelia had gone below with Riley, and William determined to go after her.

A group of the lieutenants approached him. Sidney spoke. "I was thinking, sir. Perhaps that Frenchie captain's had a change of heart after spending the night in the brig. With your permission, I'd like to question him again."

"Very well, Mr. Fletcher."

By the time William arrived at the lower gun deck where the sailmakers worked, Amelia was nowhere to be found. He descended to the orlop deck and looked in the sick bay and then the operating theater, but she was in neither place. As he walked through the doorway from the surgeon's work area, he heard someone clearing his throat. The noise was faint beneath the creaking of the pumps and the carpenters' hammering.

He stepped back into the theater for a lantern and then followed the noise into the dark area at the stern of the ship, above the hold. In the gloom, he saw Corporal Thorne standing at attention against the bulkhead. The marine presented his arms and saluted then tipped his head to the left. William's gaze moved in the direction the man had indicated. The captain stepped closer and heard another sound, one that caused his gut to sink. He raised the lantern and saw that Amelia sat on the deck wrapped in her blanket, sobbing.

William crouched next to her, placing his hand upon her back. Gasping breaths wracked her body, and he felt completely helpless. "You need sleep, Amelia. Come." He held on to her arms, but she didn't try to stand.

She attempted to speak through her tears, and William understood nothing except for the word *nightmares*.

He stood, bending down to lift her, and then carried her through the ship, up the companionways, and across the deck to his quarters. She rested her head upon his shoulder, and he could feel the moisture from her tears on his neck. Sitting next to her on the sofa, he pulled her against him and wrapped his arms around her. She wept against his chest as he smoothed her hair.

Eventually the sobs slowed, and William found himself muttering words that he hoped were calming. "Everything is all right now, Amelia. I have you." He was amazed at the phrases that came from his mouth. He had never comforted anyone in such a manner. "Don't worry anymore," he soothed. "You will feel better once you've slept."

Amelia whispered, "I am too frightened to sleep." Her breath caught in a gasp. "When I close my eyes, I see . . ."

He understood perfectly. "I know. It is the same for any of us. War is hell, Amelia. It is my deepest regret that you witnessed it firsthand."

"I just want to go home." She spoke through her gasping.

"Shhh. You must rest. Shall I ask the surgeon to fetch something to help you sleep?"

"No. Please do not leave me, William."

Shortly after, Amelia's head grew heavy against his chest, and her breathing deepened. He waited until he was certain she was truly asleep then carried her into his private cabin and laid her in his berth. He arranged the blanket to cover her then carefully untied the laces and removed her boots. Dried blood was spattered on them and on the bottom of her skirt and petticoats. William lifted a strand of hair off her face, and Amelia sighed softly.

He stood for a long while, holding her small boots and watching her sleep. The things she had said warred with each other in his mind. "I just want to go home," and, "Please do not leave me." What were Amelia's true feelings? Would he be able to make her happy in England? Between her father's suit, a traitor, and the French battleships, would he even have the opportunity to try?

Chapter 17

Amelia woke slowly, feeling as though she had not slept at all. Her head ached, her eyes were swollen, and she was famished. Looking around the darkened room, she was confused. Where was she? This was definitely not her cabin. For one thing, there were curtains on the windows, and— She sat up suddenly, recognizing exactly where she was. She scrambled out of Captain Drake's berth. Her heart was pounding.

William had brought her here while she slept? Tucked her into his own bed? Laid her head upon a pillow that smelled just like *him*. A hot blush stole up her neck and spread across her face.

She remembered her collapse after the funeral. It had been too much to bear—all the death, the pain of the injured, and the sorrow on William's face. She had tried to remain strong and allow herself to shed a quiet private tear, but once she had let loose the tight hold she'd kept on her emotions, they gushed forth in a torrent that she had been unable to control.

And then William had been there. He'd held her as she wept and sobbed and generally lost all her credibility as a rational person. He had spoken soothing words, and in his arms, the fear of what she might see when she closed her eyes abated, and she'd finally allowed herself to sleep, knowing that he was near.

Hearing voices outside the room, she became self-conscious. She had behaved like a ninny. A woman taken with the vapors and prone to hysterics. She had always prided herself on the fact that she was not the type of woman to fall apart or to act in an insensible fashion. What must William think of her?

Amelia walked to the window and pushed aside the curtain. It did little to lighten the room. The dense fog continued to cover the skies.

She wondered how long she had slept. Was it evening? Or had an entire day passed?

Her eyes were beginning to adjust to the gloom, and she saw that her trunk sat next to the captain's washstand. Checking once more to ensure that the door was firmly closed, Amelia quickly changed out of her bloodstained dress and petticoats and put on fresh clothing. She washed her face and hands, cringing when she saw the dark brown color of dried blood beneath her fingernails.

She looked into the mirror and took stock of her appearance. There was nothing to be done for the swollen eyes and splotches on her cheeks from her spell of weeping. She brushed her hair out and arranged it. A little water rejuvenated the curls around her face. Overall she felt much better and much more in control of herself now that she was fresh and clean. She searched around the room for her boots and found them next to the door, cleaned and polished.

Voices still carried through the door. She was reluctant to disturb them, but she was also quite hungry and curious about the state of the ship and crew after the battle. She pulled the door open and stepped into the captain's sitting room.

William sat at the table, and his lieutenants sat in various positions around the room. The mood was somber and made even more so by the dark fog outside the stern windows. When he noticed her entrance, Sidney stopped talking, and all of the men stood.

"I am sorry to interrupt. I . . ."

Sidney smiled, and she was surprised by the weariness in the man's face. "It is a welcome interruption."

William stepped toward her, and she felt the familiar heart fluttering that always accompanied his presence. "You look much better this afternoon, Amelia."

"I did not mean to displace you from your cabin, sir." She felt very uncomfortable discussing her sleeping arrangements with all the men watching her.

"Please, do not concern yourself. Your own cabin is quite uninhabitable at the moment, and I have commandeered another for myself."

"Mr. Fletcher's, I should hope," Amelia said, raising an eyebrow at Sidney.

The corners of Sidney's mouth turned up in a tired smile.

"Naturally," William said.

Amelia bobbed in a small curtsy. "Please carry on, gentlemen. I apologize for interrupting your conference."

William walked with her to the door and opened it, following her out of the room and closing the door behind him. He nodded to Corporal Ashworth, who saluted upon seeing them. Amelia shivered and wrapped her arms around herself. The dark fog that surrounded them muffled the noise of the waves. Looking across the ship, Amelia found she could scarcely see the main deck. The sounds of the pumps and flapping of sails were eerily disembodied and floated from every direction.

William's brows were drawn together. "Please promise me you will eat, Amelia."

"Do not worry yourself. I shall make my way to the galley immediately." She laid her hand upon his chest. "And have you eaten today, William? Or slept?"

He placed his hand over hers. His eyes were tired, and beneath them, dark smudges stood out on his tanned skin. His face was unshaven, and she saw lines around his mouth that had not been there a few days earlier. "Yes. I have eaten."

From the corner of her eye, she saw Corporal Ashworth step discreetly away.

"Please take care of yourself," she said. "A captain must have his wits about him."

William lifted her hand and placed a kiss upon her palm. "I find that I quite enjoy knowing that you worry for me, Amelia. A very selfish thing, is it not?"

She closed her eyes briefly as the heat from his kiss spread over her skin. "It is not selfish, sir. Every person deserves to feel as if there is someone who cares for him."

He held her hand, pressing her palm against his prickly cheek. "And do you care for me, Amelia?" His voice was low, and for an instant it seemed as if his confidence slipped, exposing vulnerability in his dark eyes.

"Yes. I believe I do." She stood on her toes and kissed his cheek then turned and walked across the deck. Corporal Ashworth followed. Amelia glanced back once before descending the companionway, but the captain and the entire quarterdeck had been swallowed by the dark fog.

Amelia's breathing was quick, and her cheeks were flushed. She paused to collect herself for a moment on the middle gun deck. Heat from William's kiss still warmed her palm. And the memory of his face—how could she have ever considered this man cruel?

Once she was calmer, she noticed the men working by the lantern light to clean the decks with "holy stones"—so called because their shape resembled a Bible and the sailors kneeled as if in prayer as they scrubbed the decks. The holes she had seen in the bulkhead earlier were nearly all patched, and the carpenter's mates were painting the new wood to seal it from the moisture that would settle and cause the wood to rot.

Amelia continued to the galley, and Slushy greeted her when she entered. "And how are ya, miss? A tough business yesterday. I'm glad to see ya safe." He brought a basket of biscuits and set it before her with a jar of marmalade.

"Thank you, Slushy. I am glad to see that you are safe as well."

Amelia rapped her biscuit on the table and began to eat. She watched the other mess captains and the ship's boys working. There was no conversation, no friendly teasing, and Slushy's singing was conspicuously absent. A somber mood permeated the entire ship. It was sobering to think that these men—and boys—had endured such a thing.

Leaving the galley, she and Corporal Ashworth walked to the surgery theater.

Dr. Spinner was folding the bandages they had washed after the battle the day before. "I thank you for your assistance yesterday, Miss Becket. It was much needed."

Amelia acknowledged his thanks with a small bow of her head and a smile. "And how do you do today, sir?"

"I am well. We have lost three more patients since this morning, and there are some I fear will not last the night."

Upon hearing this, Amelia's heart became heavy. "And how can I be of use to you, Doc—" But her words were cut off by a crash that shook the ship and nearly knocked her off her feet. Before her mind had time to comprehend what was happening, another crash followed the first.

"We are under attack." Dr. Spinner called over the crashes and sounds of men running and yelling. Amelia realized his arm was around her waist and his hand upon her arm, steadying her.

How could it be? There was no call to battle stations, no ringing of the bells.

Amelia joined the throng and ran up the companionway, the noise and smells of battle growing louder as she neared the main deck—irregular gunshots, the clang of metal upon metal, screams, and crashes.

"We've been boarded," someone yelled.

When she emerged onto the deck, she saw in the fog the shadows of men hurling around. Some fought with knives, others with axes that did immeasurable damage. A musket fired near her, and she ducked. When she turned, she saw a man slash another with a knife and then fling him overboard as he screamed.

But she had only a glance before Corporal Ashworth caught up to her and grabbed her around the waist, pulling her back below deck.

Amelia fought against him, furious that he would stop her. "Corporal, you must release me. I must return to the deck."

Corporal Ashworth did not answer. When they reached the orlop deck, he took Amelia's hand and pulled her toward the stern and into the small, dark area above the hull. His grip was tight, and he pressed her into the darkest corner of the stern rather roughly.

"Corporal," she said. "You are hurting me." She strained to get past him.

"Apologies, miss, but I cannot allow you up on the deck. Not when men are fighting. They'll cut down anyone in their path when they're taken by battle madness. Even a lady."

Amelia leaned back against the bulkhead, and Corporal Ashworth released her.

"What do we do, Corporal?" The images she had seen in her quick glimpse upon the deck swam before her eyes.

Amelia listened to the sounds of combat, attempting to hear anything that would tell her what was happening. Her heart was pounding. Sailors called orders, some in English, others in French. The sounds of battle drifted down to her—crashes of men and objects hitting the deck, the screams of the wounded. What of William? She had no doubt that he was leading the men. That he was fighting for his life this very minute.

Amelia hadn't realized she was crying until she tried to speak. "We must do something."

Corporal Ashworth only stood still, hands upon his weapon, listening.

As suddenly as it had begun, the commotion ended, and the silence that followed was nearly as terrifying. Footsteps sounded on the companionway steps.

"Your captain has surrendered the ship. All able bodies report to the deck immediately," called an unfamiliar and heavily accented voice.

"Surrendered?" Amelia said. "Impossible. Captain Drake would never—"

"Come, miss," Corporal Ashworth said, and the resignation in his voice caused a wave of fear to creep up her spine.

She followed the corporal up the companionways to the main deck, and the sight she witnessed caused her to cover her mouth with her hands.

Her gaze swept across injured sailors, blood, and shipmates lifting bodies and limbs. Large grappling hooks dug into the gunwale of the deck, scratching ugly holes in the wood and connecting the *Venture* to a French warship that floated disturbingly close but still partially concealed in the fog. The soldiers that stood guard around the deck wore the deep-blue, high-waisted coat, with its contrasting white lapels, and the white trousers of the French navy. Even as she stood next to him, Corporal Ashworth was disarmed and marched to join the other marines under guard beneath the quarterdeck.

But what caused her to tremble was the sight of the captain and the officers upon their knees with their hands tied behind their backs and French muskets trained on them. A man paced in front of them. With epaulettes on his shoulders and a rounded felt cockade hat that bore a red and white rosette, he was obviously the leader.

William was speaking, and from the expression on his face, he wasn't complimenting the French captain on the curls at the ends of his long, thin moustache.

Bolstering her courage, Amelia stepped across the deck toward the man, just as he pulled back his hand and struck William across the face with enough force to snap his head back.

William glared at him, and Amelia stepped up her pace.

"Monsieur!" she managed to cry before she was stopped by a group of soldiers with their muskets pointing directly at her.

"What is zis?" The French captain waved his hand at the soldiers, and they lifted their weapons and stepped back. "Mademoiselle, I did not realize we had a lady on ze ship."

Amelia's gaze darted to William, and he narrowed his eyes, shaking his head slightly.

"Capitaine Philippe Valiquette at your service." The French *capitaine* continued. "And may I ask who I have ze pleasure of speaking to?" He curled his mustache around his finger as he spoke.

Amelia opened her mouth to answer, but William spoke first. "This is Lady Lockwood, bound for England. I hope you realize, sir, that you are transporting a foreign dignitary and will treat her as such."

Amelia stared at William for a moment, trying to read his expression. The corner of his lip was split, and a trickle of blood dripped down his chin. He gazed back at her steadily, until her attention was recaptured by Capitaine Valiquette.

"Lady Lockwood. *Enchanté, madame.* I shall of course personally see to it that you are set aboard a neutral ship bound for England." He held her hand and bowed over it. From the side of his mouth, he spoke to one of his officers in French, "After I have collected the ransom that the lady's family will undoubtedly pay for her safe return."

The other officer laughed, and Amelia smiled at them politely, giving no indication that she had understood, even though she was sorely tempted to rip her hand out of his and strike him the way he had hit William.

"Monsieur, Captain Drake has French prisoners that have been treated by the ship's doctor and now rest in the sick bay. He has treated them with every kindness while in his care, and I am sure you are a gentleman that would reciprocate this courtesy to him and his crew."

"*Oui*, madame. I should not want zem harmed before zey are taken to madame le guillotine." He turned his face toward the English officers. "Especially zis brute of a captain."

Amelia opened her mouth to unleash a tirade upon the capitaine, but another slight shake of William's head stopped her.

Her head reeled. William and his officers were to be executed. She did not know whether to plead with the capitaine or to scream at him. Either method would probably have the same effect of simply angering him.

Capitaine Valiquette still held her hand and was studying her face. "It will be delightful to have your company, Lady Lockwood. I would be pleased if you would join me aboard my ship for dinner zis evening."

The officer who the capitaine had spoken to before said something in French that caused Amelia's ears to burn and both men to laugh. Apparently the capitaine did not have the most pure of reputations when it came to entertaining women in his quarters.

Amelia considered telling them that she would rather face the guillotine herself than spend the evening with Capitaine Valiquette and his curling mustache, but she knew she must remain in his good graces if she was to have any hope of helping William and his men. She needed to think of a plan, and she needed the freedom to do it. Convincing the capitaine that she was a harmless woman whom he did not need to keep under guard was her best chance to do anything useful. And based on what she'd heard the officer say, a bit of flirting would not hurt her efforts.

She gave the capitaine her most engaging smile and slid her hand into the crook of his elbow. "Thank you, monsieur. I would like that very much."

He lifted her hand, planted a kiss on her fingers, then set it back upon his arm. Amelia glanced at William. His jaw was clenched as he watched them.

Capitaine Valiquette kept his hand upon hers as he gave orders in French. Amelia listened closely, hoping her face did not reveal the fact that she was concentrating on his words, hoping to learn some information that would help William and his men. The British marines were to be incarcerated upon the French ship, and the officers locked up in the brig of the *Venture*. Their weapons were to be confiscated and stowed in the bow near the brig.

Most of the French soldiers would remain on board the English ship, supervising the repairs and keeping her crew in line, with the orders that any insubordination would result in the guilty party being immediately shot and tossed overboard with no questions asked.

The capitaine was most excited about the larders aboard the *Venture*, as apparently the supplies on his ship were quite low. As Amelia listened, another French sailor reported the extent of the damage to their ship. It seemed that while the French army may have been stingy with rations, the extra sails aboard their ship were plentiful and in good condition. The officer predicted that they should be able to sail both ships to France on the morrow.

Amelia watched as the officers were ushered below deck at the point of their enemies' bayonets. William turned his head, surveying the destruction surrounding him, and for a brief instant, his gaze met hers. Seeing the tension in his eyes, her heart clenched. She must do something.

Amelia was relieved when Capitaine Valiquette finally relinquished his hold on her arm.

"Madame, I shall send for you in two hours." The capitaine twirled his mustache and smiled.

"Thank you, sir. I shall be looking forward to it." She curtsied and batted her eyelashes.

Capitaine Valiquette kissed her hand once again, which Amelia felt was taking entirely too many liberties, and they parted. She walked as calmly as she could up the gangway to the quarterdeck and into the captain's quarters. Once she was inside, she shut the door and sat hard upon the floor, holding her head in her trembling hands.

With the marines and officers locked up and the crew under armed guard, Amelia was their only hope. And the idea didn't exactly fill her with confidence.

Chapter 18

Amelia couldn't let William and his men face execution. The very thought nearly caused her to stop breathing, and she thrust it from her mind. It would help no one if she were to panic. She must concentrate.

They were in French waters, and she suspected it would take less than a day to reach the mainland once the capitaine decided to set sail. The ships would be separated, and all hope of regaining the *Venture* would be lost without the marines. That left just her tonight. She had two hours to think of a plan. But what could she do? Various strategies came to mind, and she subsequently discounted each. She couldn't overpower the soldiers or damage their ship. She realized she had very little to offer in the way of espionage skills.

What were her talents? Sewing sails? Managing a plantation. Neither would be of any use. Sugar. She definitely knew sugar, but how would understanding the proper use of sweetener accomplish anything? Just as she started to discard this thought, an idea began to take shape. She did know sugar, very likely better than nearly anyone. And she could use that. But how to set the plan into action?

Amelia hurried into Captain Drake's private sleeping quarters and shut the door. At the very bottom of her trunk lay her fanciest satin dress. She chose it not only to impress Capitaine Valiquette—he would be easy to distract with a pretty gown and a bit of eye batting—but because of the full skirts, with their layers of ruffles and flounces. The many petticoats she would wear beneath it would perfectly conceal the items she needed.

Hurriedly pulling out her small sewing kit, Amelia set to work stitching the hems of her petticoats together in a manner that created hidden pockets beneath the dress. Once she finished, she realized that over an hour had already passed. She pulled on the strings of her short stays corset; tied the strings above her waist; and then slid the dress over her head, reaching behind herself awkwardly to fasten the buttons and wishing, not for the first time, that she had a lady's maid aboard.

Once she was tied up and buttoned in, she stepped onto the quarterdeck and walked down the gangway, knowing that she attracted plenty of attention in her bright blue dress. She smiled and waved to the French guards as she made her way down to the orlop deck, although inside, her heart was pounding. What if someone stopped her and demanded that she return to her room? She mustn't look suspicious. Forcing herself to walk, not run, down the companionway, she found the doctor at work in the operating theater.

"Hello, Dr. Spinner," she sang. "I will be just a moment." She winked at him quickly and hoped he would understand not to question her.

The doctor's eyebrows rose when he saw her dress, but he just said, "Very well, miss," and returned to the patient whose arm he was suturing.

Amelia hurried past the guards to the dispensary cabinet and found the bottle she needed. She bid farewell to the doctor and hurried out of the theater with a few smiles and waves, marveling at the fact that nobody suspected her capable of any deception just because she was a woman. They probably assumed she was procuring smelling salts to prevent herself from having hysterics or some other such womanly malady. Once she was alone in the companionway, she bent down and slipped the bottle into one of the hidden pockets in her petticoats.

She wondered how much time had passed, hoping she still had at least twenty minutes before the capitaine sent for her. Sweeping into the galley, she found Slushy, and glancing around to ensure that there were no guards, she pulled him into the purser's storeroom and shut the door.

"Slushy, I need your help."

Reaching into her petticoats, she pulled the laudanum from the hidden pocket. "We must get this into the French soldiers' rum."

Slushy's eyes opened wide. He glanced at the door then pulled her to the far corner of the room. "Miss, I'm sorry about the captain. I am. But this just won't work, and we'd be killed for even attempting it."

Amelia felt her throat begin to constrict. "Slushy, please. You don't need to do anything; I just need a few bottles of rum. If I'm caught, I'll say that I acted alone. Please help me."

Slushy folded his arms and leaned back against the wall. His eyes had softened. "I know you're desperate, miss. I'd do anything to help the captain. But this . . . it's not a good plan. They'll taste that stuff. It's bitter as—"

Amelia interrupted him. "But we have treacle. It won't completely cover the taste, but it will help disguise it. Please, Slushy. The French captain's sending the officers to the guillotine. This is our only chance." She held on to his hand. "Just a few bottles, please?"

Slushy looked down at where Amelia was squeezing the life out of his hand. He looked into her face and must have seen something there because he sighed. "Very well, miss." He walked to the cupboard at the side of the room and pulled the key from his pocket.

Amelia rushed to pull a jar of treacle and a cup from the shelf and sat on the floor. She poured a large dollop of the treacle into the cup and opened the laudanum. The smell alone was enough to make her eyes water. She carefully drizzled a small amount into the cup and, using the wooden spoon Slushy handed her, began to mix the two together.

Amelia had learned from the doctor that even a very small amount of the potent medicine was enough to render a man unconscious. She dipped her finger into the mix and touched a bit onto her tongue, wincing at the still bitter taste of the laudanum, and added more of the sugary syrup. She knew she couldn't sample it very often during the process unless she wanted to find her own senses dulled, or worse, wake up hours later on the floor of the storeroom.

Once she was satisfied that the bitterness of the tincture was sufficiently disguised, Slushy helped her add the mixture to bottles of rum, pouring a bit back out to taste again. She swished a small amount around in her mouth before spitting it out—not caring that Slushy saw such an unladylike act. The taste proved that the sweetness of the rum and treacle had worked precisely as she'd thought it would, and while the rum tasted a bit different, the bitterness of the laudanum was concealed. Amelia hid the laudanum in her petticoats, not wanting to leave any evidence that might implicate Slushy.

In all, they had tainted twelve bottles of rum. After they hurriedly replaced the corks, Amelia slipped three bottles carefully into her petticoats, padding them with cloth to prevent them from clanging against each other. She carried one in her hand, and the other eight were to be delivered to the French soldiers aboard the *Venture*. Slushy planned to ask the ship's boys and mess cooks to pass the word to the English sailors to avoid the rum at all costs.

Using a barrel for support, Slushy stood and held his hand out to pull Amelia to her feet.

She swayed her hips and walked around experimentally, ensuring that the bottles would not bang against each other and would remain hidden beneath her skirts. Before she left, she wrapped her arms around Slushy. His embrace was tight, and she realized that he was worried for her.

"You take care of yerself, miss. And teach them Frenchies a thing or two."

"Don't you worry, Slushy." Amelia's voice shook. She had been so sure of this plan, but now that she was about to leave the safety of the galley, she realized that she was truly afraid. What if she was discovered? She did not believe that she would even have the hope of waiting until they reached France before she was executed.

She walked up to the main deck, holding her face in a smile even though inside she felt like she would shatter. But she could not fail. William's and his men's lives depended upon it. And she could not let them down.

The officer that Amelia had seen the capitaine speaking to earlier caught her eye when she stepped onto the main deck. He walked toward her.

"Bonjour, madame," he said, continuing in stilted English. "I am Jacques. If you please, I will bring you to Capitaine Valiquette's quarters."

"Bon-jewer, Jacques," Amelia replied, purposely slaughtering the French pronunciation badly enough to make the man's nostrils flare. "Mer-cee." She followed him to the gunwale, where a board had been laid between the two ships. The board slanted downward since the French ship rode lower in the water than the *Venture*.

Amelia handed Jacques the bottle she held then grabbed her skirts tight as he helped her step up onto the plank behind him. The ships were not steady. They bobbed with the waves, and Amelia gripped Jacques's hand probably more tightly than was necessary as she walked and slid down toward the other ship. A sailor at each end held the board to keep it from slipping off the rails and plunging them into the ocean. She focused on the lanterns on the opposite side, glad that it was still foggy and she could not see how high she was above the water.

When she reached the other ship, she stepped down onto the deck with Jacques's assistance, again maneuvering her swaying skirts away to keep the bottles from bumping into his ankles. From what she could see in the near darkness and the fog, the French ship was smaller than the *Venture*. Few soldiers stood upon the decks as she walked past, and those that did merely smiled and tipped their caps to her.

They reached a door. Jacques knocked, and upon hearing the voice inside bidding them enter, he swung open the door and bowed as Amelia entered.

Capitaine Valiquette stepped toward her and took her hand, kissing it. "Madame, you look *très belle* tonight."

The hair on the back of Amelia's neck rose. She could all but feel the capitaine's eyes skim over her, and she fought down a small wave of panic. Jacques was going to leave her alone with this man, and who knew what thoughts the curling-mustached capitaine had on his mind? She remembered the British officers kneeling upon the deck of their ship, hands bound, and the cruel way the Frenchman had struck William. She clenched her teeth and steeled up her courage. This French capitaine would regret ever challenging the *Venture* and Captain William Drake.

"Thank you, Capitaine," she said, trying to sound demure instead of terrified.

Jacques handed the bottle to Capitaine Valiquette, telling him in French that Amelia had brought it with her.

"I do hope you enjoy rum, capitaine. This bottle is from my own sugarcane plantation in Jamaica," Amelia said. She gave him what she knew was a flirtatious smile.

Capitaine Valiquette dismissed Jacques and pulled the cork out of the bottle, filling the two goblets that sat upon the table. He pulled out a chair for Amelia, and she sat carefully, adjusting her skirts around her. He pushed her chair in and trailed his fingers down her arm before taking his own seat next to her.

Amelia felt a sudden urge to wash her skin where the capitaine had touched it.

A steward entered with a tray and placed their meals upon the table, pulling the coverings off the plates and setting their napkins into their laps.

The capitaine dismissed him and indicated for Amelia to begin her meal.

Amelia had to force her eyes away from the capitaine's goblet and cut a small bite of pork. Her appetite was nonexistent, and she hoped he didn't notice her hands shaking.

"This is delicious, Capitaine," Amelia said, willing him to pick up his goblet.

"Please, let us dismiss with the formalities. You must call me Philippe." He smiled, cut a large piece of meat, and pushed it into his mouth, chewing noisily.

"Then, Philippe, I hope you will call me Amelia." She tried not to stare at the way his mustache wagged up and down as he chewed.

"Amelia. It is a lovely name." When he grinned, she was able to see that he had not entirely swallowed his pork before baring his teeth. If her nerves weren't already making her stomach queasy, Philippe's table manners would have done the job nicely.

She lifted her goblet. "To new friendships, Philippe."

He picked up his own goblet and took a drink, sloshing the rum around in his mouth to clear out any remaining food before he swallowed in a gulp and belched loudly.

Amelia kept her lips closed as she tipped her drink toward her then dabbed her napkin on her mouth. "And how do you find the rum, sir?"

"Very good," he said, taking another swallow. "It has a . . . different . . . flavor."

"Yes, it is the treacle. An old family recipe." She winked at him and then wished she had not when he slid his chair closer, brushing his leg against hers. Amelia was beginning to feel a bit alarmed. Not only because he had moved so near but also because the capitaine's ankle was disturbingly close to the bottles hidden in her skirts. And he'd had two large gulps of the rum. Was it having no effect? Had something gone wrong? Perhaps she had misjudged the dosage or not been aware that rum somehow affected the potency of the medicine.

Philippe ripped off a large mouthful of bread with his teeth and began to gnaw on it.

Amelia reached across the table for the bottle. "Here, allow me to refill your drink, Philippe."

Taking another large swig of rum, he swished it around in his mouth with the half-chewed bread and gulped the entire glob down his throat with some effort. Amelia was quite impressed that only a small squirt of rum escaped his lips. Capitaine Valiquette was truly a marvel of deplorable etiquette.

"Very good rum, would you not agree, Amelia?" Was it her imagination? Or did his eyes look just a bit sleepy?

"Oh, thank you, Philippe. I am so pleased that you like it."

Philippe placed his hand on the back of Amelia's chair, and she froze. How was this man still conscious? And how would she possibly defend herself if he got any more familiar?

"Amelia, you will enjoy traveling aboard my ship." His face was horribly close to her own, and she found that tainted rum lent his breath a quite putrid aroma. "Ze French, we are gentlemen, not unshaven savages like the English captain and his sea dogs."

Amelia blinked. She pursed her lips and attempted to control her anger by focusing on the drop of rum that hung precariously from the tip of one of the capitaine's mustache curls. "Sir, I am afraid you are quite mistaken. The captain and his men have been very gracious to me."

Philippe took another noisy swig of rum, gulping it down. "Bah," he said, and she wrinkled her nose, wishing she had learned her lesson the first time and held her breath when his face was so near.

He blinked slowly before he continued speaking. "I should have blown zis ship from ze water, but ze reward for a man-of-war is too tempting. And it will be very satisfying to send ze famous Captain Drake to meet le guillot—" Capitaine Valiquette's eyes rolled back in his head, and he slumped forward onto her shoulder, nearly knocking her to the floor.

With an enormous effort, Amelia heaved him back into his chair and hurried into action. She had no idea how long the captain would be unconscious. As quickly as she could, she removed two of the bottles from her petticoats and set them upon the table. Then she turned and began to search his quarters. Every noise she heard sent a chill of dread through her. At any moment a member of the crew could enter the cabin and she would be discovered.

Taking the lantern into the captain's sleeping area, she searched his trunk and found what she was looking for: pistols. She also found a bag of powder and shot and quickly slipped it all into the pockets in her petticoats. She lifted the capitaine's sword, but it was too long to fit beneath her skirts, so she continued to search until she found a sharp dagger.

Quickly looking at the capitaine's desk, she seized any documents that she thought might prove detrimental to the French and folded them up, hiding them in the pockets beneath her skirts. She hurried back to the dining area and searched the captain's person, nervously poking her fingers into his pockets and inside his regimental tunic. She discovered a small pistol, which quickly joined the others.

Amelia turned and gave one more sweeping glance around the room. Her eyes lit again upon Capitaine Valiquette, and her anger at his words returned. How dare he insult her captain! And her shipmates. Amelia retrieved the small dagger she had found, and acting with a bravery that she would never have been capable of had her fury not been fueled by his rudeness, she grabbed hold of the capitaine's waxed mustache and sliced it off. She repeated the action on the other side, placing the stiff curls into her pocket.

She extinguished all but a few candles in the room, hoping that nobody would check on the capitaine if they believed him to have retired for the night. Then she picked up the bottles from the table and opened the door, speaking loudly as she turned back toward where the capitaine sprawled unconsciously in his chair. "Thank you, Philippe. Dinner was wonderful. Good night."

Closing the door behind her, she stopped the first soldier she saw. "Capitaine Valiquette asked me to deliver this rum to his officers."

The man held up his lantern. He squinted and tipped his head, regarding her for a moment. Would he believe her? She smiled and batted her eyes a few times, and his gaze moved back to the bottles in her arms.

"Merci, mademoiselle." He took the bottles and led her to the plank between the ships.

Amelia held her skirts as she carefully stepped up the plank in the pitch-blackness. The lantern on the *Venture* glowed in the fog, seeming so much farther away than it had when she'd come the other way an hour earlier. Wind whipped upward between the two ships, nearly causing her to lose her balance. The pistols and last bottle were heavy in her petticoats, and her heart nearly thudded out of her chest. It was only a matter of time before Jacques or another officer discovered Capitaine Valiquette. Would they believe he merely had too much to drink? She could only hope that she would be able to set the next part of her plan into motion before her deception was discovered. But there was no turning back now. Her failure would result not only in her own death but assure William's as well, and that was all the incentive she needed to continue.

Chapter 19

William sat upon the deck and leaned his shoulders back against the bars of the brig. *His* brig on *his* ship. He had never felt so angry and so helpless. Sidney sat next to him, and the other officers either stood or sat in the small space surrounded by iron bars. None of them spoke. William felt their despair. It weighed heavily upon him, like a boulder pressing down on his chest. He had done the unthinkable: surrendered his ship.

The French had come upon them in the fog and boarded the ship, completely taking the *Venture* by surprise. They had attacked without mercy, using axes, pistols, swords, and bayonets. When William had seen the extent of the bloodshed and realized that fighting would only yield more, he ended it the only way he could—by relinquishing his sword to the French capitaine. And now, instead of his crew being slaughtered, he and his officers faced execution.

He hung his head forward. And what would happen to Amelia? Now that the capitaine believed her to be a traveling dignitary, she had a better chance of arriving safely in England. But what then? He was no longer concerned with the blasted jointure arrangement. If William was to be killed, at least he knew that Amelia would be provided for, even if it meant she would bear his brother's name. An ache grew in William's chest when he thought of her. Would he ever see her again?

This very moment, she would be eating dinner in the ridiculous mustache-twirling French capitaine's quarters. William could only hope her title would ward off any of the man's unwanted advances. He clenched his hands at the very thought of that buffoon touching his Amelia.

Sidney bumped William's shoulder with his own, distracting the captain from his maudlin contemplations. "You made the correct decision, Captain."

William glanced at him. "A strange sentiment from a man destined for execution."

"If we had continued to fight, more lives would have been lost. You thought only of your men, not your own reputation or pride. It was the correct decision."

William rubbed his eyes with his fingertips. "Thank you, Mr. Fletcher."

"I feel proud to have served with you, Captain. And proud to call you a friend." Sidney's voice was low, and he looked across the brig as he spoke.

"Come, man. All is not lost. You speak as if we're heading to the executioner today."

Sidney lifted his shoulders in a shrug. "I did not want to forget to tell you."

From the periphery of his vision, William studied his oldest friend. Sidney had always been exactly where he was now—at William's side. Despite his penchant for flippancy, Sidney was a loyal companion and even now supported William.

William felt his throat begin to constrict. "It has been a privilege to serve with you, Mr. Fletcher. It is a fortunate man indeed who has such a friend as yourself."

Sidney nodded once and continued studying the opposite wall.

The captain watched the guards. The three French soldiers had confiscated the English officers' weapons and then escorted the prisoners at bayonet point to the section of the ship that housed the brig. The guards had shoved and spit on them and hurled what William assumed to be insults as they'd pushed the officers into the brig and locked the padlock on the door. The room was well lit by lanterns that hung from the ceiling so the guards could maintain an effective watch over their prisoners. But once the officers were locked in, the Frenchmen had promptly ignored them. The guards were currently seated on barrels, using a large crate as a card table. The lack of discipline shown by the enemy soldiers was deplorable. Sitting down on duty? Gambling?

Just as William was pondering the miracle that Napoleon had thus far experienced a fairly successful campaign with such a poorly trained army, the door to the room opened, and Amelia stepped in wearing a stunning blue dress and carrying a bottle of rum. She closed the door behind her.

William gasped. *No! What is she doing?*

But Amelia did not even spare the incarcerated officers a glance. Instead, she focused her attention on the French soldiers, who had risen to their feet upon seeing her. She spoke to them in French, and though William could not understand her words, he saw that the soldiers relaxed. Amelia sat upon the crate with them, laughing at something one of them said. She opened the bottle, and the men passed it around, obviously very grateful for the spirits—and for the enchanting company.

William felt as though a clamp had been fastened about his insides. Amelia must be hoping to intoxicate the soldiers and somehow overpower them. It would never work. One bottle of rum would not do anything but impair the Frenchmen's judgment and possibly loosen their inhibitions, especially with a lovely young lady in their midst. She was most certainly putting herself into a situation which she would quickly find out of her control.

William stood. "M'lady. You mustn't—"

One of the guards picked up his musket, stepped up to the bars, and raised the butt of it to use as a club while William continued his protests.

Amelia hurriedly stepped between them, saying something in French to the guard and giggling. She linked her arm through his and turned to pull him back toward his friends. But with her other hand, she found William's and slipped something into it without the Frenchmen noticing. She and the guard took their seats once again upon the crate, and Amelia continued to charm them with her batting eyelashes and French chitchat.

William turned his back to the bars, faced Sidney, and opened his hand. The two of them leaned close, and by the light of the swaying lanterns, they peered at what appeared to be two thick hooks sitting in William's palm.

Sidney lifted one and studied it for a moment before he broke into laughter. The first good humor William had seen from him in days. After a quick glance at the guards, Sidney stifled his glee, but his eyes continued to shine with mirth.

William raised his eyebrows in question.

Sidney held the hook above his lip and pretended to twirl it. William looked back at the object that remained in his hand. The capitaine's mustache? He glanced back over his shoulder at Amelia.

"How—"

Sidney continued to grin. "None of us should have ever doubted the ingenuity of Miss Amelia Becket." He held the half mustache up again and spoke in a nasally voice, "Especially zis brute of a captain."

William turned his attention back to Amelia. He could hear the sound of quiet laughter behind him as Sidney apparently shared the joke with the others. A surge of energy took hold of the officers as the cloud of despair began to disperse.

One of the soldiers sitting with Amelia slid down to sit on the deck, resting his cheek against the crate. Was the man sleeping? Another took a long drink of the rum and toppled onto the floor.

Amelia did not appear surprised. Her focus was on the last soldier. Although William could not understand the man's words, the Frenchman appeared to be nervous. His voice rose as he pointed to his shipmates and then to the bottle of rum. Amelia was attempting to reassure him. Her voice was calming, but the man refused to be placated.

The soldier reached for his bayonet but grasped only air. His movements were sluggish. He blinked slowly and reached again, only to be stopped by Amelia's voice and the pistol she held pointed at him.

The tension in the room instantly rose. Amelia's eyes were narrowed, and her voice was sharp, but her hand shook. She lifted the bayonet and moved it out of the man's reach, speaking a litany of words that William did not understand but which resulted in the soldier loosening his buckle and removing the ring of keys attached to his belt. Amelia snatched the keys from his hand and stepped toward the brig.

She began to work the keys in the large lock, holding the pistol beneath her arm. "The marines are aboard the French ship," she said quickly to William. "The capitaine and hopefully most of his officers should be either sleeping or very near to it. The French soldiers are aboard the *Venture*, and your weapons are stowed in the bow."

William leaned his head closer, resting his hand upon her shoulder. "You should never have endangered yourself in this way."

She tried a different key, wiggling it as she spoke. "I find, Captain, that I prefer your head where it is."

The lock clicked, and William saw movement from the corner of his eye.

"Amelia! Behind you!"

Just as Sidney pushed the gate of the brig open, the French soldier stumbled toward Amelia with his dagger raised. She turned but too late, and he slashed the knife downward into her side.

Amelia screamed and staggered back against the bars. Sidney quickly dispatched the man, and William pushed through the gate of the brig, pulling Amelia into his arms.

When he looked into her face, William saw that it was deathly white. He turned his attention to her injury and saw blood spread from the gash in her side.

She winced in pain. "William, go! The laudanum will wear off quickly."

Blood was seeping from the tear in her dress and beginning to drip onto the floor. Lieutenant Wellard handed William some rags. He took them, pressing them against Amelia's wound. She breathed in sharply.

"I will not leave you, Amelia." He clutched her close to him, even as he felt her legs refuse to support her. He lowered her to the ground to lean against the crate, his arms still around her.

"William." Her voice was alarmingly soft. "I do not think the wound is deep. But if you do not defeat these Frenchmen, we shall all face the guillotine. It would not matter if I was the Queen of Sheba; no title will save me once my deception is revealed."

He was torn. He could see the truth in what she said. It was the only way to save her and his men, but the thought of leaving her bleeding upon the deck was inconceivable. Standing, he lifted her into a shadowed corner. He pulled off his jacket and folded it, tucking it gently beneath her head.

"I brought pistols." Amelia winced again as she clutched the rags to her side. "In my skirt." She pulled on her skirts to reveal the pockets in the hem of her petticoats, and William was dumbfounded as he pulled out two pistols, a dagger, and a bundle of documents.

He brushed the backs of his fingers along her cheek. "You are amazing, Amelia. The men of this ship, and even His Majesty the King, owe you a debt of gratitude for what you've done."

"I did not act out of patriotism. And though I care for the crew of the *Venture*, I confess, it was only their captain that I thought of." She reached to press her hand against his cheek. "You must go. Find Dr. Spinner, and I shall be well."

William glanced toward where his men stood awaiting his orders; then he turned back to Amelia, cupping his hand behind her neck and pressing his lips against hers. The warmth of her response was nearly his undoing. He pulled away. "I will not fail you," he whispered before brushing one last kiss across her lips.

He stood and strode to where the officers waited. Sidney held one pistol, and the other officers had claimed bayonets and knives from the guards. William kept a pistol for himself and handed the other to Lieutenant Wellard.

"Men, I believe we owe it to Miss Becket to show those Frenchies that they attacked the wrong ship." He opened the door and charged into the night to reclaim what was his.

Chapter 20

Amelia heard voices echoing from far away. She struggled to understand them, feeling as if she were swimming toward the surface of the sea but unable to reach it. She finally gave up the battle and slipped back into the deeper water.

The voices came again, but this time they sounded nearer. She recognized Dr. Spinner's clipped tones, followed by William's low responses. Gradually she began to understand what they said.

". . . luckily not deep. If it hadn't been for that corset, it would have been much worse. As it is, I was able to stitch up the wound cleanly. She is just sleeping off the effects of the laudanum now."

"I thank you, Dr. Spinner. Mr. Fletcher, please inform the other officers of Miss Becket's condition. They have been quite concerned."

"Aye, aye, Captain. And I must say that I have found another reason to appreciate ladies' undergarments. Not that one was needed."

"You're dismissed, Mr. Fletcher."

Amelia forced her eyelids apart, trying to bring the room into focus, but it was too hard to keep them open. She shifted and sucked in her breath at the pain in her side. She immediately felt a hand upon her forehead.

"Amelia," William said softly.

She struggled to open her eyes again, willing the room to stop spinning.

"Are you in pain?" he asked.

"A bit," she whispered. Her mouth was so dry. "But I do not want any more medicine." She glanced around the room before she closed her eyes again, realizing that she was lying upon a table in the operating theater. She vaguely remembered Dr. Spinner finding her in the dark corner near the brig and inspecting her wound by lantern light. At her direction, he had found the laudanum in the secret pocket of her petticoat and held her head up as he tipped the bottle into her mouth. She had choked on the bitter taste and fumes and then remembered no more.

As her mind became more alert, she jolted. "William, the ship. You've reclaimed the *Venture*."

William's hand brushed down to cup her cheek. "Yes. Thanks to our daring sugar saboteur."

Amelia leaned her head against his palm. She closed her eyes again. "I am so glad you are safe, Captain," she said and drifted back to sleep.

***

The next time Amelia woke, her head felt much clearer and the sun was shining through the curtained windows. She recognized that she was in the captain's quarters, but instead of rushing out of the berth as she had done previously, she allowed her mind to wander to the evening before. More specifically, the moment William had kissed her. Her first kiss. The mere memory of his lips on hers sent tingling shivers across her skin and caused her toes to curl.

If there had been any doubt that she was in love with Captain Drake, that one small action had put it to rest. Despite the pain of her wound, the kiss had felt like warm sunshine spreading over her. Had it been the same for William?

She thought back to the words he had said. *I will not fail you.* Not exactly a declaration of love. A small ribbon of doubt wove its way into her thoughts. Had he merely kissed her because he thought she might succumb to her wound? He hadn't known that it was not her lifeblood pouring out onto the floor. Or perhaps the kiss was a result of his excitement at the chance to reclaim his ship.

She pulled her blanket up, holding it against her cheek as she turned onto her side. How did William feel about her? He had been charming, to be sure. They had developed a friendship and had even waltzed. But she had been the one to kiss him twice upon the cheek. She had told him that she cared for him. And he had never said the words in return.

It would be wise not to allow himself to develop feelings for her. If the legality of her dratted signature next to his brother's was validated, it would be immoral—not to mention illegal—for him to love her.

Two months ago, widowhood and the benefits it brought with it had felt like a prize she had won, but now she would give anything—her plantation, her freedom—if only she could undo the action. If only she had not become Lady Lockwood. Amelia choked back her tears. She had cried quite enough over the last few days.

She reached her right arm across her body and tenderly touched the wrappings the doctor had applied around her torso. Carefully, she pushed herself into a sitting position, and while it was painful, it was not unbearable. Beneath her blanket she found that she wore a man's white shirt over her blue gown. Upon further inspection, it was apparent that the gown was torn and damaged beyond repair. The corset she'd worn beneath it was missing. She assumed the doctor had removed it to apply her sutures.

Though she was weary, Amelia decided against allowing herself to fall back to sleep. She was anxious for details about how the officers had reclaimed the ship, and she also worried about what dreams she might have now that she was not relying upon medicine to put her to sleep. She climbed out of the berth and moved to the washstand. After washing her face, she brushed her hair, despite the difficulty of lifting her left arm, and finally allowed the curls to fall naturally over her shoulders rather than arranging them. Peeling off the bloodstained dress while keeping her left arm close to her side, she slipped on a fresh gown and was attempting to fasten the buttons down her back with one hand when a knock sounded at the door. She opened it.

William stood in the doorway, dressed in his full-metal regimentals. She raised her eyebrows, wondering why he wore his formal uniform, and then she noticed that he held his Bible. A fresh wave of sorrow settled over her. *Another funeral.*

"I heard you moving about. Are you in pain, Amelia?"

"No. Just a bit tired."

"And do you need assistance with . . . anything?"

Her face colored. "Actually, if you don't mind, would you fasten my gown?" She turned around and swept her hair out of the way.

William stepped closer and made quick work of the buttons, the brush of his fingers sending tingles flowing over her skin. She turned around, shaking her hair back over her shoulders and feeling suddenly shy. "Thank you, Captain. If you find that ruling an earldom does not agree with you, I believe you might choose to seek a career as a lady's maid." She glanced at him and saw a small smile lifting the sides of his mouth.

He stepped aside and indicated for her to precede him into the sitting room.

Amelia stepped back into the cabin, pulled her blanket from the berth, wrapped herself in it, then made her way into the outer room and sat in her favorite spot upon the window bench, pulling her stockinged feet up on the seat next to her.

William stood next to her and arranged the blanket, pulling it to cover her legs. "I have sent Riley to fetch some breakfast. And Corporal Ashworth will be outside your door if you have need of anything. Please do not feel as if you must attend the services today. It is more important that you rest."

Amelia nodded. Getting dressed had drained her energy. "I am sorry, William. I know the funerals are difficult, especially for the captain."

"It is difficult for everyone. But it is an honor for me to pay tribute to these men and their sacrifice."

A knock sounded on the door, and Riley entered, carrying a breakfast tray and setting it on the table. His face lit up in a smile when he saw Amelia. "The whole ship has been worried about you, Miss Amelia. I'm glad to see you feeling better."

She tried to muster a smile of her own but was finding it increasingly difficult to keep her eyes open.

"Please eat, Amelia," William said.

"I shall in a bit. I just want to rest for a moment."

Amelia leaned her head against the window and closed her eyes. She heard William and Riley leave and imagined the captain standing upon the deck, reading the verse of scripture, and the bodies being tipped into the water. Strange images filled her mind, distorted pictures of fighting, of dismembered soldiers, of blood dripping onto the floor of the operating theater, of bodies floating in the sea. Screams of dead and dying men filled her ears, and Amelia woke with a jerk.

William stood over her, his hands upon her shoulders, as if he had shaken her. His brows were drawn together. "Amelia, wake up. You are dreaming."

Her eyes darted around the room, and she realized she was trembling.

"It's all right, now." William sat upon the bench next to her feet. He held on to her hand. "You are safe."

"I must have fallen asleep," she said, still trying to push the images from her mind.

William looked into her face, frowning. "You did not eat."

"I am not hungry." She noticed that the captain's coat hung upon the chair at his desk. "How long did I sleep?"

"A few hours. It is nearly time for the afternoon watch."

"I did not realize I was so tired." She stifled another yawn and bent her neck, which was sore from leaning in such an awkward position.

William helped her to stand and led her to the table. "Please, try to eat."

She obediently picked up a biscuit and rapped it upon the table before taking a small bite.

He sat next to her, pouring water from a pitcher into two cups and setting one in front of her plate.

"I am sorry to have missed the service," Amelia said. "How many?"

"Seventeen." William rubbed his eyes with his fingers. "We lost many more, but when the French had control of the ship, my men were not given a decent burial."

Amelia set her biscuit upon her plate. "It would have been many more, Captain, if you had not surrendered the ship when you did."

"I believe, Amelia, that the honor of saving English lives is due to you."

"Any man aboard the *Venture* would have done the same."

"You give yourself too little credit. No man aboard would have been able to do what you did."

"I was just lucky the capitaine did not consider me a threat."

"A mistake he will not make again, I wager. The man may never trust another woman as long as he lives." William took a drink. "At least he will not allow any near his mustache."

Amelia smiled. "And in what condition did you find the capitaine and his officers?"

"Most were sleeping like babies. Those that weren't were easy enough to overcome, as I believe they'd had too much to drink."

Amelia's smile grew. "I am so glad the plan worked. I feared the laudanum would be discovered."

"You should not have done it, Amelia."

Amelia's smile fell from her face as she saw William's expression. His eyes bore into her, and she could not believe the fury she saw in them.

"Sir?" She shrunk under his gaze. "I only thought to—"

"You were very nearly killed. You put yourself in unnecessary danger, and what would have happened if you were exposed?"

Tears burned the back of her eyes. "Are you angry with me, Captain?" she asked in a small voice.

"Yes. No." William stood and began to pace.

Amelia suddenly felt like a child who had misbehaved. She had not expected this, so she hung her head, hoping he would not see her tears.

He finally stopped and pulled his chair closer to her, raising her chin. "Amelia. I cannot begin to thank you for what you did. It was brave and brilliant, and it terrifies me to think that you put your life at risk for—"

"For my shipmates, Captain." She kept her eyes lowered.

"I would never have forgiven myself if anything had happened to you." He wiped the tears from her cheeks with his thumb.

"I would never have forgiven myself if I had not tried. These men, this ship, it has become . . . I care for them, William, for all of you."

He raised her chin even higher, so that she was forced to lift her gaze to his face. He stared at her for a moment. Then his eyes dropped to her lips, and Amelia's pulse began to race. Would he kiss her again? They sat frozen for a heartbeat, and then William stood, stealing with him all of the warmth in the room.

"I must take the noon bearings on the quarterdeck."

Amelia swallowed and pulled her blanket tighter around her shoulders. The doubt that she had felt earlier returned, causing a quiver in her stomach.

"I am sorry I spoke in anger. I was out of line," William said.

"I understand."

He pulled on his jacket and walked toward the door.

"Captain?"

He stopped and turned back to her.

"If you had told Capitaine Valiquette that you are an earl, he would have no doubt spared your life."

"And abandon my men to face the guillotine alone?" His eyebrows were raised; his expression told her the very idea was completely ludicrous.

Amelia nodded. "I thought you would say that. You are a good captain, William."

He looked at her for a moment, as if he might say something, then nodded stiffly and left the room.

Amelia finished her biscuit but could not bring herself to eat anything else. She wandered around the room for a moment, stopping at the captain's desk.

Sealed envelopes were piled into a neat stack next to a ledger on one side of the desk. The book was opened to a page with a list of names. A piece of paper lay beneath a quill. It appeared to be the beginning of a letter. She glanced at the words:

To the family of Edward Baker,

I regret to inform you that Mr. Baker was killed in battle on the evening of the third of October, 1809, when an enemy force . . .

Amelia glanced back at the stack of envelopes and remembered what William had said—seventeen buried today, in addition to those lost earlier and those whose bodies were not recovered. Her heart ached as she thought of all those letters and all those families who would never see their loved ones, and she moved back to the window bench, feeling as though she had intruded on something private.

When William opened the door, Sidney was with him.

". . . but both missives were exactly the same, Captain. How many others are out there? And who might have . . ." Sidney's voice trailed off when he saw Amelia.

He hurried to her. "If it isn't the mustache bandit." He grinned and pulled an envelope from his pocket. "I shall consider these bits of waxed facial whiskers as some of my greatest treasures until the end of my days. I do not think I shall ever be able to look at a mustachioed man the same."

Amelia laughed and then quickly stopped, wincing and holding her side.

"Are you quite all right? Shall I send for the doctor?" Sidney placed a hand upon her shoulder.

"It is a good reminder to contain my merriment within ladylike bounds."

"Then we shall all be sorry to be denied the sound of your laughter. I have found myself quite dependent upon it and may suffer from withdrawal." Sidney placed his hand upon his heart dramatically.

William cleared his throat. "And are we to have a conference, Mr. Fletcher, or should I return in an hour when you are finished making a fool of yourself?"

Sidney winked at Amelia and walked to the table where William waited.

"Would you prefer if I left you alone, Captain?" Amelia asked.

"No. I would prefer for you to remain where I can keep an eye on you and assure myself that you are not sabotaging any Frenchmen or pointing pistols at guards." William spoke gruffly, but his eyebrow raised the tiniest of ticks, and Amelia's heart warmed, relieved.

She settled back in the window bench and watched the waves as William and Sidney discussed the status of the ship. The conclusions of their conference were thus: Sidney would captain the French ship, returning to London alongside the *Venture*; the reward for delivering a captured ship would be divided up among the men. With the other ship's supplies and sails, they should be in London by the next day.

An unpleasant rolling feeling began in Amelia's stomach when she thought of leaving the ship and setting foot in a strange city where the only person she knew was her father. She thought of how much she would miss this vessel and its crew. They had become like family to her. And to think that she had feared them when she had arrived, thinking they were nothing but savage sea dogs. And how she had misjudged their captain. He was nothing like the horrible, beastly man she had judged him to be upon their first acquaintance. She had never known anyone as thoughtful or seen a man care about his crew the way William did.

Amelia stood. Any more musing and she would certainly drive herself to tears. "I think I shall take a walk about the decks," she said when she saw that William and Sidney had also stood and were looking at her.

After bundling up in her coat, shawl, and blanket and declining an offer of company, she made her way out onto the quarterdeck and then down the gangway to the main deck. It had taken a large amount of energy to walk as far as she had, so she found a crate to sit on, shivering in the cold.

As she watched the crew reattaching sails to the yards and repairing the wood of the gunwale, Riley came to sit next to her.

"Just think, Riley. Tomorrow you will be sitting at your mother's table with your little sisters, eating potatoes and beef covered in gravy."

"It's true, Miss Amelia. And it will be good to be home."

"I shall miss your company."

"And I will miss yours too. It's been nice to have you aboard the ship."

They sat quietly for a few moments before Riley excused himself to return to his duties. Just as Amelia began to wonder how she would ever be able to climb the steps of the gangway to return to the captain's cabin, William found her and, supporting her with his arm around her waist, assisted her back to the cabin. He seemed to have an uncanny ability of knowing when she needed him. Her gratefulness was tinged with sorrow as she realized they would be in London tomorrow, and the idea of losing William's constant presence was so painful that she did not let herself form the thought fully.

Chapter 21

Amelia spent the remainder of the afternoon repacking her dresses and other clothing and resting in the captain's sitting room. William tended to matters on deck and listened to reports concerning the state of the ship. They ate a quiet supper together, though it was not an uncomfortable sort of quiet. When it became too dark to watch out the window any longer, Amelia moved to sit upon the sofa. William continued writing letters and recording in the ledger.

She thought about how contented she felt spending a quiet day with William but, as usual, pushed the thoughts from her mind. It would not do to dwell on things that could not be.

William came to sit on the chair next to her. "You are looking fatigued, Amelia. Perhaps you should retire."

"I am very tired. But I confess I am quite afraid to sleep. When I dream . . ."

William lifted his hand as if to touch her face but apparently thought better of it and instead rubbed his thumb over his bottom lip. "I shall remain here in the sitting room tonight. Will that help?"

She nodded. Her throat was suddenly scratchy. It was becoming more apparent that her affection for the captain was very much one-sided. It would be better once she did not see him every day. Her heart would have a chance to heal. The sooner she left this ship—and William—the better she would be.

Amelia spent a restless night in the captain's berth. She was freezing, and when she finally drifted to sleep, her dreams quickly turned into ghastly nightmares that jerked her awake and left her terrified and covered in sweat. At one point during the night, once again waking with a start, she immediately heard a knock upon the door.

"Amelia?"

"I am all right, Captain. There is no need to worry." She fought against the tremors that shook her body.

"I heard your cries. Do you need—Shall I enter?"

"No. Thank you, William. I am sorry I woke you." She heard him move away from the door, and she spent the remainder of the night tossing in the berth, not permitting herself to sleep.

The sun finally began to shine through the window. She rose and dressed as warmly as possible then left the room, intending to see if she could catch a glimpse of England.

Amelia found that despite her lack of sleep, she felt her energy returning. Fortunately, her injury did not hurt quite as much as it had the day before. But it had still been a struggle to dress and arrange her hair. She did manage without help, though, and that was reassuring in itself.

As she left the cabin, she was met by Corporal Thorne, who stood next to the door inside the sitting room.

"Captain Drake was called onto the deck and asked me to stay close if you should need, miss," he reported.

Amelia thought this was the longest sentence she had ever heard from the man. "Thank you."

"I am glad to see you are well, Miss Becket."

"Likewise, Corporal."

She ate a biscuit with some marmalade that she had found upon the sideboard table. Stepping out onto the deck, Amelia felt the fluttering returning to her stomach. The ship was sailing through a large harbor that narrowed to meet the mouth of a wide river.

Various ships surrounded the *Venture*, and Amelia looked on, fascinated at the different vessels and their inhabitants. While they were yet in the harbor, she spotted the French ship, with Sidney upon the upper deck. Captain Drake was speaking to the signal lieutenant, who used colored flags upon the mast to signal to the other ship, which raised its colored flags in return.

The HMS *Venture* joined a crowd of ships, large and small, that sailed in and out of the largest port in the world. Amelia walked down the gangway and watched from the main deck as they traveled up the wide River Thames and neared what was unmistakably the city of London.

The boatswain called out to the men, "Reef the sails!" and sailors climbed the riggings, untying the sails and rolling them up to bind them to the yards. The order was called to lower the anchor, and Amelia immediately felt the vessel's momentum halt.

When the French ship was close, cables and grappling hooks were used to connect the two vessels, and Sidney gave the order for the crew of his ship to board the *Venture.*

As she looked up the river at the noisy city covered with a layer of haze, any excitement she had previously felt upon embarking on her adventure was replaced by uncertain dread. The *Venture* had come to feel like home. It was a small community unto itself, one in which she did not have to worry about her father, the jointure settlement, or the strict rules of polite society. She had been welcomed by the crew, and they had never looked down upon her when she had not arranged her hair properly or not worn her gloves upon the deck. She felt as though she shared a bond with her shipmates that could never be replicated. They had fought for her, protected her. She had held their hands, whispering words of reassurance as they wept and bled. Together they had watched friends die and had buried them in the ocean. Few people would understand the relationship between shipmates, and for Amelia, once she stepped upon the shore, this world would no longer be hers. Her throat began to constrict, and she blinked away the pesky tears that had formed in her eyes so often of late.

Her mind returned to William. This brotherhood had been his life, and he too would leave it behind in London. The captain loved his ship. He loved his men, and now he was off to be an earl far away on a lonely estate. Amelia's heart was heavy as she thought of how he must be hurting.

As she turned away from the deck to compose herself, she spotted a small craft heading toward the ship. A group of marines pulled on the oars, and an admiral stood in full uniform: a blue frock coat with gold-trimmed lapels, the gold-ornamented epaulettes of an admiral, a white waistcoat, and a bicorn hat. For a moment, Amelia held her breath, wondering if her father had come to meet her, but as the boat drew closer, she didn't recognize the man. She was not surprised, but it did sting a little.

The admiral's boat was attached to the boat pulls, and the sailors heaved on the pulleys until the admiral and his guard of marines swung onto the davits and were piped aboard by the boatswain's whistle.

William met the admiral, and he, Sidney, and the other lieutenants went to the captain's quarters.

Judging by the ship's bell, over half an hour had passed when Riley found Amelia on the deck and summoned her to meet with the admiral and the captain.

When she entered the room, the men stood. William introduced her to Admiral John Griffin. The admiral was probably near the age of Amelia's father. His hair was gray and his face wrinkled from a life spent on the decks.

"It is a pleasure, sir." Amelia curtsied.

"The pleasure is all mine, Miss Becket. And upon hearing Captain Drake's report, I should like to extend my deepest gratitude for your actions in securing this ship. From what he has told me, none of these officers would be alive now if not for your bravery."

Amelia felt her cheeks redden. "Captain Drake is too kind, Admiral. Each member of the crew was a vital part to the success of the voyage. I did not do anything that one of my shipmates would not have done in my place."

The admiral tipped his head, scrutinizing her. "And do you consider yourself a member of the crew, then, miss?"

"Yes, sir."

"His Majesty's navy would be fortunate to have more sailors like you, Miss Becket. It has indeed been my pleasure to make your acquaintance." He turned back to William. "And now, I believe we should continue this report and discuss . . . the other matter ashore in conference with the Lords of the Admiralty. With Miss Becket's permission, I shall see her safely to her father's home, and then I shall meet with you, Captain Drake and Lieutenant Fletcher, in the admiralty chambers at three this afternoon. Perhaps, Miss Becket, we can have a cabin boy accompany us to your father's home?"

Amelia nodded at the admiral after glancing at William to see if he would insist upon accompanying her himself, and her stomach dipped uncomfortably when he did not.

"I should like to address my crew first, sir," William said.

The admiral nodded. "Of course."

Amelia accompanied the lieutenants to the main deck, leaning upon the railing as she walked down the gangway. She did not think she would be able to climb the stairs many more times today.

At the captain's command, the boatswain blew his shrill whistle and called, "All hands on deck!"

Amelia moved to stand next to Riley and waited until the hammering of feet upon the companionway had stopped. The main deck was filled, and as she looked around, her heart was warmed when she saw the faces of many people she now considered friends.

Captain Drake, Admiral Griffin, and First Lieutenant Fletcher stood on the quarterdeck. The shrill of the boatswain's whistle quieted the men, and William stepped to the rail, looking down at his crew.

He swallowed thickly before he spoke. "I have had the very great honor of captaining the *Venture* for the past three years." His voice carried over the sound of the waves crashing against the hull and over the muted noises from the other ships around them. "In that time, I have found myself surrounded by the best of men in the worst of times. War has a way of proving a man's character. Cowards show their true colors when threatened, and brave men perform in astounding ways. This crew has proven itself time and again to be the best in His Majesty's navy, and I would challenge any man that claimed otherwise."

William stopped talking, his eyes sweeping over the men on the deck. "Before I disembark, I have some commendations to present. Admiral Griffin has delivered appointments for Mr. Gifford and Mr. Hill. You are hereby promoted to the office of lieutenant, effective immediately. Mr. Hobbs, you are promoted to gunner."

The midshipmen patted their shipmates on the back and congratulated them for successfully passing their examinations.

The captain's voice rang out once more. "And there is one more commendation that I wish to confer. Miss Becket, would you please join me upon the quarterdeck?"

Sidney stepped quickly down the gangway, and Amelia took his arm, leaning on him as she ascended the steps. When they reached the upper deck, he led her to where the captain waited. Amelia's legs began to tremble, and she wondered whether to attribute it to her injury or to the feel of nearly fifteen hundred eyes upon her.

William spoke again. "Miss Becket joined this ship as a passenger, but as you all know, she has proven herself as loyal and brave as any member of this crew. Each of us owes our lives and our freedom to her ingenuity and courage. I should like to present Miss Becket with a midshipman's patch. It is well earned." Captain Drake handed Amelia the white patch, with its golden button and loop of rope that the midshipmen wore upon their collars.

She took it from him and studied it for a moment before pressing it to her heart and looking up to see William's face.

He nodded once, his demeanor remaining solemn, but she saw the corners of his mouth pull very slightly.

"Thank you, Captain," she said, feeling heat spread through her chest.

The crew cheered, causing the tears that had begun to burn in Amelia's eyes to threaten to spill over. Taking Sidney's arm again, she returned to the main deck, where she was bombarded with well-wishes and smiles.

The boatswain piped for silence once again. William stood quietly for a moment before speaking. "Before I step down, my last action as captain is to confer the ship to First Lieutenant Sidney Fletcher, hereafter to be known as Captain Fletcher." William cleared his throat and swallowed before he continued. "A more suitable man for this command you shall not find, and I could not leave the *Venture* in better hands. It has been my pleasure to serve with each of you." William turned to shake Sidney's hand and then Admiral Griffin's.

The entire crew erupted into applause and cheers, and Amelia, ladylike or not, joined them. Sidney pressed his finger and thumb into the corners of his eyes, swallowing hard, and followed William as he climbed onto the davit and swung into a dinghy with a crew of marines. They were lowered and rowed away without a glance behind, leaving Amelia feeling very much deserted.

Leaning on Riley, she made her way to the captain's quarters. She hurried into the cabin, not allowing herself to look around and wax sentimental. If she could just leave the ship, she would no longer feel so sorrowful. She quickly donned her bonnet and gloves, wrapped her blanket around her, and slipped the midshipman's patch into the ribbon with William's letter and Tobias's embroidery. She checked to make sure that the pouch for Anna was still packed away safely then closed her trunk and joined Riley on the quarterdeck, where they waited next to the davits for the boat that would take her to London and to her father. Admiral Griffin joined them before long, having finished touring the ship and assessing the extent of the damages.

The boat was lowered, and the marines rowed toward the docks. The dirty river was bordered on either side by more buildings than Amelia had seen in her entire life, the buildings so close together that they were nearly on top of each other. Although it was midday, the smoke in the air filtered the sunlight eerily, as if it were twilight.

When she stepped onto the docks, she was hit by a wave of noise and confusion. People yelled and pushed. Carriages moved through the crowds. Children ran between and beneath the masses. And the smell: smoke, horses, humanity. Everything around her moved too fast. It was overwhelming, and she was glad she had Admiral Griffin's arm to hold on to.

Just as Amelia took Admiral Griffin's hand and settled into his waiting carriage, she heard a voice calling the admiral's name. Turning, she saw a young girl with a large white box tied with a blue ribbon, running toward the trio.

Admiral Griffin stopped in front of the girl and spoke to her for a moment before taking the box from her; then reaching into his pocket, he handed the girl a coin.

She curtsied and disappeared back into the crowd.

The admiral and Riley climbed into the carriage, and the admiral handed the box to Amelia.

She raised her eyebrows, but he indicated for her to open it.

Untying the ribbon, she took off the lid and pulled aside the layers of paper to reveal a folded garment.

When she removed it from the box, she saw that it was a blue cloak trimmed with golden fur. She gasped. It was so thick and warm and beautiful.

She leaned forward and wrapped it around her shoulders, tying the ribbon below her chin and marveling that anything could feel so soft. "Admiral Griffin, did you—"

"No, Miss Becket. It was not I. But seeing your reaction, I'll confess to wishing I'd thought of such a gesture."

Amelia searched through the box and the paper inside. "There is no note."

"I think, miss, that you should ease your mind. I doubt that even this young boy would have trouble identifying the giver of such a thoughtful gift. I'd wager a certain captain is concerned that his Jamaican shipmate will find London quite a bit less temperate than her island home. " The admiral winked, and Amelia pulled the fur of the cloak up around her flushed cheeks as she looked out the window.

Her mood was instantly lightened.

The carriage drove through the cold streets, and gradually the houses became much grander and farther apart. Large walls surrounded the structures, and elaborate wrought iron gates blocked out unwanted visitors.

It was in front of one of these elegant-looking structures that the carriage halted, and Amelia quickly bid Riley farewell, pecking a kiss on his cheek. The admiral held her hand as she stepped from the carriage, and then he offered his arm to walk with her up the front steps.

The door was opened by a rather cross-looking bald man. "I am sorry, but the admiral is not home at present."

"Thank you," Admiral Griffin said. "This is Admiral Becket's daughter, Miss Becket, just arrived from Jamaica."

The butler's eyebrows raised. "I was not told to expect a visitor."

"The admiral's own daughter is hardly a visitor. Please send a man to the carriage to fetch her trunk."

"And what is your name?" Amelia asked the butler.

"Hastings, miss," he said before yelling into the dark house for someone to assist the carriage driver.

The admiral turned to her. "I think you should be very well taken care of, Miss Becket." He raised his eyebrow toward Hastings, who appeared not to notice. "And I shall see to it that young Riley is delivered to his home as well."

"Thank you, Admiral Griffin."

"It was indeed a pleasure, miss. And I hope our paths shall cross again while you are in London." He bowed his head before turning to leave.

Amelia imagined herself running after him and begging him to return her to the *Venture*, but mustering her courage, she turned and followed Hastings into her father's house.

A large staircase rose in front of her. All of the windows were covered with heavy drapery, and the walls were papered in a dark pattern. The entire effect was one of gloom and cold.

"May I take your cloak?" Hastings asked, though he spoke with no politeness. His words seemed to come straight from a handbook of "manners appropriate for a butler."

Amelia unwrapped her cloak from her shoulders and handed it to him, immediately noticing the chill it no longer protected her against.

The butler looked at the blanket she wore over a sailor's oilskin coat and raised his eyebrows slightly.

She took off the coat carefully—her injury was still tender—and gave it to him with her gloves and bonnet, but she retained the blanket around her shoulders. He held the oilskin coat with his nose slightly wrinkled before handing the wrappings to a young maid who had appeared. She scurried away, apparently to hang them in a cloakroom somewhere.

"Since you weren't expected, a room has not been prepared." Hastings sighed and looked at Amelia as if her presence was going to cause him an exorbitant amount of extra work. "And we have no lady's maid on staff."

"I understand, Hastings. Please do not worry yourself."

"I shall send the housekeeper, when she has the time, to instruct a chambermaid to see to your accommodations."

"Thank you."

"You can wait in the library if you'd like." Hastings waved toward a doorway behind him. "And I suppose you'll be wanting something to eat." He sighed again. "I will ask Cook to see to it."

"And when is my father expected home?"

"I really could not say. The admiral does not keep regular hours. He will return when he sees fit."

"And is there no way to notify him of my arrival?"

Hastings looked up at the ceiling as if asking for divine guidance in answering such ridiculous questions. "I shall tell him as soon as he returns."

"Thank you." Amelia followed Hastings into the library, where he lit some candles and built a fire in the fireplace, then he left her to her own company.

The sorrow she had held at bay broke free, and she buried her face in her hands, missing her spot upon the window seat aboard the *Venture*. And even more, missing the man who would know exactly what to say to comfort her.

Chapter 22

WILLIAM STOOD AT ATTENTION NEXT to Sidney in the Lords of the Admiralty boardroom. Behind them, large windows spanned nearly the entire wall. On the opposite side of the chamber, charts and maps were rolled and hung from rods above a massive mantelpiece; inside burned a roaring fire. Forty feet above him, an ornately carved ceiling crowned the historical room. To his left, the ticking of the prominent clock ensconced in a carved marble bookshelf sounded loudly as Admiral Griffin and the ten men on the board of the Lords of Admiralty sat silently studying William and Sydney.

Finally, one of the admirals spoke. "It is a severe accusation that you make, Captain."

"I speak only as I find. The evidence is in front of you." William waved his hands to indicate the missives recovered from the French ship. The documents sat on the table next to the HMS *Venture*'s mission papers, which the admirals had passed around the boardroom table while William had given the report of the voyage.

"It could be a horrible coincidence," a small admiral wearing a powdered wig said. "We do not know whether the mission was issued by the traitor—"

"Don't be daft, man," another much larger and much louder admiral interrupted. "The script upon each of the missives is the same as that upon the mission papers. And who would have known the *Venture*'s location better than the person who had ordered it?"

"Surely, sirs, there is a documentation process?" Sidney said. "It should be possible to determine what person, or persons, issued the mission orders."

A tall, wiry admiral wearing wire-rimmed glasses slammed his hand upon the table. "The orders were approved by this board. To accuse one of the Lords of Admiralty is treachery."

Sidney stiffened, and William could practically feel waves of anger flowing from his friend. "With all due respect, sirs," Sidney bit off the words, "because of these orders and the subsequent betrayal, I watched good men hacked to pieces by French boarding axes—"

William put his hand upon Sidney's shoulder, hoping to calm him.

Admiral Griffin spoke. "Nobody is being accused. We all seek the same answers."

The men in the room seemed to all speak at once, some visibly upset. William caught Admiral Griffin's eye, and the older man shook his head slightly, cautioning William to remain silent.

The Lord High Admiral rose from his place at the head of the conference table, and the room immediately quieted. "It is obvious that the mission was compromised, and none wants to acknowledge that it could have been done by one of our own." He motioned to a clerk who stood in a corner of the chamber. "Find the office from which these orders originated. I want the name of each person who would have had access to this information as soon as possible."

The clerk picked up the documents in question and scurried away.

The large admiral spoke again. "We know that only a select group of men are privy to the confidential orders given to a man-of-war. Aside from those in this room, only the commanding officer and likely one or two others with whom he may have consulted."

"There is one among that party who is involved in a legal suit with Captain Drake," Admiral Griffin said, and all eyes turned to William.

"Is this true, Captain?" asked the Lord High Admiral.

"Yes, sir. Admiral Becket and I are involved in a suit of a personal nature."

"That does cast a different light upon the case. And might I ask what the suit is in regards to?"

"It is a discrepancy in the matter of his daughter's alleged proxy marriage to my late brother." William's muscles tensed. He did not want Amelia's name associated with this business in the least. The very idea of the admirals discussing her made him clench his teeth. He watched the men shrewdly, judging their reactions.

At that moment, the clerk returned with a stack of papers, which he handed to the Lord High Admiral, whispering to the admiral for a moment, pointing at something on one of the papers and then lifting the stack and pointing at another. The admiral listened carefully and then spoke to the group.

"It appears that our suspicions are not wholly without foundation. Admiral Becket did issue the orders, and it seems that he somehow managed to get them approved without actually presenting them to this council."

At the words, every man in the room burst into angry dialogue, the noise ringing through the high chamber. The very idea that they had been duped outraged the board.

The Lord High Admiral held up his hand for silence. "There is obviously a flaw in the order of operations, and Admiral Becket has used it to his advantage. How he was able to accomplish this and send a ship upon a mission without the proper authority behind him will be investigated thoroughly. Yet there is another factor we must take into consideration. His actions, if exposed, will cast doubt upon our competence as a board. The entire British navy and even the government will suffer because of it. During wartime, citizens must have complete confidence in their leaders. We have seen the results in France when the government is mistrusted."

The powder-wigged admiral spoke. "And the evidence is not yet irrefutable. An argument could be made that Admiral Becket did not have any idea of the contents of the missive, just as we did not."

"The man's character is not unknown to us. While a brilliant leader and strategist, he has been known to act . . . unethically," said the tall admiral.

"Unethically?" The large admiral spoke again, his booming voice echoing throughout the chamber. "Placing wagers upon a fixed horse race is acting unethically. Admiral Becket behaved in a treasonous manner, risking hundreds of lives to enact revenge against a man over a simple matter of jointure. He has betrayed his country and must be punished."

"Yes, but a man of his standing will still be very difficult to convict," the spectacled admiral pointed out.

Sidney shook with suppressed rage.

William spoke up. "And, sirs, I would hope you would be sympathetic to the fact that he has a daughter. Her reputation will undoubtedly be soiled should he be tried and hanged as a traitor."

The Lord High Admiral looked at William shrewdly. "One would think, Captain, that you of all people would be thirsting for revenge in this case. Would you truly let the man walk free to spare Miss Becket a blemish upon her family name?"

Admiral Griffin spoke then, and William was again grateful for the man's calm head. "Miss Becket has proven herself to be quite the reverse of her father, and Captains Drake and Fletcher feel some loyalty to her. Surely after her heroism aboard the HMS *Venture*, she does not deserve to be branded with the label of traitor because of her father." He stood and faced the board. "Perhaps there is an arrangement that can be made that will satisfy all parties. I have heard rumors of a very remote outpost in Zanzibar that may have need of an admiral in residence . . ."

An hour later, William, Sidney, and Admiral Griffin left the boardroom.

"I thank you, Admiral," William said. "Your compromise was a stroke of genius."

"I believe that Admiral Becket will be quite surprised at receiving his new assignment within the next week."

The men shook hands.

William was relieved, but he couldn't help but think the orders couldn't come soon enough. The very thought of that man near Amelia put him on edge.

"It was my pleasure, Captain. Or perhaps I should call you my lord?" Admiral Griffin's mouth turned up in a small smile. "The British navy has lost a good man, sir." The admiral turned to Sidney. "And you are bound for Portsmouth today?"

"Yes, sir. I must see to the ship's repairs."

"Congratulations on your promotion, Captain." Admiral Griffin shook Sidney's hand and left to return to his office.

William was emotionally exhausted. He found his mind traveling to Amelia. He wondered how she would greet him. Cheerfully, most likely, and she might share some bit of humor that would relieve the strain of his day. He felt himself longing to be near her, but before he could seek her company at her father's house, he had a meeting with his solicitor.

He and Sidney walked through the admiralty complex and to the waiting carriage.

Once they had climbed inside, William leaned back against the leather seat and studied his friend. "You have been unnaturally quiet, Sidney. Something is distressing you."

"I merely wonder why Admiral Becket would go to the trouble of sending a ship for his daughter and then sabotage its return. There are much easier ways to go about ridding the world of William Drake, if you'll pardon me for saying so. But why risk his own daughter's life?"

"I admit I have wondered the same thing. If it was a simple matter of winning the case of his daughter's jointure, her death would nullify the entire proceeding." Speaking the words caused his chest to ache. He wanted nothing more than to conclude the meeting with his solicitor quickly and hurry to see Amelia.

Sidney tapped his finger against his lip thoughtfully. "He could not guarantee that she would have survived the attack, especially if the ship had been sunk. It does not make sense, does it?"

William and Sidney rode in silence to Sidney's family home. After bidding his friend farewell and wishing him a safe trip to Portsmouth, William continued to his townhouse on James Street. The solicitor, Mr. Campbell, was already waiting in Lawrence's—now William's—study. The man had been the solicitor for William's father and was easily in his seventieth year. Deep wrinkles spread across his face, but judging by the older man's disposition, William guessed the lines had been formed equally by smiling as by pursing his brow as he perused a document.

Mr. Campbell jumped up to greet William and shook his hand as soon as he entered the room. "It is good to see you safely ashore, my lord."

William marveled at the man's ability to move in such a spry fashion at his age.

"Thank you. And I am sorry to have kept you waiting." He indicated for Mr. Campbell to be seated and sat himself in the large chair behind the desk, feeling as if he were impersonating a lord. "And what news do you have regarding the suit against Admiral Becket?"

The solicitor leaned back in the chair, crossing one ankle and resting it on his other knee. "We are scheduled to present before the magistrate in four days. I have consulted with a barrister who will represent your case in court. With his assistance, I have been able to discover a great many things, all leading me to believe that your brother and Admiral Becket had a scheme in the works. The admiral's solicitor has been most reluctant to release the documents to confirm my suspicions, but with an order of compliance from the magistrate, we should be able to gain access to the papers."

"What sort of scheme?"

"I shall know more in the next few days, but there are clear indicators that your brother may have created a new will. Whether of his own choice or under coercion, I am not sure."

William stood. "A new will? In that case, these proceedings should be easily finished."

"The will does not specify the Lockwood family in the will, but if my research is correct, it does bequeath many of his lordship's holdings to another."

This was not possible. William's mind spun, and he did not even know what questions to ask. "How . . . ?"

"As I said, my lord, we shall know more as the documents are turned over."

This could not be. Lawrence would not have done something so underhanded, something that would hurt his family so cruelly. William did not realize he had begun to pace until Mr. Campbell spoke.

"And how did you find the daughter?" the solicitor stood in front of his chair, and William realized the man must have stood when William had. He would have to remember that people would not sit when he was standing now that he was Lord Lockwood.

William indicated for Mr. Campbell to resume his seat and then moved to an armchair in front of the desk to sit next to him. "I am certain Am—Miss Becket had nothing to do with the deception."

Mr. Campbell's wise eyes narrowed slightly. He studied William for a moment before he spoke. "And perhaps there is more reason than that of your brother's jointure for you to not want Miss Becket's name associated with your brother's."

William had a sudden urge to loosen his cravat under the man's scrutiny. "Yes, I would prefer for Amelia not to be legally considered my sister."

The solicitor leaned closer, his expression serious. "Then, Lord Lockwood, you must listen very carefully. It is imperative that nobody has any reason to believe that any sort of feelings exist between you and Miss Becket. It would damage our case if there is even the slightest indication of affection or even friendship between you. I suggest, nay admonish, my lord, if you should find yourself in Miss Becket's presence, you treat her with indifference, even coolness. This town is known for its listening ears and loose tongues. Especially among servants."

"But, sir—"

"It is the only way, my lord. If we are to convince a magistrate that you have been wronged by Admiral Becket and that his daughter was not legally joined to your brother, rumors of a relationship between you would serve only to discredit the suit." The solicitor smiled, deepening the wrinkles around his eyes. "Would you not do anything in your power to dissolve this supposed union and free Miss Becket from your brother's name?"

William nodded. He was disappointed that he would not be calling on Amelia for the next four days, but he understood. And he would not let his desire to be with her *now* destroy the hope he had of being with her *always.*

Chapter 23

Amelia spent the remainder of the morning in the library, alternating between looking out the window at the foggy, cold city and moving back to sit near the fire. So far, London had completely fallen short of her expectations. It was damp and dreary, and even though she had not expected her father to run to her with open arms, she had at least imagined he might have a few words to say to her or at least give his staff warning of her arrival.

Cook brought a meal at midday, and Amelia found that she did not have much of an appetite, so instead of eating, she set out to find the housekeeper or someone who could direct her to a dressmaker's store. If she was going to remain in this frozen city, she would need to purchase some warmer clothing.

Carrying a candelabra, she ventured up the dark staircase to the upper story of the house. The wooden railing was carved with ornate patterns, and the carpet was rich and thick. She realized it was really quite a beautiful residence, if only the dark drapes had been opened and there wasn't such a sense of foreboding covering the entirety. It was as if everyone held their breath. And it didn't take much imagination to discern what—or who—kept such a sense of apprehension nigh.

Hearing noises at the end of the hall, she followed them and came upon a girl—the maid who had taken her cloak. She was putting linens on a bed in the farthest bedroom. Amelia's open trunk sat upon the floor near the uncovered window, and her dresses hung in the closet.

When her presence was noticed, the young girl curtsied.

"Apologies, miss. I was just preparin' ya room. 'Is 'ere's the brightest room in the 'owse, and I thought ya'd like the view."

It took Amelia a moment to understand the girl's accent.

She must have taken Amelia's silence for displeasure, for she began to wring her hands. She curtsied. "If ya please, I'm Frye."

"How do you do, Miss Frye."

"Just Frye, miss. I've nearly set this place t'rights and shall be outta yer hair quick as a wink." She picked up a rag and began dusting the windowsill.

"Actually, if you don't mind, Frye, I was hoping for some assistance. I do not know my way around London and am in desperate need of some warm clothing."

"'S true, I've unpacked yer clothing, and ye'd need to wear all them delicate things on top o' each other just to keep off the chill."

"I was hoping you might spend a few hours with me this afternoon. Is there a dry goods store nearby?"

"Aw, ye'll not want ta be goin' to no dry goods, miss. Ye'll be needin' a proper dressmaker or modiste, and a shoemaker—those slippers ye've got won't keep yer feet warm. Then a glover, a haberdasher for ribbons and woolen stockings, a milliner for bonnets. 'Twill be an entire day, and ye'll need a footman just to carry all yer purchases."

Amelia was taken aback. In Jamaica, everything she needed would have been purchased in one store or from traveling merchants. She felt intimidated by the prospect of visiting so many shops just to buy some new clothing.

"And would you accompany me, Frye?" Amelia pulled her blanket closer around her shoulders, trying to stop her teeth from chattering.

"I'm no lady's maid, miss, but I'll help ye as I can." Frye's lips pursed, her nose creased, and her eyes squinted slightly, giving her a worried look, "But the master don' like it when we leave wi'out 'is 'pproval." She glanced past Amelia and out the door, as if the admiral might somehow overhear her.

Amelia was not surprised, although it did sadden her a bit when she thought of how cruelly her father must treat his staff for Frye to act in such a way. "Perhaps, Frye, I shall speak to my father when he returns home and ask for his permission—and for the use of a carriage?"

Frye's face slackened with relief. "Thank ye, miss."

Frye finished making up the room and left Amelia to herself. She sat upon the bed, grateful for the blankets and quilts that Frye had left, and examined her surroundings. The drapes had been pulled back from the window, leaving only a sheer covering. When she looked out, she saw that she did have a beautiful view of the street below, and it continued down the tree-lined road to some gardens that would likely be lovely to walk in during nice weather. It still amazed her to see trees with no leaves.

Next to the closet was a desk, and Amelia saw that her ribbon-tied parcel with the captain's letter, her midshipman's patch, and Tobias's gift sat upon it next to the oilskin pouch she had promised to deliver to Anna. Amelia resolved to do so tomorrow, when she hoped to have use of a carriage.

She wandered around the house a bit more that afternoon, exploring the dimly lit rooms by candlelight. After she returned to her room, she noticed it was becoming darker outside.

The clopping of hooves pulling a rattling carriage was becoming a familiar sound, but unlike the others she had heard throughout the day, this noise stopped in front of the house. She hurried to her bedroom window, certain that William and perhaps Sidney were coming to pay a visit. But as she looked down to the walkway below, she saw instead her father. The admiral was leaning heavily upon his footman, who was assisting the admiral from the carriage and up the steps to the front door.

Amelia took a deep breath, wincing at the pain it caused in her side, then walked down the hall, descended the stairs, and met Admiral Becket in the entryway.

"Father." She stood awkwardly at the bottom of the stairs, not knowing exactly how to greet him.

He stopped, leaning on the footman and studying her with bleary eyes. "Still the spittin' image of your mother, aren't ya?"

She noticed that his words were slurred but didn't let it deter her. He was the only family she had, and even though their relationship had never been close, she found herself nearly desperate for his approval.

"Welcome home, sir. I trust you had a good day?" she said, doing her best to smile.

He shrugged out of his cape, practically throwing it at the butler and, teetering, plodded into the library to sit heavily in one of the chairs.

Amelia stood uncertainly in the doorway until he looked up and motioned with a quick flick of his wrist for her to join him. She sat upon the chair next to his.

"I got word last night that the *Venture* would be in port early this morning, but the magistrate could not be persuaded upon to hear our case for another four days. The sooner the matter is settled, the better."

Amelia felt her stomach grow heavy. Her father had known she'd arrived in London earlier that morning but had not come to greet her until now—nor directed that a room be prepared for her. She still managed to find a smile somewhere deep inside.

"It will be nice to spend some time with you, sir, before I return home."

The admiral snorted and motioned to the butler, who quickly filled a glass with some sort of liquor and handed it to her father. "If only you weren't so much like your mother," he said. His eyes glazed over as if he was no longer aware that she was in the room. "Women destroy everything I attempt to create." He took a deep drink and wiped his lips on his sleeve, glancing at her. "It seems you couldn't even manage to maintain an arrangement when nothing was actually required of you aside from your signature."

"I hardly think I can be blamed for Lawrence Lockwood's untimely death, sir. Or the fact that his heir doesn't appreciate that a stranger has laid a jointure claim to his estate."

The admiral turned his entire attention on Amelia, and his expression was terrifying. His fists clenched, and for a moment she thought he would strike her. "You must do everything in your power to get that settlement. The papers are signed. It is all legal, and I have invested an excessive amount of time and effort. If you fail at this . . ."

He left the words hanging in the air, and Amelia felt cold waves of dread flow down her scalp and over her skin. Any hope she'd had of a nice evening meal with her father suddenly seemed like an absurd fantasy.

She stood. "I am quite tired from my journey, sir. I shall bid you good night."

The admiral dismissed her with a wave of his hand.

Amelia stopped at the door. "Sir, tomorrow I should like to have use of a carriage to purchase some clothing more suited to the colder climate. If—"

"Fine, whatever you need. You must not embarrass me in court dressed like a colonist. You have money to spend?"

"Yes, sir."

"Of course—the plantation. Very well. Do not bother me again."

Amelia walked through the door, pausing at the bottom of the stairs and leaning her hand upon the rail as she struggled to get her emotions under control.

She heard her father's voice from the library and took a small step back to where she could partially see him through the doorway. He sat facing away from her, staring into the fire and muttering. Amelia could scarcely make out his words.

". . . should have learned my lesson . . . not acted rashly again . . . certain death would leave no room for dispute . . . won't be swindled like before . . . rightfully belongs to me."

For some reason, his words chilled her. What was he talking about, *before*? She began to feel sick at the implications in his ramblings, and she hurried up the stairs, determined to put as much space between her and her father as was possible. When she arrived at her room, Frye was just setting a tray of warm rolls and soup on her desk. Amelia realized that aside from a ship's biscuit this morning, she'd not eaten all day and wasn't sure she had the stomach for it now.

Wrapping up in her blanket, she picked apart some rolls, ate a bit of soup, and finally gave up on the hope that William would visit.

After she changed into her nightclothes, she watched the gaslights illuminate down the street, amazed at such a thing. Perhaps William had too much to occupy his day. There would be matters of his estate requiring his attention. And of course he would need to report to his commanding officers on the particulars of the voyage. Yes, that must be it. His day was filled with duties.

Amelia forced away the doubts that had plagued her. If she did not have the hope of seeing William, of him returning the love that she had for him, there was nothing to tie her to this cold, foggy island, and she would leave as soon as she could.

She piled some quilts on top of her traveling chest and, wrapping her blanket around her shoulders, sat upon it, leaning her forehead against the window. In the dark, she could just imagine that she was in the captain's sitting room on her window bench, with the sound of the timbers creaking and the waves lapping against the hull. She could almost envision William on the other side of the room, calculating his charts or entering information in his logs. If only he were here. He would know how to banish her nightmares. He would make everything right. She hoped with all her heart that he would visit tomorrow.

The sleepless nights were beginning to catch up with her, and though she hadn't intended to, she closed her eyes. Again, her dreams were filled with horrors and death and fighting, and now her father was added into her world of terrible nightly visions. What had he meant when he'd said he would not act rashly again? Her imagination became her enemy as it magnified every horrible thing she had witnessed.

She awoke to Frye shaking her. "Miss, yer wakin' the 'ousehold with yer screamin'."

Amelia sat up, realizing she was drenched in sweat and trembling. "I'm sorry, Frye."

"Come, miss. You wash up an' change yer nightclothes, and I'll fetch ye some tea."

Amelia pulled off her soaked clothing and dressed in a dry chemise and nightgown. The tea settled her nerves, and once she had convinced Frye that she was indeed feeling better, Amelia was left alone. But she did not sleep. How could she when she might again awaken the entire household with her nightmares?

One notion had entered her mind, and she could not shake it. Had her father been talking about the plantation, claiming it was rightfully his? And when he spoke about *before*, he couldn't have possibly been referring to her mother's death, could he? Even *he* was not so wicked as to—But the thought would not leave her mind. Her father had arranged a marriage, and a few months later, her husband had died. Then Amelia had found herself, on his orders, in enemy waters, where she had been lucky to survive herself. She banished the idea. Her father was rude, calculating, and typically inebriated, but unpleasantness did not make one a murderer.

Chapter 24

THE NEXT MORNING DAWNED COLD and cheerless. Amelia had managed to keep herself awake through the remainder of the night and now set about getting herself ready for the day. Her injury was healing, and she found it didn't hurt as badly to lift her arm to arrange her hair. She took extra care, ensuring that curls flowed over her forehead and down her temples and neck. She wanted to look perfect when she saw William.

After she was certain her father had left for the day, she had breakfast downstairs in the dining room and waited, wishing it was not improper for a lady to call upon a gentleman.

Just as she determined that he would certainly call upon her that day, the bell rang. Amelia's heart leapt in her chest. She straightened her skirts and sat up tall as Hastings entered the room. But instead of announcing a caller, he held out a silver platter that contained only an envelope upon it.

She recognized William's script, and after thanking Hastings and waiting as patiently as she could for him to leave her alone, she opened the envelope and removed the folded paper inside.

Miss Becket,

I am very sorry to tell you that I shall not be able to see you until the legal affairs existing between us are settled.

William Drake, Lord Lockwood

Amelia swallowed at the lump that was expanding in her throat. What could William possibly mean by such a note? Did he truly not want to see her? If such was the case, it would have been better if he had sent no note at all. She blinked back the tears that were threatening to spill from her eyes, and the doubts that had begun aboard the ship grew.

William had not told her good-bye when he'd left the *Venture*. He had not promised to call upon her or given her any indication that he would—but the image of his face appeared in her mind. Memories of their time together: the way he had held her as they waltzed, their closeness as they had watched the whales, and the feel of his kiss. Had the entire experience been one-sided? Had she merely been a diversion, and he had intended to end any sort of association once they were in London?

Amelia put the letter away. If that was what William wanted, she would see him in four days at the trial and then would waste no time putting both him and England behind her. She gathered her cloak, gloves, bonnet, and the pouch for Anna then asked Hastings if he would be able to obtain the address of a Miss Regina Foster.

Hastings lifted his eyebrow slightly. "The carriage driver will deliver you to Miss Foster's residence, miss. No directions will be necessary."

"Thank you, Hastings. I shall return soon, and I have asked Frye to accompany me upon my outing."

"Very good, miss."

After a short drive, the carriage stopped in front of the largest residence Amelia had ever seen. Even the Colonial Offices in Spanish Town were miniscule compared to this monstrosity that towered over every other building on the square.

The footman held her hand as she stepped out, still unable to take her eyes off the structure. "Are you certain this is Regina Foster's home?" she asked.

"Not likely to mistake it for another, miss." He tipped his hat, and Amelia pulled her cloak closer around her shoulders.

"Ne'er thought I'd see the day I'd be walkin' up the front steps to the Fosters' 'ouse," Frye muttered under her breath.

Amelia rang the bell, and the door was answered by a man with ridiculously straight posture. He looked down his nose at her, apparently unable to bend his neck to make eye contact. "Miss Foster is not at home at present." He began to close the door, but Amelia stopped him.

"Excuse me, sir. I have come to call upon one of her servants. A chambermaid named Anna Wheeler."

The stiff butler looked at her for a moment, and then his eyes moved to Frye. "It is not usual for domestics to receive callers." He began to close the door again.

It was all Amelia could do not to shove the door open. "I have come bearing news of her grandfather's death. Surely with the mistress from home, Anna might be spared for a moment to receive condolences?"

The butler blinked slowly then finally stepped back, opening the door completely, and Amelia and Frye stepped into the grand entryway.

Amelia had to employ all of her self-control to keep from staring about the hall with her mouth agape. She was surrounded by opulence that she could have only imagined, from the shining chandelier in the center of the elaborately carved ceiling down to the marble floors. The space in between was equally stunning, with a golden-framed mirror, vases full of flowers adorning nearly each flat surface, and luxurious pieces of furniture.

Frye had no such reservations. "Dash my wig, an' if this place didn't cost a lumpin' pile o' spankers!"

The butler's face remained haughtily irritated. "May I take your wrap?"

"Thank you." Amelia handed him her cloak, and Frye removed her own coat, which the butler took, his nose wrinkling in a clear indication of disgust.

"And who shall I tell Anna is calling?"

Amelia was tempted to introduce herself as Lady Lockwood. It would certainly wipe a bit of the smugness off Mr. Ramrod-Straight-Back's face, but the last thing she wanted to do was complicate matters and stir up questions about her legal suit, so she said, "Amelia Becket, daughter of Admiral Becket."

"Perhaps your . . . lady's maid would like to wait in the kitchen?" The butler waved to a servant Amelia hadn't noticed, who led Frye away.

Amelia was shown into a sitting room that was every bit as grand as the great hall, and she took a seat upon the sofa. It was not long before a young, slight-looking girl with pale skin and hair entered the room, looking anxious.

"Anna?" Amelia's eyes burned. The girl was no doubt related to Tobias. Same kind eyes, same mild manner.

Seeing the girl's nod, Amelia continued. "My name is Amelia Becket. I just arrived in London yesterday, and . . . I was on the same ship as your grandfather."

Amelia berated herself for not putting more thought into what she would say once she arrived. "Would you like to sit down?" she asked, patting the seat next to her.

Anna sat on the far side of the sofa, barely resting on the edge.

Amelia pulled Tobias's pouch from the pocket in her skirts and held the small parcel in her hands. Her throat was constricting. She hadn't realized how difficult this would be. Anna looked so vulnerable and gentle. "I do not know whether you have been informed that your grandfather was killed in a battle?"

Anna finally spoke. Her chin trembled, and her eyes began to fill with tears. "Yes, I received a letter from Captain Drake this morning."

Despite the circumstances, Amelia still felt the flutter in her chest when William's name was mentioned. A feeling of warmth grew inside her when she realized that he had attended to the matter of notifying the families of the death of their kin as soon as he had gotten into port.

"I was with Tobias as he died, and I do not think he suffered." She handed Anna the pouch. "It was his final wish that you should have this."

Anna took the pouch and held it for a long moment before untying the leather strings and peeking inside. She poured out a handful of gold coins and unfolded a beautiful picture embroidered upon a piece of sail. An island scene with palm trees and flowers. Anna spread the cloth upon her legs, tracing the stitches with her fingers.

"I am truly sorry for your loss, Anna. I considered your grandfather a dear friend of mine. He spoke to me of you often and loved you very much."

Anna's face crumpled, and she began to sob.

Amelia scooted across to the other side of the sofa and pulled the younger girl into her arms, stroking her hair and allowing a few tears of her own to fall.

"What is this?" A shrieking voice shattered the tender moment.

Anna jumped to her feet, and Amelia looked to the doorway of the sitting room, where a very beautiful, very elegant, and very angry woman stood. The woman was Amelia's own age, Amelia guessed, with honey-colored curls and a scarlet dress that was more lavish than any Amelia had ever seen. Even in the young woman's fury, she posed in a way that showcased her gown and figure to its fullest potential.

"Who are you? And what are you doing in my house?" she demanded. She continued without waiting for an answer. "And, Anna, what in the world gave you the idea that you were permitted to sit upon the furniture?"

Anna struggled to speak through her sobs. "I am sorry, miss." She hurriedly pushed everything back into the pouch.

"You take too many liberties. I am to attend a dinner party this evening, and instead of preparing my gown, you are—"

"It won't happen again, miss."

Amelia was furious. "I assume you are Regina Foster," she said, fully aware that she had no right to speak in that tone to a woman so clearly her superior. "I apologize for occupying Anna's time, but I merely came to convey my condolences upon her grandfather's death."

Regina turned her full attention to Amelia. Regina's lip curled as she looked Amelia up and down, perusing her colonial dress.

"How dare you speak to me?" She glared at Amelia.

Anna took a step closer to Regina. "Please, miss, she—"

But Anna was cut short by a slap across the face from her employer. "Prepare my attire for this evening immediately or you can consider yourself terminated."

Amelia was overwhelmed by rage. "Anna," she said to the retreating girl, who held her hands over her cheek. "I cannot imagine any reason for you to continue to be treated in such a manner by this woman, who, by her very actions, has shown that she does not possess the slightest bit of refinement. I should very much like for you to come with me, as I have need of a lady's maid and would never behave toward you in such a vulgar manner."

"What makes you think you can presume to rob me of my servant, you . . . peasant?" Regina's voice was a screech.

Amelia spoke calmly, though in order to do so, she could feel herself trembling. "I am merely extending Anna an offer of employ that she can either accept or refuse with her own discernment."

As Amelia began to walk out of the sitting room door, she started to speak again. Her voice was not quiet and demure and she held her gloved hands clenched at her sides, but she prided herself on the fact that she had not yet lost her temper. "And might I add that I have never been treated in such a discourteous manner by anyone—and I was recently held prisoner on a French warship." She paused and turned to Anna. "If you should decide to accept my offer, I am willing pay you double your present wages. I shall wait outside in my carriage for your decision, as I have no intention of spending another second in this vile woman's presence."

"I do not think that is an option for you, as you are not welcome in my house. I will not associate myself with a person of low breeding such as yourself!" Regina yelled, and her voice rang through the main hall.

Sweeping past Regina Foster, Amelia strode down the wide hall, intending to demand her cloak and her maid, but she stopped short in the entryway, where the butler stood next to a tall, handsome gentleman.

The man was frozen in the act of handing his walking stick and hat to the butler, and both men stared toward the women, their eyes wide in astonishment.

Miss Foster had followed Amelia out of the sitting room, and upon seeing the men, Regina's demeanor instantly transformed into one of a proper young lady. "Your Grace," she said with a sweet smile and a deep curtsy. "How lovely to see you. My dear friend and I were just having one of our silly arguments. I insisted that her tan skin and freckles are so much more appealing than my own milky white complexion, but she of course does not agree."

Amelia tilted her head and looked at Regina with half-lidded eyes. The duke did not appear to be a simpleton; surely he had heard the insults the lady of the house had screamed at Amelia.

"Ah, I will indeed never understand the ways of the gentler sex," he said finally, breaking the awkward silence. "And, Miss Foster, would you do me the honor of introducing me to your friend?"

Regina froze, caught at the height of rudeness. She had not even asked her guest's name, and Amelia certainly was not going to offer assistance.

Miss Foster was rescued by her butler. "M'lady, shall I have Cook serve the tea for you and Miss Becket in the conservatory?"

"Thank you, Lucas."

Regina turned back to the duke and batted her eyes. Amelia was amazed by the difference the handsome gentleman affected in the woman. "Miss Becket, allow me to introduce His Grace Charles Bramwell, Duke of Southampton."

Amelia dipped in a low curtsy, and the duke took her hand. "Do I have the honor of addressing Miss *Amelia* Becket?"

"Yes, Your Grace."

"What providence! I had intended to call upon you today as one of my morning visits." He must have seen Amelia's puzzled expression because he continued. "Miss, I owe you a great debt of gratitude, as you are the reason for the safe return of a favorite nephew, Corporal Jonathan Ashworth. Since yesterday, I have heard of little else and would like to invite you to a gathering tomorrow night, a ball."

The duke turned to Regina, whose lovely features, Amelia was delighted to see, were marred by a scowl. "And of course, I have come to invite my dear friend Miss Foster as well."

As if by magic, Regina's brow smoothed, and her demure smile returned. "Of course I shall attend, Your Grace. There is nothing I should like better."

"And Miss Becket, I am sure you would disappoint my nephew and myself immensely should you not be there."

"I thank you for your invitation, sir, but I do not think such a thing will be possible. As you know, I arrived in London only yesterday and have no suitable clothing, nor a chaperone."

A charming smile lit up the duke's face. "I shall remedy the dilemma with the aid of my very grateful older sister—Corporal Ashworth's mother, Lady Vernon—who should love nothing more than to spend the day assisting you in your wardrobe and the evening serving as your chaperone."

"I—"

"And there shall be others there of your acquaintance, Miss Becket. The earl of Lockwood and Captain Sidney Fletcher."

Regina's eyes widened ever so slightly. "The earl of Lockwood. I have not seen him in ages. What grand company we shall have, Your Grace."

If Amelia had thought her dislike for Miss Regina Foster could not possibly be any stronger, the sound of William's name on her perfectly pouty lips plummeted the woman into the realm of pure loathing.

"If Lady Vernon would be truly willing to assist me, Your Grace, then I shall be delighted to attend."

Chapter 25

AMELIA WALKED UP THE STONE steps at the front of the Duke of Southampton's London residence with Lord and Lady Vernon. Lord Vernon was much like his son, long limbed and a bit awkward, but he compensated with a cheerful disposition and smile. His wife was smallish and a bit plump but every bit as amiable.

When the door was opened and their outer clothing borne away, Amelia looked around at the entry hall. It was beautiful and very elegantly decorated, though without the ostentatiousness of Regina Foster's home. The duke apparently had very fine taste, and his sense of style was sophisticated without being overdone.

"Come along, dear. You look beautiful," Lady Vernon said, gently leading her charge to where the duke stood greeting his guests. Amelia could not help but glance around the hall, searching for William.

The past two days had been a whirlwind of dressmakers and fittings and shoemakers and jewelers. Lady Vernon had even insisted upon making a stop at a sweetshop. Amelia had never seen so many wares for sale and so many beautiful things. She had been overwhelmed and immensely grateful for Lady Vernon's assistance, as Amelia would never have been able to accomplish such a monumental task on her own.

She wore a satin dress in a rust-orange color that Lady Vernon had insisted looked perfect on her, with long gloves that rose past her elbows. Amelia suspected Lady Vernon wanted to hide as much of the tanned skin as possible. A gold chain with a simple pendant hung at Amelia's neck, and her new lady's maid, Anna, had taken the time to weave cream-colored pearls into Amelia's dark tresses. She felt like a princess.

As soon as the duke saw them, he strode across the hall, kissed his sister upon the cheek, greeted his brother-in-law with a hand clasp, and took Amelia's hand, bowing. "Miss Becket, I cannot tell you how delighted I am to see you tonight and how lovely you look."

She dipped in a curtsy. "Thank you, Your Grace."

"Where is my Jonathan, Charles?" Lady Vernon asked. He will be anxious to greet Miss Becket."

"He awaits you in the ballroom. Come, Miss Becket." The duke held out an arm for Amelia and led them into the ballroom.

The room was every bit as tastefully decorated as the entry hall. The wooden floors were polished to a shine, and beautiful furniture stood against the wainscoted walls in small clusters, perfect for visiting.

Amelia scanned the crowd, hoping to see William, and when she finally did, her heart slammed into her ribs. He stood at the other end of the room, talking to Regina Foster. Her arm was linked in his. She smiled sweetly at something he said and cast her eyes downward.

"Please do not make yourself nervous, Miss Becket," the duke said, and she noticed that her hand was clenched rather tightly on his arm.

"I am sorry, Your Grace." She forced her eyes from William and looked at the duke. "I confess I have never attended such a grand assembly. We have nothing so fine in Jamaica."

"I count myself fortunate, then, that you should have nothing to compare this gathering to. This time of year, London is frightfully dull, and just wait until you see a real ball with all the *ton* in attendance." He smiled and nodded to guests as they passed but did not release Amelia's hand.

She glanced again to where William stood and noticed that Sidney had joined them and was laughing with Regina.

The duke must have followed her gaze. "Oh, but of course you would want to see your friends." He led her across the room to William and Sidney.

They both turned to her when she and the duke joined them. Regina curtsied to the duke and leaned the slightest bit closer to William.

"Lord Lockwood. Captain Fletcher. Miss Foster. How lovely to see all of you. I do hope you are enjoying yourselves," the duke said.

After hearing their assurances that they were indeed having a lovely evening, the duke continued. "And I know that you have all made Miss Becket's acquaintance."

William and Sidney each inclined their heads, and Amelia dipped in a small curtsy, suddenly shy around these men who she had considered to be her dearest friends just a few days earlier.

When she dared lift her eyes to William's, she saw that his face was set and his jaw clenched. She looked to Sidney, who covered for William's rudeness by taking her hand.

"A pleasure, as always, Miss Becket. And you look very pretty this evening."

"Thank you. And how have you spent your time in London, Sid—Captain Fletcher?" she asked.

"I have been in Portsmouth since the day after we arrived, miss, and only returned this morning."

"And the *Venture*?"

"The repairs will take time, but we hope to have her shipshape in a few weeks."

"I am glad, sir," Amelia said.

She turned to William. "And have you been in Portsmouth, as well, your lordship?"

"No. I have not."

"Oh. I am surprised that I have not chanced upon you in London, sir." From the corner of her eye, Amelia saw Regina smirk but did not let it deter her.

"I have been quite occupied, miss. Did you not receive my note?" William looked at her intently; his eyes narrowed ever so slightly, and she did not need to wonder what message he was trying to convey. He was not interested in her and wanted to spare her the humiliation of having to tell her such a thing.

She blinked at the prickling behind her eyes. "I did, sir." She swallowed as she saw Regina tug upon William's elbow.

"If you will excuse me, Miss Becket." He inclined his head once again.

"Of course."

Sidney took her hand. "I am glad to see you are well, miss," he said. He opened his mouth as if to say more but glanced toward William and excused himself.

The duke apparently did not notice any awkwardness in the meeting, and if he did, he did not comment upon it. "There he is," the duke said, motioning to someone she immediately recognized.

In spite of the painful encounter and the added distress of seeing William with the woman she considered the lowest form of humanity, Amelia's face lit up in a smile. "Corporal Ashworth! How very wonderful to see you."

The corporal strode across the room in his gawky manner but dressed in immaculately clean regimentals. He took her hand, and Amelia immediately felt a bit of her apprehension abate. This was the man who had guarded her with his life, who had spent every hour on duty for over six weeks protecting her, and she felt a swell of affection upon seeing him, as she supposed one might feel toward a brother.

"Miss Becket, it is a pleasure to see you. You are feeling well?"

She knew he was referring to her injury but would never say such a thing aloud. "I am well, sir. And I nearly did not recognize you, as you did not present arms or snap to attention when I entered the room."

"If it would make you feel more comfortable, miss, I shall remember to perform the proper ceremony upon seeing you."

"Next time, then." She winked before remembering that was hardly proper behavior for a lady.

Corporal Ashworth's smile grew, and she decided it was well worth it to flout propriety once in a while if it produced such a result.

"And, Corporal, I am afraid I have monopolized your mother for the past two days."

Corporal Ashworth kissed his mother on the cheek. "I assure you it has been a delight for a woman with only sons to spend some time fussing over a young lady."

Lady Vernon patted her son on the arm. "I love my sons dearly, but it has been quite a diversion to have a young lady to pamper, Miss Becket. I do hope you enjoyed yourself as much as I did."

The Duke of Southampton was the perfect host, introducing Amelia to everyone who came to pay their respects. She finally made her way to where Lady Vernon had taken a seat, and Amelia was introduced to still more people. She knew she would never be able to remember all of the names and titles, so she focused instead on not looking across the room to where William stood, tall in his black waistcoat, talking with Sidney and a group of men.

At a signal from the duke, the music in the room changed slightly, and gentlemen began to seek out partners for the dancing that would soon commence. Next he turned to Amelia. "Miss Becket, as you are quite the loveliest lady here, and my special guest, I should like to request your hand for the first two dances."

"Thank you, Your Grace. It will be an honor."

As the duke led her onto the dance floor to stand at the head of the company, she glanced toward William, who had yet to acknowledge her. He was leading Regina onto the floor, and Amelia swallowed hard against the constriction that grew in her throat.

She turned her attention to the duke, hoping that her conversation was rational, as her mind was drawn to the smiles exchanged between William and Regina.

The duke was an excellent dancer, as was to be expected, and once Amelia was able to concentrate, she found him quite a gracious partner. He asked about the voyage and the battle, though, from his questions, it was apparent he had heard most of the details from his nephew.

She noticed many of the young ladies watching him and realized that she had a very sought-after companion. Not just because of his title but because the Duke of Southampton was handsome and charming and likely the most eligible bachelor in the city.

When the dances ended, he led Amelia back to sit with his sister and confirmed that she would save the dinner dance for him. She had sat for merely a moment before her hand was claimed by Corporal Ashworth, who told her that he was disappointed he had not had a chance to dance with her in the wardroom on her birthday.

The memory of that night and the emotions that accompanied it flooded into her mind, and she did her best to force them out, glancing again to where William danced with yet another lady. Even Sidney avoided Amelia's eyes as he and his partner passed in the set.

After dancing with Corporal Ashworth, Amelia took her seat next to Lady Vernon. The young lady realized that she had not quite healed sufficiently to engage in so much physical activity, so she declined a number of potential partners. Instead, she spent the next hour answering questions from various people who pressed her for details about the battles. It seemed that word traveled fast throughout London society, as many people already knew the story but were eager to hear her retelling of it.

Before long, she had quite a group gathered around her, and it was with a bit of shoulder tapping and "pardon me's" that the duke made his way to the center of the crowd as he returned to claim her for the dinner dance.

When the music started, Amelia recognized it as a waltz.

Whispering started around the room. Despite what William had told her, based on the reactions she saw around her, a waltz was apparently still scandalous in London. The music stirred memories of her birthday night, being held in William's arms and feeling as though she was floating on air. That was the night she had fallen in love. She hesitated, looking for William. Seeing him bow, take Regina Foster's hand in his, and then place his hand upon her back caused a flare of jealousy that nearly took Amelia's breath away. Her heart was racing, and she was starting to feel a bit light-headed.

Amelia paused, and the duke inquired if something was wrong.

"I'm afraid, sir, that I do not have much experience with a waltz." She tried to control the tremor in her voice, hoping he would attribute it to nerves. "Jamaica is still a bit old-fashioned."

"I should have realized. I myself was required to obtain special permission in order for a waltz to even take place tonight." He placed her left hand upon his shoulder and took her right hand in his, whirling her onto the floor. "But I cannot think of anyone I would rather waltz with. I think you shall love it, Miss Becket."

It was true. She loved the dance, the feeling of being held close by someone, of her skirts whirling around her ankles, of moving around the entire dance floor uninhibited. The waltz was magical, but she did not enjoy it, not when each time she caught sight of William and his partner, tears threatened to spill from her eyes and she clenched her teeth, holding the tears back.

The dance finally ended, and the duke led Amelia to the head table, where he sat her at his right, in the place of honor.

Glancing down the table, she saw that William sat next to Regina. His eyes met hers but only briefly, and he gave no sign of acknowledgment before turning back to his partner.

Amelia's eyes burned. She took a sip of water, hoping to calm herself, resolving not to look in William's direction for the rest of the night.

Across the table sat Lord and Lady Vernon and their son. And on the other side of Amelia sat a very robust man with ruddy cheeks who the duke introduced as James Dunford.

"Commander Dunford is to set sail for the West Indies this very week. I assumed the two of you would find much to discuss," the duke explained.

"And where are you bound, sir?" Amelia asked.

"Grenada," he said. "I'm after the spices that are worth their weight in gold here in England. His Majesty's trade embargo has served to make many a merchant a wealthy man."

"Surely you mean to make a stop in Jamaica. You'll not find better sugar, and I can guarantee you a fair price." She smiled. "Though I do not think this is an appropriate place to discuss matters of business."

"Perhaps." He pursed his lips. "Jamaica, eh? The idea is tempting, and sugar is nearly as valuable as any spice with this dratted war." He took a drink from his glass goblet. "And how long do you intend to remain in London, Miss Becket?"

Amelia fought to keep her eyes from straying down the table. "I do not know, sir. I suppose it is for my father to decide, though I have grown quite homesick."

"Surely you would not leave so soon," the duke said.

"I have no plans in either direction, Your Grace."

"I should feel your loss most personally, as I should like the opportunity to know you better, miss."

Amelia blushed. "Your Grace, I am not sure if London . . . agrees with me. I am not used to such finery—or such cold weather."

"But you must agree that the society is preferable to anywhere, do you not?" Lady Vernon said.

"It is true, I have been fortunate to make the acquaintance of truly amiable people in my short time here." *And some not so amiable.*

"If you decide to return soon, miss, I shall be happy to transport you aboard my vessel, the SS *Louisa*," James said. "We set sail at noon in two days' time."

"Thank you, sir."

At the conclusion of the meal, Amelia walked with Lady Vernon as the ladies withdrew to the drawing room for tea while the gentlemen remained for port and masculine discussion.

"And are you feeling quite well, Miss Becket?" Lady Vernon asked quietly as they walked. "You seemed a bit pale after the waltz."

"I do not think Miss Amelia Becket should worry that she has grown too pale," Regina Foster said loudly as she walked past them.

Lady Vernon shot a glare toward Regina and led Amelia to a corner of the room, as far as possible from Miss Foster, motioning for a maid to pour Amelia some tea.

"I am quite well, my lady. Thank you for your concern."

"And do not fret about the sharp tongue of that woman," Lady Vernon said. "It is hardly a wonder that she has had three Seasons and not managed to ensnare a husband—even with the enormous fortune her father left her."

"I do not know if that will be the case much longer," said another woman, sitting near them. "It seems that Regina and Lord Lockwood have developed quite a friendship tonight."

Amelia set down her tea. "I am sorry, Lady Vernon. I am actually feeling a bit dizzy. Perhaps I should make my excuses and—"

"Of course, dear. It is a wonder you have been able to keep such energy all evening."

"Is it true that you were injured in a naval battle, Miss Becket?" asked the woman sitting close to them.

Lady Vernon shooed the woman away and helped Amelia to stand. Then she linked her arm through Amelia's and led her from the drawing room, calling for her carriage and their cloaks.

"I am sorry, my lady. I shouldn't want you to miss the party on my account."

"Do not fret, Miss Becket. I shall send a servant to notify my husband and then deliver you safely home and return in time to play cards before I'm missed."

As the women waited in the entry hall for the carriage, Sidney walked from the dining room and strode toward them.

The very sight of him made tears well up in Amelia's eyes.

"Miss Becket, might I have a word with you before you depart?"

Lady Vernon narrowed her eyes. "Captain, as you can see, Miss Becket is quite unwell."

"It shall be for just a moment, my lady." He led Amelia a short distance from Lady Vernon.

"Amelia," he said softly. "I overheard a servant telling Lord Vernon that you were ill. I am so sorry that things are . . . the way they are. I cannot bear to see you upset."

"I'm afraid that I was just mistaken about a particular . . . relationship, Sidney."

Sidney turned to face her directly, looking intently into her eyes. "The person in question's feelings are much the same as they've always been, Amelia."

"That is quite enough," Lady Vernon said, helping Amelia into her wrap. "There will be plenty of chances for visiting once Miss Becket is feeling better. Good night, Captain."

"Good night, m'lady, Miss Becket." Sidney held Amelia's gaze for a moment longer before looking away. What had she seen in his eyes? Was it pity?

Sidney had obviously been politely telling her that whatever she had thought existed between her and William had been very one-sided. He was doing her a favor, really, keeping her from making a fool of herself, and she wondered who else may have noticed. William had never cared for her the way she had for him. All the doubts she had were confirmed by Sidney's words and William's actions. William's feelings were the same as they had always been, and now she had only to be regretful that she had let her own develop to such an extent.

She thought about Commander Dunford and his ship leaving the day of the trial. She would see William that day for the last time, and the outcome of the trial did not matter. If William truly did not care for her, there was no reason for her to remain in England and no reason for her to ever set foot upon its shores again.

Bundled up in Lady Vernon's carriage, Amelia leaned her forehead against the window and let her tears slide down her cheeks, loving the warm cloak that encircled her and wishing it could somehow heal the part deep inside of her that she feared would never stop hurting.

Chapter 26

William leaned forward in the leather chair at his club, resting his elbows on his knees. He took another drink of the amber liquid that he had hoped would calm his tension, but so far it had not been effective.

Sidney leaned back in the chair next to him, crossing one ankle to rest upon his opposite knee.

Since it was not the Season, the club was fairly empty, but a group of men still sat near enough for William to overhear their conversations. Most spoke about the duke's ball the night before, and of course, many spoke of a certain bright-eyed brunette from Jamaica who had become the talk of the town.

William gritted his teeth.

Sidney, no doubt sensing the storm brewing just beneath the surface of William's calm exterior, shifted forward in his seat, placing his foot upon the floor. "The hearing is tomorrow morning," he said in a lowered voice. "Patience, old boy."

Patience. William had had enough of patience. The ball the night before had been torture. He hadn't known Amelia would be there. When he'd seen her enter the room looking all the world more exquisite than he could have imagined, his mouth had dropped open. If it had not been for that annoying woman, Regina Foster, he was sure he would not have been able to prevent himself from crossing the room and sweeping Amelia into his arms, thereby ruining not only her reputation but his suit against her father.

As it was, he should probably thank Regina for her distraction, as bothersome as it was. She had clung to him like a barnacle on a ship's hull the entire night, and the only relief he'd found from her incessant eye batting and lip pouting was when the women withdrew after supper. He had tired quickly of her not-so-disguised insults toward the other ladies in the room and found himself longing for someone he could have an actual conversation with. Someone witty and clever, who would never put on a coy performance just to impress him. Someone whose smile had the power to chase away despairing thoughts. Someone who was comfortable with herself, who did not give a fig whether her hands got calloused repairing a sail or whether her nose got freckled in the sun upon the deck. And he could think of only one lady who would ever fit the bill: his Amelia.

A man came to sit in their corner. He shook both their hands. William searched his mind for the gentleman's name. The man had been at the ball the night before, and they had even conversed for a moment. The man was older, probably the age William's father would be if he were still living. William also noted the man's round belly and colorful waistcoat. *Charles Porter*. William would have to do better with names if he was going to make a decent earl.

"How do you do this afternoon, Mr. Porter?" Sidney asked.

"Very well, Captain Fletcher. How long do you expect to be quartered in London, sir?"

"The *Venture* has been moved to Portsmouth to undergo extensive repairs. It seems the previous captain allowed quite a lot of damage—" Sidney broke off his words, laughing at William's glare. "We expect to receive orders within the next few weeks. I have a crew who will be quite anxious to set sail by that time."

"Very good," Mr. Porter said. "And how did you gentlemen enjoy the duke's ball last night?"

"Delightful, was it not, William?" said Sidney.

William took another drink before answering dryly, "Yes, delightful."

"You seemed to be enjoying yourself very much with a certain lady of means, Lord Lockwood."

William raised his brow, but before he could answer, Sidney cut in. "I think there were many lovely young ladies among the company."

"If I were a young buck like the two of you and not a confirmed old bachelor, I should think there was only one lady at the ball worthy of my attention."

"And who is that, sir?" Sidney asked.

"Why, Miss Amelia Becket, of course." Mr. Porter took a sip of his drink and set it down on the low table that sat between the three men. "She was by far the most engaging lady I have had the pleasure of conversing with in quite some time." He crossed his ankles and folded his hands over his round waist. "And I hear the duke has already been to visit Miss Becket this morning. Quite a compliment so soon after paying her such particular attention at his ball. And did you see the two of them waltz? A handsome couple to be sure. I should not be surprised—"

But William did not hear the rest of Mr. Porter's statement. He slammed down his glass, sloshing liquid over the table, and stormed from the room, leaving Sidney to make his apologies.

William stepped down the front steps of the club and quickly sent his carriage driver home, opting to walk the mile through the cold streets. The cool air would hopefully clear his mind and rid him of the image of Amelia in the duke's arms as they waltzed around the ballroom.

He clenched his fists, seething. Of course other men had noticed her. They would have been blind not to. She had been surrounded nearly the entire night by admirers.

Only a few more hours and this entire business with her father would be solved. And from the news his solicitor had given him, it seemed as if it would be over quickly. But was it too late? Had he already lost her?

***

The next morning, William paced in front of the magistrate's chambers. He had met early with Mr. Campbell, who had introduced William to Mr. Grant, the barrister who would represent the earl's case. Each of the men was very capable, and William had full confidence that the matter would be handled well. The two men sat upon a bench conversing, heads bent over a stack of documents. But William paced, finding that even eighteen years of military discipline did not give him the patience to remain still when something so crucial was at stake.

When the bailiff opened the door to admit them into the chambers, William saw that Admiral Becket, the man William assumed was the admiral's barrister, and Amelia were already seated at one side of a large table.

They all looked up when the men entered, but Amelia quickly cast her eyes back down. William repeated his mantra. *Patience. It is nearly finished.*

William and his council sat at the other side of the table. He was grateful that this matter was to be handled privately instead of in a public courtroom.

The bailiff pounded his staff upon the ground. "Hear ye, hear ye. All rise for the Honorable Clarence Thurston, Esquire."

They all stood, and the magistrate entered the room, his black robes swishing around him and a curled white wig upon his head. He sat at the head of the table, and then he motioned for the rest of the room to be seated.

"Are all parties present?" the magistrate asked, and upon receiving an affirmative answer from both groups, he continued. "As I understand it, we are here to settle a matter concerning the legality of a marriage license signed by one Lawrence Drake, earl of Lockwood, now deceased, and a Miss Amelia Becket." The magistrate turned to Amelia. "And am I to understand that you are the woman in question—Miss Amelia Becket?"

Amelia opened her mouth to answer but was cut off by her father.

"Sir!" Admiral Becket interrupted. "By referring to her thus, you already favor our opponent. My daughter shall be known in these proceedings, and henceforth, as Lady Lockwood."

The admiral's barrister was attempting to quiet the bellowing man, and the magistrate narrowed his eyes, focusing on the admiral. "Sir, your barrister shall represent you, and I do not permit such outbursts in my chambers. If I want to hear you speak, I shall question you directly."

Admiral Becket's face grew red. He inhaled as if to unleash another tirade, but a few whispered words from his barrister stopped the admiral, and instead, he glared at each person in the room in turn, including Amelia.

William clenched his jaw.

The magistrate cleared his throat. "And am I to understand that . . . the admiral's daughter signed the marriage license in Jamaica and Lord Lockwood signed the same document in England, but no wedding was ever performed?"

Admiral Becket's barrister spoke. "Unfortunately, Lord Lockwood's commitments in India, followed by his untimely death, prevented such a thing, sir."

"I see." The magistrate wrote upon the papers in front of him. "And, young lady, you argue that such a ceremony is unnecessary, and this document, as a contract, entitles you to the rights of jointure as Lord Lockwood's widow?"

Why is he questioning Amelia?

Amelia looked at the magistrate for a long moment. "I am sorry, sir. I do not know exactly how to answer that question. I did sign the document, believing it to connect me in marriage, by proxy, to the late Lord Lockwood. But upon his death, the disagreement over jointure has been raised by my father and the current Lord Lockwood."

He turned to William. "And Lord Lockwood, you seek to discredit this woman. To expose her as a fraud and declare this document illegal."

William looked at Amelia, but her gaze did not rise to meet his. He swallowed before he answered, hating his words, but knowing he must say them. "Yes, sir."

He heard Amelia's quick intake of breath.

"And, young lady, you have no opinion in the matter?"

Amelia glanced at William and then at her father, whose face was angled away from the magistrate, preventing the presiding authority from seeing the threat in his eyes. She took a breath, looked away from the admiral, and spoke to the magistrate. "I was not coerced into signing the document, sir. I did so of my own free will, but I have since come to regret it. I have no desire for an inheritance that does not belong to me."

At her words, the admiral sprang to his feet, spluttering in a rage. The other men in the room jumped up, afraid that he might strike his daughter. Out of habit, William reached for his sword, then cursed the fact that he no longer wore it as part of his regimentals.

The magistrate banged his gavel upon the table, and with the help of the bailiff, Admiral Becket was returned rather forcefully to his seat.

"One more display like that, Admiral, and I shall have you removed."

Amelia remained standing, not bothering to wipe the tears from her cheeks, and William felt his heart compress.

"Sir." She spoke to the magistrate in a quiet voice. "If you would please excuse me from the remainder of the proceedings. I do not believe my presence here is necessary."

The magistrate studied her for a moment. "Even though the verdict is to determine the entire course of your life?"

"The verdict will be determined with or without me present, sir."

The magistrate nodded. "Very well then. You are excused."

Amelia hurried from the room, and though it broke William's heart to see her hurting, he was glad that she would not have to witness the remainder of the proceedings.

She had been incredibly brave, and he was certain that her father would not treat her kindly when he returned home. William determined to get there first.

The magistrate spoke again. "And now, I should like to hear the evidence presented by the barristers. Admiral, your representation may begin."

Admiral Becket's barrister, Mr. Stanley, was a young man with a hook nose. He stood and took a breath before speaking. "Your Honor, Admiral Becket's daughter and the late Lord Lockwood, both of sound mind, endorsed a legal document with their signatures. The marriage certificate was legally obtained, and such a contract is legally binding. The admiral is guilty of no deception, and while he acknowledges the great tragedy of the earl's early death, it does not nullify the agreement."

The barrister resumed his seat next to Admiral Becket, and the magistrate wrote some notes before turning to William's side of the table. "And Lord Lockwood, your counsel may present a counterargument."

Mr. Grant stood, and while he did not speak as quickly as his opponent, his words were clear and firm. William was again grateful to Mr. Campbell for choosing this man.

"Your Honor, not only was no marriage ceremony performed but there is no evidence that any effort was ever made to do so. And, sir, if I may . . ." Mr. Grant took a document from Mr. Campbell and handed it to the magistrate.

Admiral Becket began whispering furiously to his barrister, who only shrugged his shoulders.

The magistrate perused the document for some time before turning back to Mr. Grant. "And would you care to explain this, sir?"

"By court order, Lord Lockwood's solicitor was able to obtain this document, which we believe to have been drafted mere months before the unfortunate death of the earl's brother. It is, as you can see, a will, bequeathing the entirety of Admiral Becket's daughter's plantation to the admiral upon either Miss Becket's or her husband's death. Such a thing, sir, cannot help but call the admiral's character into question, as it appears he had devised some scheme with the late Lord Lockwood."

"Admiral Becket, this information is quite condemning. Do you have an explanation?"

The admiral's face turned red. "How dare you accuse me of such a thing! You have no proof." He pointed to the magistrate. "I have done nothing illegal, and I insist upon a new magistrate. One who is not so obviously biased. Tell me, sir, how much gold did Lord Lockwood lay in your palm to ensure his victory?"

"Bailiff, remove this man from my chambers immediately. He will be detained in a cell overnight."

"I am an admiral in His Majesty's navy!" Becket screamed as the bailiff dragged him from the chamber.

Mr. Stanley rubbed his eyes.

The magistrate took a breath before speaking. "Lord Lockwood, it is completely within your rights to begin criminal proceedings against Admiral Becket concerning your brother's death."

It was the plantation. That was the admiral's design all along. It was unbelievable that the man would go to such lengths to obtain it. A thought crept into William's mind: had the admiral somehow been responsible for the death of Amelia's mother as well? William hoped that question would never be addressed in Amelia's presence.

Hearing Mr. Campbell clear his throat, William realized that the magistrate was awaiting an answer. "Sir, a military court has already begun investigating the admiral."

"Very well then. And how would you prefer to proceed with the matter at hand? Should you like your brother's marriage annulled?"

"No, sir. I do not wish to ruin the reputation of the lady. I should like the entire matter discredited. As if it had never happened."

"As the marriage was never solemnized by the church, I shall make arrangements immediately as per your wishes."

"Thank you." The relief that washed over William left his muscles feeling weak.

The magistrate rose, and the remaining men in the room stood as he exited the chamber. Mr. Stanley followed closely behind him.

William shook the hands of Mr. Campbell and Mr. Grant. "I cannot thank you enough for how you handled this matter."

"There will be time for that later, Lord Lockwood," Mr. Campbell said, a twinkle in his eye. "I should think you have a visit to pay and news to deliver to a particular lady."

William did not have to be told twice. He walked out the door and discovered Sidney waiting for him in the entrance hall of the courthouse.

"And . . . ?" Sidney asked, walking rapidly to keep up with William. "Are you going to tell me the verdict?"

"The magistrate's decision was in our favor." William climbed into his carriage. "And if you would like to accompany me, I am going to pay a visit to Amelia Becket."

When they reached the admiral's residence, William leapt from the carriage and practically bounded up the stairs. Sidney, for once, was more reserved.

William rang the bell and tapped his foot upon the step as he waited.

A butler answered the door, and William told him they had come to visit with Miss Becket, glancing past the man into the house in his eagerness to see Amelia.

The butler looked annoyed with the two men. "Miss Becket is gone."

"We can wait." William said. "When do you expect her to return?"

"You misunderstood me, sir. Miss Becket is *gone*. She took her trunk and her maid and left over an hour ago."

"Surely she plans to return. Where would she go?" William felt the beginnings of panic gnawing at his insides.

"I think not, sir. The carriage driver conveyed her to the docks." As the man closed the door, William heard him mutter, "And as for myself, I shall enjoy a good night sleep without Miss Becket's nightmares waking the whole house."

William turned. "Sidney, we must get to the docks!"

But Sidney was already running down the walkway to the carriage, calling orders to William's driver to get them to Greenwich as quickly as possible. The men climbed inside, and William raked his fingers through his hair.

"William, we must think. There are hundreds of ships in port. Where would Amelia go?"

"That man from the duke's ball. Mr. Dunford. What was the name of his ship?" William searched his mind. He had nodded politely that evening as the man had told them about his forthcoming voyage to Grenada, but William had been so distracted by Amelia that he had only half listened. His heart was pounding, and even now he found it impossible to concentrate as he struggled to suppress the dread that was growing heavy in his chest.

"The SS *Lilian*? No, *Louisa*," Sidney said, his brow furrowed. "But Amelia would not have left. I cannot believe it."

William remembered holding Amelia in his sitting room after the battle. She had been broken and hurt and at her most vulnerable. Now he heard the words she had said as if she were sitting next to him. *Don't leave me, William*, and *I just want to go home*. The true longings of her heart. If she believed William had left her, he had no doubt of her next move.

It was after many inquiries and a frantic search that a dockworker finally pointed down the river, where a merchant ship was sailing out toward the open sea. "'Ere's the *Louisa*, sirs. Pity it is. Ya just missed 'er."

Sidney patted William's shoulder. "I am sorry, old boy."

William's limbs felt as if they were filled with lead. He watched the *Louisa* as her sails were reefed, filling with wind and taking Amelia from him.

Straightening his back, he turned to Sidney. "Captain Fletcher, I am going to need a ship."

Chapter 27

Amelia sat in her cabin on the merchant ship. She had asked the ship's cook for some ginger to make tea for poor Anna, who was feeling the pains of seasickness.

Amelia held the cup toward her lady's maid. "Drink a bit; it will help. We have been at sea two days, and you shall feel better by tomorrow. I guarantee."

"I do not know how you can stand it, miss. The rocking of the ship is dreadful."

"One becomes accustomed to it. You shall love Jamaica, Anna. And as we get closer, it will become warmer upon the decks and we can watch for dolphins." Amelia dipped a cloth in a bucket of cool water and applied it to Anna's forehead. Then the girl lay back upon her berth to rest.

Amelia heard noises upon the decks above her and felt the familiar pain that she knew would soon be accompanied by tears at the memories that filled her mind almost constantly. She had taken to remaining below deck—under the pretense of caring for Anna—to avoid the open sea and the smells and sights that reminded her of William. Thinking of him was too painful.

Her constant sorrow had left her feeling hollow. She pulled her blanket closer around her shoulders; even that was a reminder of him.

How could she have ever let herself develop such feelings for this man? It was merely a few months ago that she had congratulated herself on the fact that she had not allowed such a thing as love to ruin a perfectly good sham marriage. She had looked upon other ladies as fools for allowing themselves to be swept away like lovesick ninnies.

As she lay back upon her own berth, her tears began afresh. She covered her mouth in order not to disturb Anna.

She noticed more noises upon the deck above her, and her heart began to race. Memories of the battles crashed over her, and it took all her strength to hold in her fear. She hurried from the cabin, not wanting to disturb Anna, who needed her sleep.

Amelia thought she would scream. The urge to hide fought with the need to know what was happening above deck. She tried to push down her anxiety as the familiar noises of men yelling and heavy footsteps running over the wooden boards nearly drove her to her knees in fear. She was creeping up the companionway on shaking legs when someone shouted, "We're being boarded!"

Full-blown terror exploded in Amelia's chest. Running up the last steps, she emerged onto the deck and saw a sleek vessel situated much too close. Men were clambering across planks to board the SS *Louisa*, and one man swung on a rope, landing gracefully upon the deck.

William. Her terror ceased, though her heart continued to pound in her ears. She did not know whether the sight of him brought more hurt or more relief, but he was here.

He strode across the deck to Commander Dunford. "My apologies, sir, but it appears that you have one of my crew among your ranks."

"I assure you I checked each man's documentation myself, sir."

William turned to Amelia, walking slowly toward her. "Miss Amelia Becket. As I am certain you are aware, desertion is a serious crime."

Amelia did not know whether to laugh or to cry. She was so happy to see him and so hurt and so . . . confused.

"I did not think my company was necessary anymore, Captain." She lowered her eyes, feeling hot tears slip down her cheeks. The relief at seeing him brought her emotions to the surface with a vengeance. "Or wanted."

William took her arm, leading her out of earshot of both crews that stood upon the deck, watching the couple. He pulled her blanket tighter around her shoulders, lifting her chin with his crooked finger. "Amelia, you are wanted. I need you. I could not bear for you to leave me, as I am quite in love with you."

William held her face in his hands, using his thumbs to brush away her tears.

"But I thought—" she murmured.

"Amelia, I have loved you almost from the moment you sullied my boots."

She smiled at his attempt at humor. "But why did you not visit me in London? And the ball. You danced with that horrible—" Her voice caught on a sob, and she laid her head upon his chest, no longer shaking. He tightened his arms around her. "I thought you understood. I had no choice. Did you not receive my note? I could not talk to you until after the trial or else I would risk losing the suit. If our true relationship was discovered, I could have lost you forever."

"Do you really love me, William?" Her voice was little more than a whisper.

"Amelia, this past week has been torture. It has shown me that I do not want to live without you. The hope of having you by my side is the only reason I am able to leave the sea. I ache when you are not with me. I cannot bear the thought of you waking from nightmares alone when I might be there to hold you. There is nothing on earth I want more than to spend every moment with you. You have stolen my heart." He stepped back and lifted her chin until their eyes met. "You have tamed an ill-mannered beast."

A small giggle pushed its way between her tears. "I am sorry I ever said such a thing, William. You are the best man I have ever known, and I am very much in love with you."

William pressed his lips upon hers, and cheers and applause sounded around them.

Amelia looked around the deck, blushing when she saw all the sailors watching. She recognized many of the smiling faces of her shipmates: Riley, Slushy, Sidney, Corporal Ashworth.

"But there is still the matter of your punishment," William said.

"I think this is hardly the place for a waltz."

"No, but it is the perfect place for Captain Fletcher to perform a wedding. After I attempt to kiss you senseless, of course."

Just before his lips met hers, Amelia whispered, "Aye, aye, Captain."

Epilogue

William Drake, Lord of Lockwood, stepped down the stairs in the manor house, tying his cravat as he walked. Entering the dining room, he saw the dowager lady and his sister had already begun eating their breakfast.

"Good morning, Mother, Emma."

They both returned the greeting with smiles.

"I trust you slept well," his mother said.

William walked to the sideboard and began to fill his plate. Her interest touched him. He had found himself surprised by how pleasant it was to belong to a family. There had not been many people in his life concerned for his welfare.

"Thank you, Mother, I did."

"And Amelia? The storm did not keep her awake?" Emma asked.

"Not at all. The night was very peaceful." He brought his plate to the table, sitting next to his mother. "She will join us in a moment."

He looked at his younger sister. "And how did you sleep, Emma?" he asked. "Did the storm disturb you?"

"No. I slept very well, thank you." She smiled at him shyly, and he wished he knew her well enough to know whether she told the truth.

Ever since he and his new bride had arrived at the manor two months earlier, Amelia and Emma had gotten along splendidly. The two women regularly spent hours together, reading or bundling up against the cold and taking long walks around the estate. Amelia had confided in him that she believed Emma had become a bit melancholy lately, but he thought it must be attributed to the cold, dark winter. And, though he would never admit such a thing aloud, he himself had noticed the house was much duller once their guest, Sidney Fletcher, had left after Twelfth Night.

William had taken only a few bites when he heard footsteps in the entryway, followed by a rush of cold air as the manor house door was opened.

The three turned toward the dining room entrance, wondering what had caused the disturbance, when they heard the distressed voice of the butler calling, "My lady!"

William sprung from his chair and hastened to the entry hall, where the butler stood in the doorway, holding Amelia's outer wrap. William pushed past him and looked out into the garden.

He saw Amelia crouched down in the deep snow. He snatched the cloak from the butler and ran into the garden, calling her name. Was she hurt? What could she possibly be doing?

Hearing him, she turned, and he saw to his amazement, a smile lit up her face. His heart softened. There was a time he'd worried he would never see her smile again.

She held a handful of snow out to him. "It is *snow*, William! I had heard of such a thing, but I have never seen it." She stretched her arms out, motioning around her. "It is everywhere. On ever branch, each stone. The entire forest is covered—like a blanket. And it is so beautiful." She shook her hand, allowing the wet clump to fall to the ground.

William wrapped the cloak around her shoulders, tying the ribbon beneath her chin.

"And cold," he said, lifting her red hand and placing a kiss on her fingers. "Come back inside. You shall have plenty of opportunities to see the snow. We have an entire winter ahead of us."

Amelia placed her hands upon his shoulders, sliding them up to the sides of his neck. He shivered as her cold palms touched his skin, and he wrapped his arms around her, noticing again how perfectly she fit into them.

"William, I did not imagine I should ever be so happy."

"Even in dreary old England?"

"I quite adore it here. But perhaps that can be attributed to the company."

Small flurries of snow continued to fall, and some flakes landed upon her cheeks. William promptly kissed them off. "Then, I wonder if you should still want to travel to Jamaica after next year's parliamentary session ends."

Amelia pulled back, studying his expression. Deciding that he was teasing, her own face relaxed into a smile. "I would not want to disappoint your mother and Emma. They are so looking forward to a tropical holiday. And of course, a long sea voyage." She tipped her head slightly and furrowed her brow. "But do you think we shall be able to leave the estate?"

"Fortunately, my wife is very wise in matters of business. She is a supreme ledger keeper, and the tenants are quite taken with her. With her help, I shall be able to leave the estate very well managed for six months until our return."

She raised an eyebrow, and her lips quirked in a smile. "I wonder, Captain, if you needed a steward more than a wife."

William tightened his arms around her, cupping her head in one hand and bringing her face close to his. "I do not think a steward would allow me to do this." His lips brushed hers softly. "And I do not know what I should do without my Amelia."

She took his hand as they walked back toward the manor house. "I could not agree with you more, William. It turns out that marriage quite agrees with me."

About the Author

Jennifer Moore is a passionate reader and writer of all things romance, helping her find balance with the rest of her world, which includes a perpetually traveling husband and four active sons, who create heaps of laundry that are anything but romantic. Jennifer has a BA in linguistics from the University of Utah and is a Guitar Hero champion. She lives in northern Utah with her family. You can learn more about her at authorjmoore.com.

The author's first book, *Becoming Lady Lockwood*, is a regency romance centered on the British navy during the Napoleonic Wars of the early 1800s.